An Ocean Apart
Lyn Behan

Behan Publishing

Contents

Dedication   V

"Over paid, over sexed and over here"   1

1. Chapter One – Yeovil, England 1944   2

2. Chapter Two – Yeovil, England 1945   13

3. Chapter Three – Jim   30

4. Chapter Four   35

5. Chapter Five   42

6. Chapter Six – HMS Ganges   52

7. Chapter Seven - HMS Ariel   60

8. Chapter Eight - The Ark Royal   64

9. Chapter Nine - Alison   68

10. Chapter Ten - Wedding Plans   78

11. Chapter Eleven   83

12. Chapter Twelve   101

13. Chapter Thirteen   103

14. Chapter Fourteen   119

15. Chapter Fifteen   132

16. Chapter Sixteen   145

17. Chapter Seventeen   155

18.	Chapter Eighteen	167
19.	Chapter Nineteen	191
20.	Chapter Twenty	203
21.	Chapter Twenty-one	231
22.	Chapter Twenty-two	234
23.	Chapter Twenty-three – 1990	248
24.	Chapter Twenty-four – 1994	252
25.	Chapter Twenty-five – 2010	257
	Acknowledgements	262
	About the author	263

This book is dedicated to my mother, and to all those parents who either by death, divorce, or adoption did not see their children grow up.

"Over paid, over sexed and over here"

During the Second World War, one and a half million American servicemen and women – about a tenth of whom were black – were posted to Britain to support Allied operations in North West Europe. By 1944, several thousands of these American troops were billeted at Houndstone Camp near Yeovil, in the west of England, in the lead up to D-Day. The cinemas, dance halls and pubs were popular places of entertainment for these soldiers. Their gifts of nylons, chocolates and cigarettes endeared them to the local girls ...

Chapter One – Yeovil, England 1944

Jean Higgins drew her winter coat around her, tucked her scarf into the collar and pulled her hat down around her ears, as she hurried from the factory where she worked.

'Wait for me, Jean.'

Surrounded by the jostling throng of workers streaming through the main gates, all eager to get home after a day's work, Jean didn't turn around; she knew it was Betty. She slowed her pace, just managing to avoid someone pushing a bike. It was too dangerous to cycle through the crowd in the blackout.

'Jean, for goodness' sake … SLOW DOWN, will you!'

Jean braced herself for the lecture to start.

'You're turning into a right bore, Jean Higgins. You never go out, just stay home knitting and reading … I'd like someone to go to the dances with, instead of having to go on my own.'

Jean sighed. Maybe I am a bore, she thought, but she couldn't help being quiet and shy, and anyway Betty might go on her own but she always came home late at night with some chap – usually an American GI. She started to make her usual excuse, but Betty interrupted.

'And don't make your boyfriend the excuse. He's probably found a new girl, a more sociable one.'

As the crowd thinned, Betty struggled to keep up with Jean's long strides. 'How long since you've heard from him? It's been ages, and he could have been killed for all you know, and meanwhile you're wasting your life. We could all be bombed tomorrow.'

'You know very well I can't go out enjoying myself while Ernie's over there fighting.'

Jean shrugged and crossed the road, dodging the many cyclists. It had been nearly a year since Ernie's last letter, but that didn't mean he wasn't still alive. 'Anyway. I'm not interested in going dancing.'

Betty snorted. 'Oh, I'm fed up with you Jean, you're no fun at all. I should get another girl to share my room, Mam wouldn't care. She and Dad would probably like to be on their own sometimes.'

Jean flinched. She'd been lucky to get lodgings with Betty's parents.

'Come on, Jean. It's Friday and we've worked hard all week. I'm sure if Ernie's still alive, he'd want you to get out and have a bit of fun. And you must have made him at least five jumpers by now!' She gave Jean a sly look. 'Monica Simonds was saying at lunch that she was looking for new lodgings ...' She let her comment hang to give it time to sink in.

'So, what about it then, come to the dance tonight?'

'I've got nothing to wear.'

'You can wear one of my dresses.'

'Be too short for me.'

'Mam'll tack a bit of a frill on the bottom in no time.'

Jean sighed. 'Oh, all right then. If your mam can do it.' She secretly hoped that Betty's mum wouldn't have time.

Two hours later and they were in a church hall which was being used for dancing – it was one activity not proscribed by the Government:

"It is not proposed to make war total misery" Home Secretary H Morrison announced in the House of Commons, *"dancing is not*

to be included in the recreations that are to be restricted to prevent interference with the war effort".

The hall was crowded and already humming with dance music and many African American GIs from the camp. Jean looked around nervously – there had been instances where white GIs had refused to go to dances where coloured men were allowed, and some cases where coloured men who were with white women had been attacked. She breathed a sigh of relief to see that so far things were peaceful. The white men were mostly local servicemen home on leave.

She found a quiet corner and settled in to watch the dancers, already regretting having come and hoping no-one would notice her in the corner – Betty had been swept off onto the dance floor.

'Would you care to dance, ma'am?'

Startled, she looked up. A large black man stood a respectful distance from her.

'Um, I ... er ...' she mumbled.

'I'm sorry.' He looked disappointed. 'I understand. Forgive me for intruding.' He moved to go.

'No, I mean, I'm not very good at dancing ...' She was horrified he might think that she didn't want to dance with him because of his colour.

She stumbled to her feet. 'I'd be delighted, but I don't know how to dance this new jitterbug.'

He smiled and held out his hand. 'I'd be honoured to show you, ma'am. I'm James Samuels, but everyone calls me Sammy.'

'Jean Higgins.'

'Pleased to meet you, Miss Higgins.' His smile reached his eyes.

She nodded, took off her coat, placed it on the seat, tucked her clutch bag under it and took his hand.

After a few false steps, she soon got the hang of being swung around, twirling and being whirled back into the safety of Sammy's arms. She couldn't help smiling and laughing, aware of the heat rising in her cheeks.

At the end of the evening, Sammy led her to retrieve her coat and bag from where she'd left them; he took her coat and held it out.

'Thank you so much, Sammy.'

'Miss Jean, may I walk you home?'

She panicked and looked around. There was no sign of Betty amongst the crowd, and she didn't want to walk home on her own in the blackout. And she didn't know this man. But part of her wanted to be with Sammy. She slipped her arms into her coat, buttoned it and tucked her clutch bag under her arm.

'No, I'll be all right. It's not far.'

'Maybe I could walk a small part of the way with you?'

She convinced herself that it would be rude to refuse. 'Thank you.'

The night air cooled her cheeks as they strolled along. He turned on his torch momentarily to see the way.

'Tell me about yourself, Miss Jean.'

'Please, just Jean, no Miss. And, there's not much to tell.'

'Well, where do you work? What do you do?'

'I'm a shorthand typist in the aircraft factory here.' She searched around for something to say to him. 'Um, have you always been in the army?'

'Yes, I joined up to learn a trade, but then Pearl Harbor happened, and now here I am.'[1]

'What trade did you want to learn?'

He laughed. 'I hoped to learn about radio and electrics but as a black man, I wasn't allowed.'

'That wasn't fair!'

As she crossed the road, he guided her to the inside of the pavement, then let his hand fall to his side. Perversely she would have liked his arm to stay around her waist. She felt the blood rise to her cheeks at the thought and missed what he said next. Luckily, they'd reached Betty's house.

'This is where I'm lodging.' She turned to him. 'How will you get back to camp?'

'There're buses.'

'Well, thank you for seeing me home, Sammy.'

'My pleasure.' He hesitated. 'I'd really like to see you again, Jean. Will you be going to the dance on Sunday evening?'

'Um, I don't know.'

'Please try. I'll be there looking out for you.'

She could just make out the gleam of his teeth in the gloom as he smiled.

'Good night, Jean. Thank you for a lovely evening.' He took a step back, opened the small gate and waited for her to go up the path. As she reached the front door, she saw him close the gate and walk away.

She lay in bed thinking about Sammy and her attraction to him when she heard Betty creeping in.

'Know you're still awake, Jean Higgins. Saw you dancing with that black soldier all night. Looked like you were having a good time.'

Jean mumbled something and turned over in the bed as Betty got in beside her. She didn't want to talk about Sammy.

***

In late May, Jean and Sammy were walking hand-in-hand at Ninesprings, a woodland park, at the southern edge of Yeovil. With a lake and swans, it was an oasis from the bombed town and a favourite meeting place of theirs and other courting couples. The beech trees had burst into a green parasol above them. Jean swung Sammy's hand and pointed to the leaves. 'In autumn the squirrels collect the beech nuts and throw the shells down on passersby,' she laughed. Seeing the doubtful look on his face she frowned. 'Truly! They do.' They found a secluded spot and Sammy spread his jacket for them to sit on.

Jean lay down, looking up at the beech leaves rustling in the slight breeze.

Sammy lay beside her and took her in his arms. 'Jean. I love you. I want to marry you, and take you home with me.' He leaned over and kissed her. 'I love you, Jean,' he repeated, 'But at the moment I can't marry you, it's illegal in my home state in America for a black man to marry a white woman, and our commanding officer won't allow it. But I'll do everything in my power to make it happen. Jean, will you marry me?'

'I love you, too, Sammy, and the answer is yes!' The past few months had made her realise how much she loved this man. Not Ernie, it had never been Ernie. She had fleeting feelings of remorse about him, but she'd never felt about him the way she felt about Sammy. And she'd gone all the way with Sammy, but he'd said it was all right. He'd been careful. She trusted him absolutely.

Ninesprings had been the last time they'd met. She'd had a letter with a photo of him in uniform the following day.

'Another letter from Lover Boy, I see,' Betty said, peering over her shoulder at the photo. 'I must say he's a handsome chap. What does his letter say?'

Jean shrugged. 'Not much.' She pushed it and the photo back into the envelope. She didn't want to discuss Sammy with Betty.

A week later, on June 5th the town was eerily silent.

As Jean waited anxiously for news from Sammy, she had another more pressing problem. Her monthlies hadn't arrived, and her breasts felt different. By the second month she knew she was pregnant. She panicked. The D-Day landings were on the radio and newsreels in the cinema, and she'd heard nothing from Sammy. She knew that sharp-eyed Betty would soon notice she hadn't disposed of any sanitary pads.

She'd managed to hide her condition, but by the time she'd missed her third period, she knew she had to take action. There was no-one except her mother she could turn to, and that thought filled her with dread. At the weekend she caught the bus to the village where she lived and walked the two miles to her parents' cottage.

Her mother was in the back yard, hanging out washing when she arrived, and merely nodded at her. 'Hello, stranger, what brings you here?' No smile of welcome.

Jean sighed. Trust her mother to somehow make her feel guilty. 'Been busy.' She'd spent every free weekend that she could with Sammy and hadn't been home for months. She put down her bag and helped her mother pegging out washing.

'Hmm. Haven't we all?'

Jean looked around. 'Where're the girls?' She had two younger sisters, both still at school.

'Down at the farm earning a bit of pocket money.' She picked up the wicker washing basket and peg bag. 'Well, you'd better come in. Kettle's on.'

In the kitchen, Jean stood looking out the window. Her heart thumped and she felt sick.

Her mother poured boiling water into the tea pot and put the cosy on it. 'So. What brings you here today, then?'

Jean thought she could say, 'because I wanted to see my loving mother', but instead she turned from the window, took a deep breath and blurted it out: 'I'm expecting.'

Her mother spun round, her eyes wide with shock.

'Oh? And is he going to marry you?'

'Yes, when he comes back.'

'It's obviously not Ernest's, so who's the father?'

'An American soldier.' She dared not say he was black.

'You slut!' Her mother's eyes darkened as she took a step forward and slapped Jean hard across the face.

Jean put a hand to her smarting cheek and blinked away tears. 'We're going to get married and he's taking me back to America.'

Her mother snorted. 'So, you fell for that old yarn. Fine example you are to your sisters!' she spat. 'And after we spent all that money sending you to a do a shorthand and typing course ... this, this is how you repay us!' She paced around the kitchen. 'The shame, the shame of it. Well, you'll just have to get rid of it, or get it adopted.'

Jean shook her head.

'And what will Ernest say when he gets back?'

Jean said nothing. She and Ernie had only ever been friends, never anything serious on her part, he'd been the one pushing her to go out with him. But he'd been a useful reason for her reluctance to go dancing.

Her mother stopped her pacing and stared at Jean's stomach. 'So how far are you gone? Not much by the look of it. I'll have to think about this.' She raised her voice. 'But for now, you'd better walk back to the village and get the next bus to Yeovil. And tell no-one! No-one! Do you hear me?'

Jean picked up her bag, held her head high and walked out the door.

She heard it slam behind her.

Two weeks later she received a letter from her mother:

I've arranged for you to work at Bridgwater Hospital.

The matron is giving you a job there until it's born.

She'll arrange for it to be adopted, and then you will come home.

I haven't told your father or sisters. You will never mention this again.

Bringing shame to a respectable family.

There was no Dear Jean, or signature.

It turned out that the Matron was a distant cousin of her mother's, who could be relied upon to keep quiet. The plan was that Jean would work there until the baby was born, then it would be adopted. Jean would return home as if nothing had happened.

She had no choice.[2]

1. As Europe plunged into conflict in the late 1930s, the US Army began to prepare for America's involvement in a coming war. At the same time, Black Americans continued their campaign for better conditions and more opportunities in the armed forces.President Franklin D. Roosevelt found himself in a difficult political position that threatened to alienate voters regardless of his stance on the issue. An agenda that was too pro–civil rights would aggravate southern Democrats, and an agenda that appeared anti–civil rights would leave him open to criticism from northern Democrats and the ever-increasing Black electorate. Roosevelt had to walk a fine line in military issues.Though the Roosevelt administration asserted that the U.S. military would continue to be racially segregated, Roosevelt planned to provide Black officers for Black Army Reserve units, allow Black soldiers to be admitted to Officer Candidate Schools, and provide equal opportunities for civilian jobs on military installations.Even with these efforts, both civil rights activists and members of Congress continued to pressure the Roosevelt administration and the Army for greater integration, arguing that the United States could not fight for democracy overseas if democracy was not practiced in the United States.

2. https://swheritage.org.uk/news/black-history-month-somerset-devons-brown-babies/

During and shortly after the war a number of children were born to white English mothers and black US Army fathers. Nationally it is thought there were about 2,000 such children, many of whom referred to themselves as the 'brown babies'. Most were illegitimate and many ended up in children's homes. Some parents applied for permission to marry but were refused by the father's white commanding officers: in some parts of the USA mixed-race marriages were illegal and so it was often impossible for the mother to move with the child to America and for the couple to marry there.But in Somerset the children were particularly remembered because from birth to the age of five many were sent to the same children's home, Holnicote House near Porlock. By 1948, there were 45 'brown babies' known to be living in care in Somerset, about half of whom were at Holnicote. The children, when interviewed in later life, generally reported that they were very happy there.

Chapter Two – Yeovil, England 1945

The glove factory hummed with the sound of sewing machines and the smell of newly tanned leather. Ellen Jones couldn't quite hear the chatter of the other women workers over the noise, as she stitched the seams of a leather glove. She reached for new pieces, her machine quiet for a few seconds, and caught some of the latest gossip.

'And that Phyllis Marten! Well, she put on a lot of weight, then supposedly went to help a cousin somewhere up the country and came back all thin! She reckoned she'd forgotten her ration book!'

There were a few sniggers and general tutting.

Ellen laid the pieces on the machine and tried to concentrate on her sewing. It was common knowledge that a few women – their husbands or boyfriends away at the war – had embarked on affairs, some with American servicemen stationed at Houndstone Camp or billeted in the town. Now the war was nearly over and the possible return of their menfolk meant that some ill-conceived babies had to find new homes ...

***

A few weeks later, Ellen woke early. She turned to look at the alarm clock on the beside-table next to her sleeping husband. The luminous hands glowed in the dark. Half past six. She missed the dim glow that the gas lamps in the street below had provided before the blackout. She slid out of bed and felt for her clothes on the chair beside it. Taking care not to wake her husband she tiptoed out, passed her in-law's bedroom and crept down the narrow stairs, avoiding the one that creaked.

She took the kettle – filled each night ready for the morning – from the range. In the kitchen she lit the gas under the kettle and went back to the living room and stood near the range, glad of its residual warmth. She hurriedly dressed, and was about to riddle the embers in the grate, when she stopped, afraid the noise would wake Tom. He needed his rest, working all day as a fitter helping to build Spitfires and being on air-raid duty at night, not to mention his Home Guard duties. Instead, she went to the kitchen, took a pinch of the precious, rationed tea from the caddy and brewed enough for one cup.

Taking her cup and saucer into the living room, she sat in semi-darkness cradling her cup, only the light from the kitchen relieving the gloom. Her feelings were mixed – nervousness at the impending visit of the woman from the agency who was coming to inspect their home, and excitement at the thought of at last having a child. All the gossip had prompted Ellen and Tom to consider adopting a baby.

She and Tom had been married for many years and in that time her only pregnancy, to their sorrow, had ended in a miscarriage. Now, at thirty-eight, it was unlikely she would ever conceive again.

She turned her head at the sound of the creaky stair. She half rose and smiled at the shadowy outline of her mother-in-law.

'Morning Mam,' she said softly. 'Cup of tea?'

'Love one, dear.'

Ellen stood. 'Sit down, kettle's boiled.'

Gladys Jones sank into the only easy chair in the room. Nominally hers. Her husband, Alfred, had his chair on the other side of the range, an old straight-backed dining-room carver chair, a thin cushion on its hard seat.

Ellen returned with the tea.

Her mother-in-law smiled. 'Nothing more to be done. Lucky we did the outside yesterday, rain's getting heavy. Might turn to snow.'

Ellen nodded. 'Once we've had breakfast, I'll give the place a quick clean up.'

Gladys had spent the previous day cleaning and polishing, joined by Ellen after she'd finished work.

The clock on the sideboard with the Westminster Chime struck seven.

'Better wake Tom.' Ellen took her cup to the kitchen and rinsed it.

'Leave Dad sleep for a bit longer, love. His chest were playing up last night.'

Ellen nodded. Her father-in-law had been gassed in the first World War.

***

As the clock chimed ten, Gladys turned from the window where she'd been discreetly watching from behind the net curtains.

'She's here! There's a car outside!' In those days of petrol rationing, a car was a rarity. 'Quick, everyone, look normal. Tom! Put that paper away.'

Her son sighed and folded up his newspaper. Not knowing what to do with it, he half rose to sit on it, then, realizing it would end up all wrinkled – the paper was so thin – he retrieved it and placed it on the table.

'Normal people read newspapers,' he muttered.

'Dad! Put that cigarette out! You know you're not allowed to smoke, and the lady won't be pleased!' Gladys fussed around her husband, waving her hand in front of his face in a vain attempt to dispel the smoke.

At the sound of a knock on the front door. Ellen took a deep breath and went to the tiny entrance hall. A square yard separated the front door and the steep stairs leading to the bedrooms. Only visitors used the front door, everyone else came in the back.

'I'll take your umbrella.' Ellen waited for Miss Prentiss to wipe her sturdy, black lace-up shoes on the doormat. When she had moved into the living room, Ellen shook the umbrella outside, closed the door and propped the umbrella in the corner behind the door.

She shepherded into the room a middle-aged woman; her grey rain coat buttoned up to the chin and grey hair scraped into a black cloche hat – all seeming to reflect the grey weather outside.

'Er...This is Miss Prentiss,' Ellen said brightly, 'She's come to assess us for the suitability of adopting a baby.' Ellen didn't know why she said that. They all knew the reason.

She turned to the woman. 'Miss Prentiss, this is my husband, Tom, and Tom's parents, Gladys and Alfred Jones. Of course, we'll soon be finding our own place to live, but with the housing shortage at the moment, the war, you know, it's been hard to get our own place. We soon will, we have our name down on the Council housing list, but anyway, it's nice for a baby to have grandparents close, don't you think?' She paused to take a breath, conscious that she'd been gabbling on.

Miss Prentiss surveyed the group through steel rimmed glasses and nodded. 'How do you do,' she said in a clipped accent. She removed her gloves and tucked them into the large grey leather bag she carried over her arm.

'Do you need us all here?' Ellen indicated her in-laws.

'Not at the moment, maybe later. First, I need to ask you and your husband a few questions about the form you filled in and then review the situation.' She looked pointedly at the table.

'Oh! Please, sit down here.' Ellen pulled out a chair.

Miss Prentiss sat and took a folder from her bag.

'Come on, Alf,' Gladys said, taking her husband's arm.

'Right,' rasped Alfred. 'Glad and I go upstairs, you talk.' He nodded at his wife and went to the stairs. With only the small kitchen and one living room, there was nowhere else to go, rain prevented them going into the garden.

Ellen turned to Miss Prentiss. 'My in-laws are so excited at having a grandchild, aren't they Tom?'

'Yes, yes! Indeed. Me Mam can't wait.'

'And your father, Mr Jones?'

'Yes, yes, him too. Wants to tell him all about pigeon racing.' Tom tugged at his shirt collar.

'Hmm. Yes, well. So, what kind of baby were you hoping for?' Miss Prentiss opened the folder and retrieved a pencil, pushed her glasses up her nose and frowned at Ellen.

Ellen looked at her husband. 'What do you mean? A baby is a baby ...Oh, you mean a boy or a girl ... well I'd like a little girl.'

'A boy,' Tom said at the same time.

'Really, we don't mind. Either. We've been trying for years now, haven't we, Tom?'

Her husband straightened a wrinkle in the chenille cloth covering the table and gave a slight nod.

'Tom here is worn out from trying, aren't you, Tom?'

Tom shuffled on the hard chair and grunted.

Miss Prentiss's face reddened. 'Well,' she said and studied her notes. 'Hmm. No pets?'

'Just dad's pigeons ...'

'Presumably they don't live inside?' Miss Prentiss raised her eyebrows.

Pencilled-in eyebrows, Ellen noted.

Tom started. 'Of course not! They have their own houses out the back.'

They were quiet as Miss Prentiss made some notes.

'Very well, so I think you've answered all my questions.' Miss Prentiss pursed her lips and closed her note book. 'Now, I'd like to inspect the premises – maybe start with Baby's room?' She stood and tucked her notebook under her arm, still holding the pencil.

Ellen shot a quick look at her husband, and took a deep breath. 'Baby's room?'

'Yes, where will Baby sleep?'

'Well, I thought it would sleep in our room in the beginning ...'

Miss Prentiss frowned. 'We like our babies to have a good routine from the beginning. Their own sleeping quarters for a start.'

Ellen hesitated. 'We only have the two bedrooms ...'

Tom nodded.

'But you can see our bedroom, if you want.' Ellen said, hoping Miss Prentiss wouldn't want to. 'This way.' She moved towards the hall. 'Be careful, the stair carpet is a bit threadbare, your heels might catch.' She glanced at Miss Prentiss's shoes. The flat heels were unlikely to catch anything, she thought.

Miss Prentiss studied the narrow flight of stairs, opened her notebook and wrote a few comments. 'Right. Well, perhaps I'll just inspect the downstairs accommodation instead.' She turned back to the living room. 'May I?'

'Of course.' Ellen watched as Miss Prentiss looked around the room. The cast iron range with a kettle on it gave out a pleasant warmth. The chairs either side, the ancient leather lounge, its cushions bulging from the piles of her father-in-law's *John Bull* magazines stuffed under them; the big old table with its chenille cloth cover and the sideboard covered with photos, the clock and other knick-knacks, including a hair brush and comb. A gilt-framed mirror above the sideboard reflected the mantelpiece over the range; the only mirror in the house, apart from the tiny hand one over the kitchen sink where the men shaved. A few pictures of rural scenes hung on the walls.

'The kitchen?' Miss Prentiss moved toward the other door in the room.

'Through there.' Ellen nodded at the open door.

Ellen suddenly felt protective of their humble Council House. It was better than what a lot of people had these days. She straightened her shoulders.

Inside the kitchen, Miss Prentiss squeezed between the large stone sink and a gas stove to inspect a room leading off the end. A gas geyser on one wall above a small bath full of damp washing – washing ready to drape on a clothes horse to dry in front of the fire as soon as the visitor left. A copper boiler, a mangle and a neat row of shoes and boots filled the rest of the room.

'Hmm,' Miss Prentiss turned her attention back to the kitchen. She glanced out the window over the sink to the garden and pigeon houses, as she passed a small table and a pantry on her way to a back door.

'Um, it's just the privy through that door and then the door to the back garden,' Ellen muttered.

Miss Prentiss knocked on the green painted privy door.

'There's no-one in there,' Ellen assured her.

Miss Prentiss opened the door and took a quick look in at the wooden-seated toilet with a chain coming from a high metal cistern. A nail on the wall held squares of newspaper. She turned back to Ellen.

'We try and match our babies with potential parents, but we have one baby ...' she paused, studied her notes, looked at Ellen and continued, 'that doesn't seem to fit with any of our prospective parents, but might suit you very well ...' She scribbled on her pad as Ellen exclaimed, 'We'll take her. Won't we Tom?'

Tom, who had stayed in the living room during the inspection, nodded as Miss Prentiss snapped shut her notebook and walked through the living room to the table. She placed the folder in her bag, took out her gloves and put them on, smoothing the leather over her fingers as she did so, then walked towards the front door, which Tom opened for her.

'I'll consult with my colleagues and let you know.' She nodded at Tom as she walked out. 'Thank you.'

As Tom closed the front door, he said to Ellen, 'Jumped up old maid, bet she's never had a bit of the old how's your father in her life!' He cackled as he moved a few steps up the stairs. 'You can come down now, Dad, she's gone,' he shouted.

A knock sounded on the front door. Ellen opened it.

'Forgot my umbrella ...'

'Oh!' Ellen gulped as she handed the umbrella to Miss Prentiss, afraid that Miss Prentiss may have heard Tom's remark.

'Going to see what the pigeons are thinking.' Tom nodded at Miss Prentiss.

***

Two weeks later Ellen returned from work to find her mother-in-law bubbling with excitement.

'A letter came for you and Tom today, looks official.' She handed the envelope to Ellen and hovered expectantly.

'Mam! It's from the agency. We've been approved!'

'Approved! Well, love, and so I should hope! Well, that's wonderful news! Does it say when we'll get her?'

Ellen frowned. 'Apparently, Miss Prentiss will be bringing baby tomorrow and hopes we'll have everything ready!'

Gladys beamed. 'Tomorrow! That's short notice, and a Saturday, too. Lucky, I got the layette ready.' She'd been busy unpicking old jumpers, carefully winding the woolen thread around the back of a chair to make hanks, then steaming out the kinks over a saucepan of boiling water. Her husband had sat patiently holding up the hanks in his hands as she wound them into the balls which would end up being reknitted into baby clothes.

'Can't wait for Tom to get home from work, he'll be so excited!' Ellen ran up the stairs to their bedroom. She'd been half afraid to do much in advance in case their application was refused. A secondhand cot occupied the narrow space beside their bed. In it two dozen freshly laundered utility nappies were stacked at one corner. A collection of baby clothes, of assorted colours, neatly folded, together with tiny nightgowns that she'd made from an old nightie she'd found in a jumble sale, were in a pile beside their bed. She took a quick look around, smoothed the cot cover and ran down the stairs.

'What else do we need, Mam? Miss Prentiss didn't tell us what to prepare.'

Her mother-in-law thought for a second. 'It'll be different from when Tom and Bert were babies.' She frowned. 'I breast-fed them, of course, but you won't be able to do that ...' Her brow darkened and her eyes reddened.

Ellen hastened to change the subject; her brother-in-law, Bert, had been killed at the very beginning of the war. 'So, I'll need baby bottles ...'

Gladys's head jerked up. 'Yes, and condensed milk ...I don't trust that milkman, I reckon he dilutes the milk he delivers ...'

Ellen thought about the milkman. He came around every day in his horse and cart, and poured milk into their waiting jugs. Now that she reflected, it did seem a little thin. No cream on top ...

'I'll run around to the shop and get bottles and tins of milk,' she said, going to the drawer in the sideboard where the food coupons were stored.

'Do that, love. I was thinking we might make Toad-in-the-Hole for dinner tonight.'

Ellen pictured the sausages in batter that her husband loved. 'Yes, Mam, good idea. Right, I'll go now, anything else we need for Baby?'

Gladys shook her head. 'Think we have everything.' She smiled at Ellen. 'It'll all work out well, Ellen, love.'

***

'What time is old dried prune Prentiss coming with Baby?' Tom asked.

'She didn't give a time, just said this morning.'

Gladys frowned. 'Well, if the mother is breastfeeding, then it will probably be after the ten o'clock feed. They keep to a rigid routine in those places.' She paused. 'Or maybe if the six o'clock feed was the last one, well, the baby will be hungry by ten o'clock. I'll put the kettle on.'

Ellen stared at her mother-in-law. She wondered how Gladys knew this, then she pictured a young mother having to relinquish her baby – give it the last feed – and suddenly she felt sick. The thought of giving up your baby ... she remembered the one time she'd got pregnant, and miscarried ... her husband's voice broke through her thoughts.

'So, I'll have time to help Dad clean out the pigeon houses ...'

Ellen started. 'No! Just wait, please, can't have you all dirty with pigeon poo ...' She took his hand.

'Okay, love.' He sighed and looked at the clock. 'Funny coming on a Saturday morning. I suppose she thought I'd be here and not at work. Lucky I'm on night shift today.'

Ellen jumped up when she heard the knock on the front door. 'This'll be her! Quick, get your dad, Tom.'

Tom remained motionless.

Ellen went to the front door, opened it and saw Miss Prentiss with a wrapped bundle in her arms. 'Come in Miss Prentiss.'

Tom stood. 'Good morning, Miss. I see you've brought our baby.'

She nodded, walked across the room, laid her bag on the table, turned towards Ellen and Tom, and slowly pulled the corner of the blanket away from the baby's face.

Tom stared.

Ellen looked at the tiny face, long black lashes rested on the brown cheeks. She saw a fuzz of black hair on the baby's head and took a step back. 'Oh! But she's, she's ...' Ellen stammered.

'I thought you would be ideal parents for this little fellow.' Miss Prentiss gave Ellen a look which Ellen thought almost malicious. She hesitated as Miss Prentiss held the baby out to her.

'It's a boy?' Ellen looked at Miss Prentiss.

'A boy? Great!' exclaimed Tom.

Gladys came to look, paused, then turned to Miss Prentiss. 'It's black.'

Miss Prentiss nodded. 'Yes. I got the impression you would welcome any baby into your family.'

Silence. Then the baby gave a little whimper.

'It's hungry,' Gladys stated. 'Poor little mite. We'd better feed him. Kettle's boiled. Obviously, no-one else is going to care for him.' She glowered at Miss Prentiss, who couldn't meet her gaze.

'So, you'll take him?' Miss Prentiss raised her head and looked at Ellen. 'The mother called him James.' She sniffed. 'No better than she should be.'

Tom's mouth opened and closed.

Feet could be heard on the stairs and Alfred burst into the room. 'So, we have grandson?' He wheezed.

'Yes,' muttered Tom. 'James, and he's black.'

Alfred stopped in his tracks.

'He's an innocent child, and we'll take him!' With a glare, Ellen took the baby from Miss Prentiss. 'Goodbye Miss Prentiss.'

'Er. There's paperwork to sign.' Freed from her burden, Miss Prentiss removed her gloves and pulled two sheets of paper from her bag.

'Get a pen, Tom. And ink.' Ellen nodded towards the side-board.

Tom fumbled in a drawer, found a fountain pen, opened a bottle of ink and placed them on the table.

With her free hand Ellen took the pen, filled it with ink and handed the pen to her husband. 'Where does he sign?'

Miss Prentiss indicated the dotted line. 'Just here.'

Tom had no idea what he was signing, but obeyed his wife.

'Blotting paper, Tom.'

Tom looked confused.

Ellen blew on his signature. 'It's alright, it's dry enough.' She thrust it at Miss Prentiss. 'Here you go. Tom, please show Miss Prentiss out.'

Miss Prentiss sniffed, took an envelope from her bag and held it out to Ellen. 'This is his birth certificate. You'll apply to the court for consent to adopt and then to the registry office to get a copy of the adoption certificate, showing you as the parents. And get a ration book for him.' She held her head high as she stalked out.

Ellen faced her husband as he returned. 'It's a baby and no-one wants him. Except us.' She strode to the kitchen. 'Is the kettle boiled, Mam?'

Tom stared after her. His father shrugged. 'Women,' he whispered.

Ellen stroked the baby's cheek and his eyes opened. 'He's beautiful,' she whispered, 'Look Mam.'

Her mother-in-law held out the bottle. 'Here you are love.'

***

A few weeks later Tom came home from work pushing an old pram.

'Look what I got from a mate at work,' he announced as he manoeuvred the bulky pram into the living room. 'You'll be able to take Jimmy for a walk now. And he can sleep in it downstairs during the day, save you running up and down the stairs all the time.' He grinned. 'I got a half bag of coal on my way, felt a bit silly pushing an empty pram.'

Ellen's eyes lit up, 'You were twice lucky. Thanks, love, how did you manage to get the coal?'

'I think the coalman felt sorry for me. He took a few pieces from different heaps.'

Ellen sighed. 'It'll help. This rationing is driving me crazy!'

'Nah, the war's nearly over, hopefully rationing won't be for much longer.' He took a few steps towards her.

'You're all black! Not now.' She smiled at him as he lifted the bag of coal out of the pram.

'I'll get Jimmy, it's nearly time for his feed. Then I'll give the pram a clean.'

They'd all adjusted to the routine of a baby in the house. Thank goodness the air raids seemed to have ceased and they no longer had to go outside in the middle of the night to the Anderson shelter that Tom and his father had built in the back garden.

Once the news got around about the coloured baby, neighbours and a few friends visited the Jones's – mostly the women, who oohed and aahed when they saw Jimmy, but privately shook their heads and wondered how it would all turn out.

'Bitten off more than she can chew,' one old neighbour predicted.

Her friend nodded sagely. 'Mor'n likely. Wouldn't take him on, meself.'

'Who do you reckon was the mother?' another chipped in. 'Could be that Maude Brown, she were cleaning out at Houndstone Camp while her mother were minding the kiddies, and her husband in some kind of prisoner of war camp ...'

'I blame them American soldiers that moved in there, wiv their cigarettes and nylons.'

'And chocolate ...'

'Over paid, over sexed and over here. That's what my old man said.'

***

Alfred Jones watched the neighbours leave, then turned to his wife. 'Suppose the old crones will be coming next.'

'Hush,' Gladys said. 'Don't call them that. They're my sisters.'

Alf snorted which set him coughing. 'Twins, hah, any good bits in them was divided between them, jumped up old bitches ...'

Sure enough, the next day they turned up, sighing and grumbling. 'Bus from Sherborne was late again,' Gertrude said.

'Late again, and that steep hill,' Beatrice chimed in. 'Now, show us your new little grandson, Glad, we heard he's ...' her voice trailed away.

Gladys called out to Ellen who was upstairs making the beds.

'Aunty Bea and Aunty Gert are here, Ellen, come to see Jimmy.'

Ellen came down the stairs, taking her time, and wondering what bitchy remarks they'd make.

'He's in the pram, asleep,' she said, coming into the room and pointing to the pram.

'Oooh, he's a lovely little chap,' Beatrice cooed as she peered into the pram.

'So good of you, Ellen, to adopt a black baby.' Gertrude said sanctimoniously.

'Yes, we give to the black babies in church every week,' Bea added, a pious expression on her face.

Ellen fumed inwardly. 'I'm about to go to the shops with him,' she said, going to the back door to retrieve her winter coat. 'Excuse me, Aunt Bea, I need to get to the sideboard for the ration books.'

***

Ellen took the ration books, tucked them under Jimmy's blanket and negotiated the pram out the front door and down the steps to the street.

She turned her face to the unexpected gleam of sunshine, feeling happy to be alive with a baby and a husband who was in a reserved occupation and had been spared from going to war.

She pushed the pram to the local shop. Mr Molan had a corner shop and sold everything except meat, bread, milk and fish. She stopped the pram outside and went in.

'Good afternoon, Mr Molan! Got a bit of cheese for me?'

He shook his head. 'Sorry. No cheese.' He smiled at her and whispered, 'Can let you have two ounces of butter though.'

Ellen's eyes lit up. 'Really? Thank you, Mr Molan.'

He held out his hand for the ration books. 'Heard you've got a baby now.'

'Yes, he's beautiful. How much is that?'

Ellen came out, tucked her things under the pram blanket, and turned to leave, just as a woman she didn't know, on her way into the shop paused beside the pram and looked in.

She gave a start, stared at Ellen, gave a bit of a snort, turned and opened the shop door.

Anger bubbling up inside her, Ellen pushed the pram back home, jolting the baby as she pulled the pram backwards up the steps to the house, and hoping the Aunts had gone.

'Snotty bitch!' she gasped when she got inside.

'Whatever's happened?' Gladys looked up from her knitting.

'A woman outside Molan's looked in the pram, saw Jimmy and gave me such a look! Snooty so-and-so! And after those awful Aunts! Sorry Mam, I know they're your sisters but they're nothing like you.'

Gladys put her knitting into the brightly coloured fabric bag beside her. 'Ah, love, don't mind them! Kettle's nearly boiled – sit down – I'll make you a nice cup of tea.'

Ellen took the baby from the pram and cuddled him. 'You're a beautiful boy, Jimmy,' she crooned, 'We all love you.'

When she told Tom later what had happened, he shrugged. 'Bound to happen, love. There are some people like that.' He sighed. 'Jimmy might have a few bumps ahead of him in life.'

Chapter Three – Jim

I don't remember much of my early life, until I was five,
nearly six. But I'll try to include all that I do recall. I'd been
at Junior school for a year by then. One lunch time a boy called
Nigel Morris, the school bully, approached me in the concrete
air-raid shelter – left over from the war years, and still in place
in the play-ground. So far, I'd managed to keep out of Nigel's
way. 'You're dirty,' he said, pointing to my legs clad in the
regulation grey shorts. 'See these?' he indicated his own skinny,
pale shins. 'Your legs are dirty. My dad said you're a nigger.'
He thrust his face into mine. 'We don't like dirty niggers,' he
sneered. I turned away, hoping to escape him but he shoved
me hard in my back and I fell onto the concrete. Struggling to
hold back my tears I scrambled up, my knees all scraped and
bleeding.

After school I went straight to the kitchen when I got home,
and filled the washing up bowl with cold water – we only had
cold water in the kitchen in those days – then took Nan's
scrubbing brush to my legs avoiding my scraped knees. Nan
called out from the living room – she was ironing, using the
flat iron heated on the range – 'What you doing, love?'

'I'm washing my legs, I fell over.'

I heard the thud as Nan replaced the iron.

'What happened?' She frowned at my foot in the sink and the
scrubbing brush in my hand.

'Nigel Morris said I was a dirty nigger, so I'm trying to wash off the brown.'

'The little devil! Don't you mind him, love. That's your natural colour. Now stop that scrubbing and let me look at your knees.'

But I was too upset. I took my foot out of the water and dried it on the towel which hung beside the sink. 'It's alright, Nan. I'll go and help Gramp feed the pigeons.' I pulled on my sock and shoe and tied the laces.

She muttered something and went back to her ironing.

Nan didn't seem too concerned, so I went out the back to see Gramp.

'Gramp! Am I dirty?'

Gramp put down the bag of seeds from which he'd been topping up the pigeons' feeding bowls and turned to me. 'What you mean?' he whispered, Gramp's voice had got worse over the years, since he'd been gassed in the first World War.

'A boy at school said I was dirty and a nigger.'

I saw Gramp's fists clench. I thought I heard him mutter, 'Miserable little tyke!'

'No, you're not!' He rasped out a few more words. 'Talk to yer dad tonight.'

I didn't know if he meant I should talk to Dad, or he would. Sometimes it was hard to understand what Gramp was saying.

***

After our dinner, Gramp beckoned Dad out the back. They were gone for some minutes then Dad came in and told me to come out back. My stomach flipped; Dad looked so serious.

'I must help Mam with the dishes.' I thought I must have done something wrong and tried to delay. But Dad gave Mam a look.

'It's alright, love, not much to do. You go and help your Da and Gramp.'

Anyway, once we got out the back by the pigeon houses, Dad gave me a stern look and said I'd probably have a lot of nasty people say horrible things to me, but to ignore them. 'Sticks and stones may break your bones, but words will never hurt you,' he said.

Gramp didn't look convinced; he butted in and muttered something.

'Anyways, I'm going to teach you how to stand up for yourself,' Dad continued, and raised his fists. 'I'm going to teach you how to box.'

I didn't like this at first, but every night after Dad came home from work and we'd had dinner, he took me out the back and taught me boxing. Mam sewed me a pair of leather gloves and stitched a bit of worn carpet on the back of each one. Dad would hold up an old cushion and tell me to punch it. He dodged around moving the cushion sideways, up and down, backwards and forwards fielding my blows.

Dad always repeated the same story: 'Used to be a boxer, back before the war – flyweight. Bloody Hitler ruined everything.'

He got me lifting old hessian bags filled with rocks, a bag in each hand and squatting. Gradually over the weeks, I got stronger. Mam used to laugh at the little bulges in my arms, 'Call these muscles?' she'd smile, pinching my arms. But it worked. I kept out of Nigel Morris's way for ages, but one day I found him with a small boy in the air raid shelter threatening him that if he didn't hand over his pocket money, he'd beat him up. In those days we used to get sixpence a week pocket money if we were lucky. I strolled over to Nigel and told him to leave the kid alone. Nigel fronted up to me, but I aimed a right hook at him, like Dad had taught me. He fell to the ground and the kid ran off. Nigel started to snivel. 'I'll tell me Dad about you,' he bawled, wiping bloody snot from his nose with the back of his hand.

'Do,' I replied. 'MY Dad's a boxer, he'll sort out your dad!' I felt strong saying these words.

'He's not your real dad, your mother was a whore!'

That floored me. The only hoar I knew was a hoar frost. A frost that resembled an old man's beard. 'Ha!' I said, 'Tell that to the troops!' The only reply I could think of. I strode out of the air-raid shelter hoping I looked more confident than I felt.

That night, when Dad began our training, I said to him, 'Dad, is Mam a hoar?'

Dad dropped his hands and glared. 'Where did you hear that?

'Nigel Morris said me mam was a hoar, and you weren't my real dad.'

The life seemed to go out of Dad. He turned to Gramp who was watching from the side lines. 'Hear that, Dad?'

Gramp shrugged. 'Better tell now, Son,' he whispered.

Dad led me over to a makeshift seat – a plank on two oil drums. 'Sit down, lad.'

I sat down and frowned at Dad.

'See, Jimmy, what happened was ...' his voice petered out. 'Maybe I should get your Ma to explain ...' He rose and went indoors. I stayed sitting, watching my favourite pigeon, Bessie, pecking at the grain. Then Dad came out again.

'Your Mam said to tell you ...'

I knew something bad was coming; a brick settled in my stomach.

'See, your real Mam couldn't look after you. So, Mam and I took you on.' His frown intensified. 'We loved you from the minute we first saw you. And we adopted you.' He must have seen my mystified look for he continued. 'That means, we took you on as our own child.' He patted my knee. 'We love you, Jimmy, you're our world. Nan and Gramp's as well.'

'But my real mum and dad?'

'Like I said, your real mum was very young and poor and couldn't look after you like we could ...'

'My real dad?'

Dad shuffled on the hard plank and scratched his head. 'We don't know about your real dad.' He went to put an arm around me, but I stood and walked away. I went to Bessie and picked her up. I stroked her and held her close. 'You're my favourite, Bessie,' I whispered. I looked up and saw Dad sitting with his head in his hands. I walked over to him, and put my hand on his head.

'Love you, Dad,' I said. We didn't usually say words like that in those days, but it was all I could think of to cheer him up.

He lifted his head and I could see the tears in his eyes. 'You're the best son a man could want,' he mumbled, and opened his arms. Reluctantly, I cuddled into him.

Gramp turned away and sniffled.

There and then I decided to find my real mum someday and look after her.

Chapter Four

A few months after this I came home to find Mam lying on the leather lounge in the living room, her hand on her stomach. She'd been a bit strange for a while, running out to the toilet to be sick and not fancying her dinner. That was alright though. She'd push her plate towards me. 'Maybe you can finish this, Jimmy.'

I was happy to oblige. But today was unusual. It wasn't like Mam to be lying down.

'You all right, Mam?' I said, on my way to the kitchen to see if Nan had made any of her special biscuits.

'Jimmy, love,' she said. 'Just come here a minute.'

I grabbed two of Nan's biscuits which were cooling on a tray and went back into the living room.

Mam patted the lounge. I sat at the end by her feet and crammed a biscuit into my mouth. I loved that old leather lounge. I used to sneak out the *John Bull*[1] magazines to look at the cartoons on the last few pages, then shuffle them back into the pile under the cushions, hoping that Gramp wouldn't notice. He kept them all in date order, he was very particular like that.

'Jimmy, dear, I've got some good news.'

I leapt up with excitement. 'We've won the pools!' I exclaimed. Every week Dad and Gramp did the football pools hoping to win the jackpot.

Mam laughed, 'Not this time, Jimmy! No, the good news is you'll be getting a new brother or sister soon.'

I stared at her and swallowed a lump of biscuit. It stuck in my throat and I coughed.

'It was a surprise after all these years.'

I saw her clench her teeth and make a face like she'd had a spoonful of cod liver oil.

'Jacky Turner in my class has a new sister and she was found under a gooseberry bush,' I mumbled through a mouthful of biscuit. 'But, Mam, we don't have a gooseberry bush in our garden.' A pity, I thought, as I liked gooseberry jam. I took a bite of the second biscuit.

Mam groaned and bent over. I didn't like the look of her. 'You okay, Mam?'

She nodded, but her face was all screwed up.

'Okay, Mam. I'd better help Gramp now.' I slid off the lounge and hurried out the back.

Gramp had Bessie in his arms stroking her. 'Go race morrow,' he whispered.

I understood he was trying to say that Bessie would be racing the next day – a Saturday.

This was exciting. Our pigeons would be put into wicker cages and loaded onto a special lorry which would take them to the starting point many miles away. Each bird would be released and the time of release noted. When the bird arrived home, we had to note the time and I would jump on my bike and pedal like the dickens to the official recording site.

Usually when this happened Gramp would get all misty eyed and tell me about how during the war pigeons were used to send messages to the front, and save many lives. He loved to tell me about the red London buses which were used in France to house the pigeons. 'They landed on a wire and a bell would ring and the soldier looking after them would get them and remove the cylinder containing the message and contact their commanding officer ...'

Gramp told me this so many times that I knew the story off by heart, so it didn't matter that he only managed to whisper half of it. I think he meant the Great War, but Dad said they used pigeons in the last war too.

I didn't pay much attention to what Mam said about a new baby. I still slept in Mam and Dad's bedroom, but on a narrow box with a feather mattress that Mam had made. The cot I'd been sleeping in had disappeared, probably to another relative, but now it had reappeared at the end of Mam and Dad's bed. It meant there was hardly any room to move. I had to climb over their bed to get to mine.

The next day, when I got up, Nan said 'Your Mam's gone to fetch the new baby.'

I nodded, not really interested, I was busy thinking about the pigeon race. But when dad came home from work, he changed from his work clothes – he worked in an aircraft factory – as soon as he came in, washed and went straight out again. I wondered what was the rush, but he came back a little later grinning from ear to ear, saying, 'We have a baby girl!'

Nan clapped her hands and turned to me. 'Hear that, Jimmy? You have a baby sister!' She turned to Dad, 'Both doing well?'

Dad nodded, picked me up and twirled me around. 'Hear, that, Son! You have a sister!'

'But we don't have a gooseberry bush!'

Dad burst out laughing. 'It was the stork,' he said.

Imagine a stork bringing me a little sister!

Well, you can see I was very innocent in those days.

Next day Mam came home with my sister. At least she looked better than a new born pigeon, but I didn't say so, everyone looked so pleased and excited. Mam held her out to me and I put my finger in the baby's hand and she grasped it. I couldn't stop a big grin spreading across my face.

'See, she loves you, Jimmy. What do you think we should call her?'

I thought about my favourite comic, *The Beano*. 'How about Minnie the Minx?'

Mam looked at Dad. He seemed doubtful. 'Minnie Jones? I was thinking Julie sounded nice. Julie Jones.'

'We'll have Jimmy and Minnie Julie,' Mam smiled.

I beamed.

After a few weeks Mam went back to working mornings and Nan looked after Minnie. Everyone said that I had a way with Minnie. When she was teething, I was the only one who could settle her. At least that's what they said, but looking back, perhaps they were just flattering me into minding her.

The next-door-neighbour's baby, Wendy, wasn't half as pretty as Minnie. Wendy always had a snotty nose and never stopped whinging and whining. Our Minnie had big blue eyes and was always gurgling and smiling. She liked the pigeons too.

Around this time Bessie didn't return from a racing flight. Sometimes a hawk would get them. Gramp told me the Nazi's had trained hawks to pick off the British carrier pigeons. 'Bastards,' he'd muttered. He got me a new young pigeon, Priscilla.

Nan had two sisters, twins. They lived in Sherborne a few miles away. They'd married two brothers, which was handy, I thought. I sometimes wondered how the brothers could tell them apart. Gertrude and Beatrice. Great Aunts Gert and Bea sometimes got the bus and came to visit Nan. I knew Gramp couldn't stand them.

'Come on, Jimmy,' he'd say to me. 'Got to clean the pigeon houses. Excuse us.' He'd nod to the aunts. The "excuse us" was said in what he thought was a posh accent, but with his breathlessness it came out more like "squeeze us" which I thought was hilarious. 'Skinny old bitches,' he'd wheeze, heading out the back.

I always had the feeling they looked down on Nan, perhaps because their husbands had a hardware business and were well off. At least compared to Nan. They sometimes brought their old clothes for us.

'Thought you might be able to wear these dresses, Glad,' Bea might say and Gerty would chime in, 'Yes, or Ellen.' Bea would smooth the material. 'They were expensive, you know. This is good quality.' One of them would sigh and say, 'Of course they're no longer in fashion.'

The other one would hastily interrupt, 'But alright for your everyday wear, Gladys, dear.' Knowing full well that they would be considered Sunday best in our house.

I could see Mam grit her teeth and thank them, but I knew the way they said it angered her. She usually made something with the material, a blouse for Nan or a dress for Minnie. Mam was brilliant at that kind of stuff.

When Minnie was about two, Gramp passed away. He just stood up one evening and announced, 'Feeling tired. Think I'll go to bed.' Then he dropped dead.

We were all in shock. Nan seemed to be in a daze and I could see Dad's bottom lip sometimes wobbled when Gramp's name came up. I didn't go to the funeral, young children didn't in those days. I stayed home to mind Minnie. People came back to the house after the funeral. Of course, the Great Aunts came with their husbands. This was the first time I'd met the husbands. They arrived in a car, which was unusual for us, but they didn't look very cheerful, well, they wouldn't be, having to live with Gert and Bea. But maybe it was their funeral faces.

We were all glad to see them go.

***

Dad kept up the boxing training, but only every few days instead of every day. I think he was getting tired.

I hadn't realised at the time that Gramp was dying. The gassing in the war must have worn out his lungs. I felt a bit guilty that I hadn't helped him with the pigeons as much as I should have, and I missed him. Missed seeing his eyes light up when I came home from school, missed his cheery croak asking what I'd I learnt that day.

Money was very tight after his funeral. It would have been hard for Dad to pay for even a simple funeral; I suspect they would have had to get a loan and pay it off every week. Some people took out an insurance policy for such an event.

Gramp must have had a small war pension, just walking out the back to the pigeon houses exhausted him. It was amazing he'd even lived this long, into his seventies. Probably Nan would have had a war widow's pension.

Dad moved my bed into Nan's room. They thought I'd be company for her. There was no electricity upstairs, we had to take candles to bed with us. I used to sit on my bed and look out the window, counting the number of lights that would come on in the few houses across the fields. The most I counted was ten. Now those fields are covered with houses.

Mam started working full time – she had a friend, we called her Aunty Joyce, her husband had been killed in the war and she had a young son and she looked after Minnie. I got the job of taking Min to Aunty Joyce on my way to school and fetching her on the way back. Nan had got to the point where she wasn't up to minding

Min; she had bad rheumatism and it was as much as she could do to cope with the house work.

There was little money for pigeon food either, so gradually the number of birds we had diminished, until only Priscilla was left. Mam made most of our clothes. She made me a bow tie in red, white and blue for Queen Elizabeth's coronation. The only thing I remember about it, apart from feeling stupid with the bow tie, was that Mam sewed red, white and blue wavy ribbon – she called it rick rack – around the bottom of one of Min's dresses. She looked so cute, holding my hand as I took her out to the street party.

---

1. John Bull This popular magazine was printed and published by Odhams Ltd and was made famous by Horatio Bottomley, (1860-1933) arguably one of the county's biggest fraudsters of his time. It started life as a penny weekly that was to become the UK's largest-selling magazine, boasting an alleged circulation of 1,350,000 on its front cover in 1916. Although highly patriotic, it took an anti-establishment stance, championing grievances of troops in World War I, even though this was illegal, under the opinionated Bottomley. In 1946, Odhams relaunched the magazine as a large format colour weekly. Its editorial strategy also changed, switching to emphasise fiction from the likes of famous authors including Agatha Christie, Nicholas Monsarrat, Alistair Maclean, J.B. Priestley and Neville Shute.

Chapter Five

One evening we were having our evening meal, when I noticed Minnie had put down her knife and fork and was staring at me, then at Mam and Dad and Nan, I think she must have been about five at the time.

'Mam,' she exclaimed. 'Jimmy's different.' She grasped one of my hands and held it against her own. 'See, Jimmy's hand is brown. My and yours are pale.' She pointed to Dad's eyes, then Mam's and Nan's. 'And all your eyes are blue and Jimmy's are brown.' She dropped my hand, jumped up from the table and went to the sideboard and standing on tip-toe, looked in the mirror.

'And my eyes are blue too!' She turned back to the table. 'And Jimmy's hair is dark and curly ...' She sat at the table, picked up her knife and fork and calmly continued eating.

Dad gave a gentle cough.

Min looked up. 'Brown eyes are nice and I like curly hair.' She smiled at me, as if to comfort me for being different.

Mam and Dad eyed each other. I could see they were thinking they would have to explain soon to Min about me being adopted. I'd actually forgotten about my idea to find my real mother and look after her, well, not really forgotten, just put it in the back of my mind as something to do when I grew up.

My colour had never been a big issue. Of course, I did get a few snide remarks but perhaps because I was good at sport and had a lot of friends, I was accepted for who I was. It had only been that

Nigel person years ago who'd been nasty to me. Looking back, perhaps word had got around that I was not to be messed with.

A few days after this, I went to meet Min from school and bring her home and she told me that Mam had explained how they'd picked me as being special and 'dopted me.

'I'm not special, Jim,' she said, mournfully, 'I think the stork just brought me, they didn't choose me.'

I squeezed her hand. 'You're extra special, Min, I remember the day Dad came home and said they had a baby girl, they were so excited!' I didn't want to explain about how the boys in my class had said babies were conceived – it sounded just too ridiculous.

Around this time there was a craze for Golliwog badges.[1] Robertson's Jams had a scheme where if you collected a certain number of labels from their jams and marmalades you could send off and get a golliwog badge. Min desperately wanted one, and eventually managed to collect enough for one. But sometime later it came loose from her shirt and was lost.

She was heartbroken. I tried to console her, saying I would try and barter for one with my prize marbles.

She stared at me, then came over to where I was sitting reading a comic. 'Thank you, Jim, but it's alright. I have my very own Golliwog.' She smiled, ruffled my hair and kissed my cheek.

It took me a few seconds to realise she meant me. *Did I really look like a Golliwog?* A round black face, big eyes and wide smile? I don't know how I felt ...

There was a bit of an uproar about these badges at some point, but they're now collectibles.

***

Just after this, when I was ten, I had to sit the Eleven Plus exam. This determined whether I would go to a Grammar school or a secondary modern. I didn't want to go to a Grammar School because I knew the uniform was expensive and I didn't think Mam and Dad would be able to afford it. Anyway, all my friends said they wanted to go to the Secondary Modern because it was mixed. Girls and boys. I liked that idea.

However, I passed the Eleven Plus and Mam said she might be able to get a second job to pay for the uniform, but instead I got a paper round that year to help. The owner of the paper shop seemed a bit reluctant at first to give me a job, but then he muttered, 'Well, it's dark early in the morning when you'll be delivering the papers, so no-one will see you.'

I kind of understood what he meant, but I didn't dwell on it. Mam got my school blazer three sizes too big. 'You'll grow into it,' she said. She stitched up the pockets so I couldn't put my hands in them. 'Only wear them down.' I had no idea what she meant.

Grammar School was okay. Mam and Dad were so proud of me. That made it all worthwhile. When I came home with my bulging satchel, Mam would clear a space at the table. 'Sit down here, love,' she'd say, 'Do your homework here.' As if I were some kind of special genius. I knew I wasn't – I had to work hard to keep up with the other boys in my class. But I was determined to do well – to make Mam and Dad's sacrifices worthwhile.

I've heard of coloured boys who suffered bullying at school, but that never happened to me. Probably because I was very tall and strong and I excelled at sport. Particularly cricket. The P.E. teacher said I might be good enough to play for Somerset when I was older. I did get called names occasionally. But then so did other boys. Anyone with the last name of White was always called

Chalky. Millers were Dusty. The Irish were Mick or Paddy and the Welsh, Taffy. It was rarely malicious.

At one match against a visiting school, one of their batsmen passed by me on his way to the stumps. 'Hey Sambo! You bowling?' He said it in a kind of sneering way.

I ignored him.

Happily, I bowled him out with my first ball.

However, it did make me think about my natural father. Of course, I'd learnt the facts of life and about genetics. One of my parents must have been black, and that had most likely been my father. The first time I heard about rape the thought crossed my mind that my birth mother may have been raped and that was why I'd been adopted. I couldn't stop thinking and worrying. There was no-one I felt able to talk to about it. But Dad must have noticed because one evening, he suggested we do a bit of sparring. I didn't feel like it, but agreed. When we got out the back and found our gloves, he turned to me and cleared his throat.

'Um, Son, I just wanted to mention a few things about growing up.' He mumbled this and his face went red with embarrassment.

I kept my head bent as I sat on the old makeshift plank and listened while he tried to tell me about the birds and the bees and how babies were born, and the bodily changes I would be experiencing. It all came out a bit jumbled.

'Mam and I have been worried about you lately,' he concluded.

I looked up.

'Mam thought you seemed a bit down. Is there anything worrying you?'

He looked so concerned that I just blurted it all out.

'Would my birth mother have been raped, and that's why I was adopted?'

He blinked and sat down next to me. It was a few minutes before he spoke.

'No. Definitely not. Your birth mother wanted you called James, so your Mam and I thought that must have been your father's name. She must have loved your father, or she wouldn't have asked that.' His voice got stronger. 'No. They must have loved each other. Definitely.'

I stared at him. He looked so earnest and I desperately wanted to believe him. I tried to smile.

'Thanks, Dad.'

'You're what's known as a love child.' He frowned and scratched his chin. 'I think that's what your Nan said you were, and she'd know.' He picked up the gloves. 'Feel like a bit of a round?'

I didn't, but thought it would get us over the awkwardness we both felt.

***

By this time Minnie was about eight years old and followed me everywhere. She would kneel on a chair beside me at the table when I was doing my homework, leaning towards me with her elbows on the table and breathing heavily over my text books. 'What you doing, Jimmy?' she'd ask and I'd have to stop and say, 'It's physics, Min. You'll have to wait until you go to secondary school to learn about it.'

'I want to learn now,' she'd pout. She'd already started Primary school.

So, I taught her. Actually, it helped me, because, when I tried to explain everything to her, it began to settle in my brain, but I was astounded at how she seemed to absorb everything so quickly. One evening doing maths homework – quadratic equations – I couldn't figure it out. She leaned over and pointed to an equation. 'See that,' she said, and went on to solve it. I don't know how I felt – a combination of awe and defeat. How could an eight-year-old be so bright? And did that mean I was stupid?

I managed to mutter 'Well done, Min!' and she sat back in her chair beaming.

Just looking at her beautiful face and that smile ... I loved her. 'You're a genius, Min,' I said.

'What's a genius?' she asked. 'Is it like Aladin and a genie comes out of a bottle?'

Mam had taken us to the Pantomime that year when Aladin was on, and Minnie had been enthralled.

I laughed. 'No, it means you're a clever girl!'

She grinned. 'I like these 'quations, Jimmy, can we do some more?'

Min had been at school a couple of years by this time and I had to fetch her from the Infants school on my way back from the Grammar school. I would see her waiting outside the school gates, shifting from foot to foot until she spotted me. We would walk home and she'd tell me all about her day.

I somehow sensed that school was hard for her. She was so bright, way ahead of the other kids in her class.

One day I could see her eyes were red, she'd been crying. 'What's up Min?'

'Nothing, Jim,' she replied. Then started crying in earnest. 'Oh, Jim, they hate me, say I'm a know-it-all!'

I squeezed her hand. 'It's just because you're so clever, Min,' I reassured her, 'Maybe just stay quiet for a bit, you know, don't say you have the answers to everything.'

Min nodded. 'I knew you'd know what to do, Jim,' she snivelled.

Of course, my chest swelled with pride. I caught her hand. 'Come on, Min, let's see what Priscilla is doing.' We raced home.

***

My first wife, Alison, once said to me, 'Weren't you jealous of Min? After all she was your parent's biological child.'

Her words hurt me, but I never felt jealous of Min. Mam and Dad gave me so much love – it brings a lump to my throat to think of them now, all these years later – and Min was such a beautiful child, not a bad bone in her body. Well, she was like that all her life.

Instead of getting their own Council house, Mam and Dad stayed on in Gramp's. I found a labouring job for the school holidays when I was fourteen. All the boxing and weight training had paid off, I was very strong, and had grown tall. Taller than Dad even. The foreman at the concrete works near us was happy to have me pushing full barrels of sand and gravel to the mixers. That was in the days before things got automated.

Because I was working, Mam took Minnie to the public library to help carry our books. It had been my job up until then. I think at the time an adult was allowed to take out two or maybe three books, but Mam had library tickets for her brother that lived in London – we hardly ever saw him – as well as Nan and Gramps, so that meant we could borrow ten books, fourteen with my and Min's junior tickets.

Often Mam brought back books that Nan and Dad had already read, which was why we had to get a good selection.

It's hard to imagine today, but back then, especially in the winter, most nights we would read. The radio might be on, Nan would be knitting, and Mam doing piece work, hand sewing gloves for what would be considered slave wages now. Nan could knit and read at the same time – as long as it wasn't a complicated knitting pattern. You knew when she found the book enthralling, because all of a sudden, she'd stop, look at her knitting, mutter and start unpicking her last few rows. Books were an important part of our lives.

Of course, the library became Min's second home. In the school holidays after she'd helped Mam, she'd make a bee line to the library, and spend hours there. A reading room and museum occupied the floor above the library.

'It's not fair, Jim,' she complained to me, 'I'm not old enough to go into the reading room, but I can see it's mostly old men falling asleep over the newspapers.'

'I think they might go there to be warm,' I'd replied.

'Hmm, maybe, but I've found a place where I can read, it's in a corner where there's a door, with a door mat. I hide there and sit on the mat with the books the librarian said I'm too young to borrow,' she hardly paused for breath, then continued, 'And Jim, have you been to the museum?'

'A couple of times.'

'Did you notice the tessellated Roman pavements from the Fosse way?'

I had to admit, I hadn't. That kind of thing didn't interest me, but Min rambled on about how the Romans had invaded Britain and built a road going from Lincoln to Exeter which passed through Yeovil. She got more and more excited as she told me all about it.

'And people have found old Roman coins in their gardens along the road.'

That piqued my interest – they could be valuable, maybe I'd start helping Dad digging the garden ...

***

One afternoon I got home from school and the great aunts were there, Nan bustled around laying out the best china, rummaging in the sideboard for linen napkins, while Gert and Bea were billing and cooing over Min.

'Oh! Here comes your little grandson, Glad!' Gert said with a false smile. 'But he's not little anymore!'

Bea nodded. 'What do you want to be when you grow up, James?'

They always called me that.

'A coal man?' Gert smirked. Or it may have been Bea. They looked so alike.

My mind whirled. I knew what she meant. Coal men shovel coal into hessian sacks, hoist them on their leather-clad shoulders and up into a cart, ready to deliver to customers. They usually had a film of coal dust covering them. Black faces.

Nan paused in setting the table and frowned.

'A fitter, like Dad,' I replied.

I saw Nan relax.

'What about you, Minnie?' The other great aunt asked.

Min was busy writing something in an exercise book, her little tongue poking out between her lips in a way that I loved. She looked up. 'I'm going to marry Jim,' she announced. And continued writing.

Gert sniggered and Bea laughed sardonically.

'You can't marry Jim, he's your brother,' they chimed.

'And anyway, he's ....' Gert's voice trailed off. I thought I heard her say, "a half-caste". I'd been called that a couple of times, but when I looked it up in the dictionary it said it meant the child of parents from different races. Well, I supposed I was.

Nan plonked a cake plate on the table. 'I got a Battenburg cake, would you like a piece, Jimmy?'

I could sense the atmosphere was tense but I didn't know why. And I loved Battenburg cake, but it wasn't like Nan to offer me a piece before the aunts.

Min looked up. 'I'm going to marry Jim, whatever you think.' Her chin jutted out and her mouth set in a hard line. She glared at the aunts.

I felt like dropping through the floor. But while everyone looked at Min, I quickly took another piece of cake. Min must have noticed as she gave me a mischievous look, and I thought she winked.

---

1. https://www.golliwogg.co.uk/robertsons.htm

Chapter Six – HMS Ganges

I was fifteen when the Royal Navy recruitment office came to our school to encourage boys to join up. It sounded attractive. It would be a secure job and not only would I be able to help Mam and Dad, but I'd learn a trade. I took the application form home and thought about it. One of the boys in my class said he was going to join up. It sounded great. I'd be able to have an education, a career and all for free! I was excited at the pictures they showed of the ships and the places where they went.

Dad was all for it, when I showed him the forms. Because I was under eighteen, he had to sign to give his consent. 'You'll fly through it!' he said, which I found funny as I wanted to join the Fleet Air Arm.

I had to go to Exeter for the interview and the tests. If you don't know, Exeter is quite a long way from Yeovil. I had to get the train, then sit for the Navy tests – maths and English – and return home the same day. To my surprise, Dad was right. I passed them all, and Mr Lester from the cement works gave me a great reference. I think Mrs Lester probably wrote it and got her husband to sign it.

The men in the recruitment office were so nice – friendly and welcoming.

On the application form I had to sign which branch of the Navy I wanted to join. I chose the Fleet Air Arm.

The whirring chop chop sound of helicopter blades had been background noise all my life. Westland Aircraft – as it was then – would be testing choppers and the Fleet Air Arm would be training crew and pilots. I would look up and try and identify the different aircraft. Wessex, Scout, and Wasp were some that I could spot. I'd sometimes cycle to the aerodrome to watch them. I yearned to fly in one, even to be a pilot, but I knew this would be out of the question for me – unless – unless I joined the Fleet Air Arm.

I had to explain to Min that the Fleet was the Royal Navy and the Air Arm the branch that had aircraft helping them.

I went to Bristol on the train for the medical, it took hours, by bus and train, crazy now I think about it. I also passed that part. Some weeks later I received a travel voucher to go again to Exeter on the train and meet up with some other boys to go to HMS Ganges at Shotley in Suffolk.

Min wanted to know all about what I would be doing. 'Will you write and tell me, Jim?'

'Of course,' I replied.

'And I'll write to you,' she declared with that pious look she had in those days.

I managed to get to Exeter station and meet the three other boys bound for Ganges. One was a right ass-hole, excuse me for saying it, but he thought he knew it all. For some reason he had the travel passes for all of us. When we got to London, we couldn't find him anywhere, and I couldn't see the other boys either, so I made my own way to Shotley. I told the ticket inspectors what had happened and they were very helpful. I said I was on my way to join the Royal Navy at HMS Ganges. They seemed quite sympathetic but maybe that was my imagination. They probably pitied me ...

What a shock when the bus which picked us up at the station stopped outside what looked like the pictures that I'd seen of concentration camps in the war.

One of the boys, he was called Alf, pointed at the towering ship's mast in the grounds. 'We have to climb that,' he said, looking smug. 'Me bruvver was here last year and he told me about it.'

Aghast, I stared at it – a replica of a war ship mast – that each boy at Ganges was required to ascend, at least once, to the top; a height of sixty feet.[1]

Alf continued, 'Youse 'ave to climb by the inclined ratlines to a point near where the lowest yard crosses the mast, that's where youse must transfer to the outward leaning futtock shrouds to reach the edge of the platform. It sticks out ten feet from the mast.' He smiled at our reaction. 'Then, once there you've got to drag yourselves up and over the "devil's elbow".'

I thought he was making this up. I'd never heard of things like ratlines and buttons, not to mention "futtock shroud", it sounded quite rude to me. I had no idea what all those names meant. I just smiled at the time, but I later discovered that was exactly what we had to do.

The man in charge turned out to be so different from the friendly men in the recruitment office. As we got off the bus, some of the boys were crying.

'Oh dear,' said the chief, sympathetically, 'Would you like a cup of tea?'

'Yes please,' sniffled one of the lads.

'Only joking,' said the chief, with a sardonic smile. Then he shouted, 'Wipe yer bloody eyes and foller me!' And marched through the gates.

'Now, lads,' he continued, 'First thing to do ... send a card home to mummy! It stops her ringing up to see if her little Jimmy has arrived in one piece!'

I really thought he meant me, but it seemed the name, Jimmy, applied to all of us boys.

We had to line up to get our hair cut – it was shaved up to where our RN caps would sit, pushed down to our ears. I had a picture of Min's face if she could see my golliwog curls falling under the barber's clippers.

Next, we got in line for our kit – jumpers, shirts, pants – the whole kit and kaboodle – all tried on behind a low curtain separating us from the women handing them out.

Then to our quarters. Mine was Benbow. This was to be our squad. A dormitory holding fifty-two beds. Each bed had a locker and our kit had to be folded and stored in the regulation way. We did all our own laundry. Fortunately, I'd watched Nan and Mam do the washing and had helped by turning the mangle, so I knew how to wash my own clothes, but some of the lads had no idea. I could feel myself getting a bit homesick as I recalled how Mam and Nan prepared for house work. They would take a square headscarf, fold it in two to make a triangle, place it on their heads with the point of the triangle over their brow, and the back on the nape of their necks. They took the ends over their ears, tied a knot over the triangle and tucked the point of the triangle into the knot. Aprons fastened and they were ready for action! I squeezed my eyes tight to stop any evidence of my emotions.

We each had a little suitcase to hold our personal items The first thing I did was to write to Min and tell her I'd arrived safely and it was all very exciting and I was loving it. Total lies of course, but Min would have been devastated if I told her that the food was awful, that I had to sleep in a long dormitory full of snoring and farting boys, that the training was brutal, marching, learning to shoot, swim and box. And embroider our names on our kit! I thought she'd smile picturing me trying to thread a needle. It was lucky, I told her, that Dad had taught me to box as I was quite the star in the ring.

I received a reply by return of post.

Dear Jim

Thank you for your letter. I am well. Mam and Dad are well and Nan.

Priscilla is well.

I am starting at Grammar school next week.

I miss you, Jim.

Love from

Your devoted sister, Minnie Jones

I had to laugh; it was so Min. I can reproduce it here as I've kept all her letters. Many years later Min told me she'd kept all of mine ...

Looking back, I can see that Ganges made a man of me, taught me how to look after myself. Disciplined me. Even little things, like polishing the brass buckles on our belts. For training, the belts were green; for formal parades we had white belts and webbing – that would be gaiters to the lay man. We had to keep the brass polish off the white belts! Spit and polish our boots. It all seemed normal in those days. Of course, I didn't tell Min those little details, only told her the interesting, exciting parts, like the weekend we had to go to Wicken Fen and clean out the waterways, canals really. It was early March and freezing cold. My toes and fingers had chilblains – it was misery. But I made it sound fun for Min. She wanted to know why Ganges was called HMS – Her Majesty's Ship – Ganges, although it was on dry land and not a ship. I had to confess that I didn't know either.

At Christmas, I had three weeks leave. It was good getting off the train and being back in familiar surroundings, but although everything about the town looked the same, it seemed different. Like me I suppose. I walked from the station up to Gramps – I still thought of it as Gramps – even though he'd been gone for a few years.

Min threw her arms around me, 'Jim! I've missed you so much.'

I gave her a hug. School hadn't yet broken up for the Christmas holidays, so she was still in her uniform. I held her out from me. 'Min! You've grown up!'

She grinned.

'How do you like Grammar school?'

'Love it, Jim!'

I could understand that, Min was so clever – way ahead of me. Grammar school would suit her.

***

After Christmas our training resumed. Some of the instructors were pretty brutal. One day we were practicing shooting with SLR 7.62 rifles. These weigh over four kilograms, nearly nine pounds. Quite heavy and awkward for a fifteen-year-old to hold up – and some of the boys were pretty puny. I'd buddied up – as they call it now – with one boy, Brian Jackson. He came from a poor family, I forget the details, but it seemed he'd not been well nourished as a child. When he couldn't hold his rifle up, the instructor kicked him with his hobnail boots. I saw it all. The instructor glared at me as if daring me to say anything. Perhaps because I was big and strong for my age, and the boxing star, they didn't pick on me. But I felt for Brian. Don't know how he stuck it really.

Some of the boys ran away; I felt like it at times, but I would never let Mam and Dad down, and I would have felt ashamed to have gone back to school as a loser.

And so it went on. When I'd joined, I'd passed the exams with full marks and it was suggested I join the Aircraft Radio and Radar section. I enjoyed this part of the training.

One weekend we were taken on a tugboat to Holland. It took twelve hours, rocking around on the rough sea, all I can remember is being sick, along with most of the others. I suppose to get us used to life on the ocean.

I managed to get through that year, I achieved climbing the mast, which terrified me – I have no head for heights. Even watching the boy climbing the mast right to the top and standing on the button[2] made me feel weak.

Our passing out parade day arrived. Dad and eleven-year-old Min came – Mam had to stay at home with Nan who wasn't well. In fact, she passed away a few days later.

It was lovely to see them. Out of the corner of my eye as we marched, I could see Min clasping Dad's hand, then she waved at me! Naturally I couldn't respond! I didn't know how she could have picked me out from all the other boys, but of course! I was the only coloured one and the tallest!

The parade finished and I had to pack and get ready for the next stage – HMS Ariel – no time to chat with Dad and Min.

Years later Min told me that that day had been the turning point in her life, when she knew …

---

1. Climbing the mast: https://youtu.be/mkmADkG13XU?si=-7 PKtd_GEsmmAnem

2. The button was a twelve-inch circular piece of timber which held the rigging for the sailing ship. It was the topmost part of the rig. Button boys were paid one shilling to climb to the top and stand to attention.

Chapter Seven - HMS Ariel

A bus took us from Shotley to Lee-on-Solent where us Radio and Radar lads would complete the next stage of our training. This was more interesting, learning about radar and electronics and all the complicated electrical stuff. But nothing interesting I could tell Min. Although, come to think of it she would have picked up all that electronic stuff faster than I did.

HMS Ariel was much like Ganges, but not so gruelling – or maybe I'd just got used to the discipline. It sounds as if Ariel was a ship, but it was a training base on land.

When I went home after the training, everything was different. No Nan. I had missed her funeral - we didn't get compassionate leave in those days – so I kept expecting to see her busy with the old flat iron, and I'd be overwhelmed with grief. That was bad enough but I'd found a changed Min. She had her hair scraped into a ponytail and wore glasses. National Health thick black rimmed ugly things. Of course, these days they're fashionable, but she looked like a startled owl.

'Min!' I said, 'What have you done to your hair?'

'Oh, Jim, this is so much better, it saves on having to get my hair cut, and it keeps it out of my eyes.'

'And the glasses?'

'I'm short-sighted, Jim, and these glasses are fine.'

'I'll pay for nice frames, Min.'

'I told you; these are fine.'

She turned away and gathered up her text books, not looking me in the eye. 'Got to study.' She spread her textbooks on a corner of the dining room table.

I sighed. Min had taken over Nan's bedroom, and I now had to sleep on the slippery old leather settee in the living room. At least Gramp's *John Bull* magazines had somehow disappeared and the cushions were about the same level, but many years of bums on the seats had given it a distinct slope towards the edge.

I began to feel that I no longer fitted into this family. Of course, Mam and Dad were the same, welcoming me and wanting to know all about HMS Ariel. But Min seemed reserved towards me.

The next day, something woke me early – the settee wasn't really comfortable enough for a good sleep. You'd think after the hard bunks at HMS Ariel, the settee would be bliss, but I kept sliding off. In the end I raised the edges by wedging some clothes underneath.

In the morning gloom I could make out Min creeping through the living room and into the kitchen.

'What're you doing, Min?' I whispered. I saw her jump and pause.

'Just making a cup of tea, Jim. Want one?'

'Yeah, thanks. Why are you up so early?'

'Studying.'

She disappeared into the kitchen and I could hear her lighting the gas under the kettle. I lay back and wondered about her.

Five minutes later she appeared with two cups and saucers. She placed one on the dining room table and held the other out to me. I raised myself onto one elbow and took the cup and saucer.

'Not used to fancy saucers.' I tried to joke. Now that dawn was breaking, I could see that her hair was loose around her face, and she didn't have her glasses on. She looked like my old Min, her curls surrounding her lovely face and no owl spectacles. But she fumbled for them and quickly positioned the arms over her ears.

'I can see you now, Jim.' She smiled.

'Is your vision really that bad?'

She shrugged. 'Mam said it was from reading books under the blankets with a torch when I was young.'

'You're still young, Min. What are you now? Thirteen nearly fourteen?'

She nodded.

'Got a boyfriend?'

'Don't be silly, Jim!' She tossed her head and scoffed. 'What about you? A girlfriend?'

I laughed. 'Girl in every port, Min, you know what they say about sailors.' Not that I'd actually been to sea at that point. I saw her frown and quickly said, 'No one special. You're my best girl, Min.'

She actually blushed and fumbled with her books. 'Got to study now.'

'Why? Min, you're so clever, learning comes easily to you, not like me.'

She pushed her glasses up her nose, took an elastic band from her wrist, gathered her hair and formed a pony tail. The surprised owl look returned.

'I want to get a scholarship,' she muttered, opening a text book and starting to read.

'Hey! Let me put the light on, no wonder you're half blind, trying to read in this light!'

'I can see okay.' We were all conscious of not wasting electricity in those days.

She stared at her text book, avoiding my eyes. I finished my cup of tea, leaned over, put the cup and saucer on the table and lay back on the settee, watching her. I must have dozed off as the next thing I knew, Mam was asking what I'd like for breakfast.

***

Mam and Dad wanted to hear all about my time on HMS Ariel and what I'd be doing next. I told them I'd be stationed at Yeovilton and carrying on with studying and training. They were thrilled to think I'd be nearby. But I didn't get home that often. A bus took us into Yeovil to the Technical College where we studied electronics one day a week and two nights. I found it difficult – lots of mathematics, which didn't come naturally to me. I wished Min were there to help me, she would have loved all that stuff.

Chapter Eight - The Ark Royal

W ell, the next thing I knew, after taking the Institute of Electrical Engineers exams – for which I only just managed to scrape a pass mark – I got an overseas posting on the newly built aircraft carrier, the Ark Royal. The Ark Royal had been famous during WW2 but had been torpedoed on 13th November 1941 by the German submarine U-81 and sank the following day. At twenty years old I was proud to be part of her new team and excited to be visiting places like Aden in Yemen and Bergen in Norway.

It was the first time at sea for a lot of boys. Some had gone partying the night before and were late starting their first post and cautioned. It was strange being in this huge vessel, narrow gangways, metal stairs, and hard bunks. I was afraid I'd get lost. And it was all so noisy! The flight deck was amazing, with the jets lined up ready for take-off. Each time a jet returns from a flight it is towed to the turn table and a lift lowers it into the hanger below. Everything must be checked and signed off. Fuel, oil, electrics, radar, radio, and a heap of other things, all done at top speed. No time to waste between flights.

An aircraft carrier flight deck is one of the most exhilarating and dangerous work environments in the world (not to mention one of the loudest). When the crew is in full swing, planes are landing and taking off at a furious rate in a limited space. One careless moment, and a fighter jet engine could suck somebody in or blast somebody off the edge of the deck into the ocean. For those who had to run under an aircraft to mechanically attach a catapult prior to launch the task was almost suicidal. They had to cope with an aircraft loaded with bombs, engines going full speed, propellers whirling just above, flames from the exhausts and jet engines. It's equally hazardous for the pilots having to take off and land on such a short runway.

The noise in the hangars when a jet is landing is unbelievable. Like the end of the world.

I had to write and tell Min all about the catapults used to launch the fighter aircraft, and the arrester wires, and how a fighter plane has a hook at the back which the pilot lowers when coming in to land. He has to align this hook with the cables which stretch across the runway. When the plane hooks onto them it would slow the aircraft down so it could land on the short runway – an art which only experienced pilots could manage. Of course I didn't tell her about how dangerous it was.

But somehow our letter writing had reduced. I think she was busy studying and I was absorbed by all my new experiences. I did tell her about how we ate – we each had a steel tray in the canteen with depressions for the food. You'd queue up and get your main course and dessert on the tray. However, if it was a rough passage, your dessert might end up with gravy on it and your dinner covered in custard! I thought she'd find that funny.

***

The high light for me was visiting Freemantle in Australia on the Ark Royal. We were there for three weeks, and the first time we were allowed ashore I went to a local pub with a few mates. I sat nursing my pint – pathetic stuff compared to British beer and they drink it freezing cold – when I noticed this blonde girl, sitting with a group of other girls; they all had this beehive hair style, well except for this one girl. Apparently, it was a sixties thing, so Alison told me later. She demonstrated it once, somehow holding a clump of hair and combing it backwards towards her scalp until it stood on end all tangled up then lacquer it to stay high. I thought it looked awful. Back combing didn't work with her hair, apparently. Anyway, with her blond curls and no beehive, Alison stood out from the rest of the girls. I couldn't take my eyes off her. I could see her glancing over at me, but I thought it was because of my colour. I quickly averted my gaze, but every time I glanced her way, she was looking at me. One of the lads nudged me.

'See the blond with the curls, Jim?'

I nodded.

'She keeps looking at you. Go and ask her if you can buy her a drink.'

Being used to people staring at me, I hesitated, but he nudged me again.

'Nothing to lose, Jim, she can only say, no!' I was actually quite shy, so reluctantly I took a deep breath and edged around the lads towards her.

'Can I buy you a drink?' I managed to mumble as I got close. She held up a glass and grinned.

'Got my poison.' She indicated a seat beside her. The other girls shuffled along to make room for me.

'I'm Jim,' I said, for the first time grateful for my dark skin which hid the heat I could feel rising in my face.

'Alison,' she said, fluttering her eyelashes.

A warm glow spread through me. Of course, much later I realized that the initial attraction was because of her likeness to Min. The delicate features and blond curls.

I didn't know what to say after that, but she took the lead. 'Want to dance?'

Now, I have never been a dancer, but I took a swig of my pint, set it down on the table, and clasped her outstretched hand.

On the crowded dance floor, I hoped she wouldn't notice that I only shuffled around, taking her hand whenever she held it out to me. "Twist and Shout" – the Beatles song at the time was all we needed.

We met every day I had shore leave, and things were getting pretty hot between us.

The last day came and her eyes brimmed with tears. 'I'm going to miss you, Jimmy, will you write to me?'

Of course, I felt the same way. We exchanged addresses. I'm not much of a letter writer so over the months the frequency of our letters gradually diminished, and I didn't spend as much time dreaming about her.

I was very occupied with work, and a new Ark Royal posting, in 1966, to Mozambique. I'd also met another girl. She didn't turn me on like Alison did, but she was nice to meet up with on a foursome with my mates. I sometimes thought girls only wanted to date me to show how daring they were and to annoy their parents.

Around this time Min got a scholarship to Cambridge. Mam and Dad were over the moon, but it meant they didn't see so much of her as she soon found a part time job there, tutoring, so not to be a burden on Mam and Dad.

Chapter Nine - Alison

A couple of years later, out of the blue I got a letter from Alison saying that she was coming to England. It seemed to be a rite of passage for Aussies in those days to spend a year or so working in England and seeing the world. She said she'd be staying in London with two other Australian girls and sent me the address and phone number, saying she'd love to catch up with me.

As I didn't have a steady girl-friend at the time I was thrilled. I managed to get a long weekend off and went to London to meet her. Apart from the time I'd gone to Ganges – and that was only changing trains – I'd never been to London. I had to ask Alison how to find her place and how to get the tube.

Since I'd seen her last, I'd applied for permission to grow a beard and it had been granted. I know! You had to ask permission both to grow and shave off a beard. Sounds weird these days but it was the rule. I think it may still be, and permission can be refused if a beard might endanger your life, for example when wearing a diving or gas mask.

I was quite proud of mine. I kept it trimmed and within the regulation 25mm. I hoped Alison would like it. We weren't allowed the so-called "designer stubble", or a scrappy beard of uneven length, or "handlebar" moustaches – not that I would! Also, the beard must not take an excessive time to grow, that is over two weeks.

Anyway, when she opened the door of the flat, she did a double take. Of course, she'd never seen me with a beard and wearing civvies.

'Oh Jim! It's you! Come on in. You remember Clare? You would have met her in Freo.'

I had no memory of Clare and where was Freo? They must have seen my puzzled look as Clare said, 'Freo – Fremantle, and you and Alison were so wrapped up in each other that you probably didn't even notice me.'

I grinned and nodded, 'Now I remember you!'

'Well, welcome, good to meet up again. Jayne's at work at the moment.' She glanced at her watch. 'Should be back in another hour.' She winked at me. 'You're welcome to stay here, if you don't mind sleeping on the couch.' She nodded to a corner of the room.

I looked at the big old sofa. It had a few blankets covering it and a cushion at each end.

'Looks comfy,' I said. 'Thanks. I hadn't thought about where to stay.'

Clare laughed. 'Well, I'd better get going, I start work soon.'

'Clare works in a hair-dressers,' Alison said. 'Notice my hair?'

I stared at her hair which was now a kind of gingery colour and wavy instead of curly.

'Um, yes, very nice.'

'You don't think so, really, do you?'

I shook my head. 'I loved it the way it was.'

Alison looked at her watch. 'Nearly lunch time, are you hungry, Jim?'

I nodded.

'Sausage, bacon and eggs?'

'Great, thanks, that would be lovely.'

Clare looked at us both and smiled. 'Well, I'm off now, see you later, Jim.'

At last, we were alone. Alison threw her arms around me. 'So good to see you, Jim!' She pulled away.

'This is my room.'

I was a bit surprised at how quickly she'd taken me into her bedroom. Not that I was unwilling, mind you. But I was a bit peckish and would have relished the fry up first.

***

Whenever I had time off – not very often as I was enrolled in an intensive training course at the time – Alison managed to arrange her shifts to coincide with mine and I went up to London to see her, so I didn't get to see much of Mam and Dad. It must have been hard for them with neither Min nor I at home, but I didn't think much about it at the time.

Whenever I met up with Alison, we seemed to spend the days in bed and the evenings out dancing. On a few occasions we went to the bar where she worked and it seemed like the men were all over her. Maybe I was extra sensitive – I can't put it into words – but I thought the looks they gave me said "what does she see in that bloke?".

I was obsessed with Alison, and she appeared to feel the same. When I was away at sea, I kept wondering what she was doing, was she out dancing with other men? Inviting them back to her room? I once asked her about her previous boyfriends in Australia, but she only laughed and made some throwaway comment, and asked me about my girlfriends. 'Nothing serious,' I told her.

When the time came for her to return to Australia, I knew I couldn't live without her. I'd got the London train as usual, although it was a bit of a trek, and I arrived at her flat in the afternoon. She had to work that night but I wanted to catch her before she left for the pub.

I knocked on the door and heard her voice say 'Who is it?'

'It's me, Jim.'

She opened the door wearing only a nightie. I suppose you'd call it a negligée these days. Of course, you can guess my reaction. I pulled her to me, my voice husky with desire. 'Alison,' I managed to say, 'Will you marry me?' I hadn't planned on saying that, it just came out.

She drew back slightly and looked at me. 'Really?'

'Yes!'

She smiled. 'Maybe, Jim.'

Well, I was over the moon. I tried to lead her to her room, my only mission to get her to the bed.

'Hold on a minute. I have to go back to Freo in two days' time,' she murmured. 'How will we manage to get married?'

'I'll try and get leave and fly out to Australia.'

She looked dubious. 'Maybe.'

'What do you mean, *maybe?*'

She shrugged. 'TRY and get leave?'

I held her tight. 'As soon as I get back, I'll organize things.' Then I had a better idea. 'Or you stay here longer and we can get married here!'

She thought for a moment, before pulling away. 'My mum and dad are expecting me and anyway they'd want to be at my wedding.'

Then the tears started. She walked towards her room. 'It's all too hard, Jim.'

'Let's lie down and think about it.' I followed her into her room, eager to get her into bed. Her room was pretty basic anyway, only a single bed, a wardrobe, bedside table and one chair.

I lay down and held out my arms. She snuggled into me ...

Eventually we agreed she would go home as planned and organize a wedding and I'd fly out. We hadn't discussed what would happen after that.

'Maybe you could transfer to the Australian Navy,' she remarked as I kissed her goodbye.

***

When I told Mam and Dad that I was getting married to an Australian woman, they stared blank-faced at me. We were in the living room. I was unsure quite what to say, so just came out with it.

'Who is she?' Mam managed to ask, putting down her cup of tea.

I couldn't meet her eyes. 'She's a girl I met when we were docked at Fremantle a few years ago. We kept in touch and then she came to England a couple of years later on a working holiday.'

'I should have brought her down to meet you,' I looked up and muttered. 'But what with my training courses and postings, well it didn't work out.' I didn't want to confess that the real reason I hadn't was that at her flat in London we could make love. That would have been impossible at Mam and Dad's place. 'She's going back to Australia and I don't want to lose her.'

'Um, is there any other reason for the rush?' Dad frowned.

I guessed he meant was Alison pregnant.

I studied my shoes. 'No, but she wants to get married in Australia. I thought I would save up and fly out and we could get married there and then come back here to live.'

They still looked confused.

Min happened to be home at the time, sitting at the table with a book open in front of her. When I looked at her, she lowered her eyes, snapped her book shut and stood.

'Congratulations, Jim,' she said, her tone hard. 'I'm just popping out to the shops – I forgot to buy something.' She turned on her heel and left.

I stared after her. It seemed university had changed our Min. But when she came back an hour later to find me about to leave, she followed me out to my car.

'That's pretty rough, Jim, springing that on Mam and Dad! Getting married! No wonder you haven't been home for ages!' She was almost spitting at me.

'Calm down, Min,' I said, putting out a hand to catch her arm. She slapped it away.

'Why didn't you bring her down before now? Ashamed of your humble beginnings? Hey? Hey?'

She stood with her hands on her hips, I'd never seen her this angry.

I was gob smacked. 'She works funny hours, and I haven't had much time off you know, postings and training courses, and what with the trains ...'

'Huh, I thought better of you!' And she flounced back indoors.

I opened the driver's door of my old banger of a car and drove off in a pensive mood.

***

A few months later I'd come home to tell them I was on my way to join an aircraft carrier for a two-month posting. But Mam and

Dad barely listened, they were all excited, Mam waving a postcard at me.

'We've had a card from Min,' she said. 'She's coming to see us today and staying the night, a friend from the University who's from Taunton is bringing her, should be here soon, and he'll pick her up on Sunday to take her back.'

'It'll be nice to meet Min's friend,' Dad said.

*Min's friend? And **he'll** be taking her back? He? A man?*

I don't know why but I had mixed feelings about this. I don't think Min had ever brought a boy home – I'm sure Mam would have mentioned it if she had. Although from what my mates had told me when I happened to be in Yeovil with them and they'd met Min they all wanted to be introduced to her. 'She's too young,' I told them, even though at that stage she'd been seventeen or eighteen. Somehow, I didn't want these men trifling with MY Min.

She had lots of friends and always seemed to be going out in a group, but had never gone steady with a boy – well, as far as I knew. She often tried to get me to join them, telling me that all her girlfriends had a crush on me. But I always refused. Min's friends were too young for me.

I heard a car draw up outside, not that I'd been lurking by the window, watching, mind! I saw this expensive looking sports car stop and a weedy looking bloke get out from the driver's seat and race around to open the passenger door.

I gasped when I saw the passenger get out. First, a high heeled shoe, then I could see no more as this weedy bloke of a man helped her out. Next thing it was Min, but not MY Min, this Min had on a mini skirt, *A mini* skirt for heaven's sake! And her hair was a halo of long blond wavy hair! At least she was still wearing glasses, but they were no longer the ugly National Health ones.

I turned from the window. 'Min's arrived,' I said, sourly.

Mam hurried to the front door and threw it open, ready to hug Min. But she hesitated when she saw the new Min, escorted by this bloke.

'Hi Mam,' Min said as she reached the front door.

'Come in love. So pleased to see you.' Ma turned to the tosser.

'Oh, this is Toby,' Min said, 'he lives in Taunton and he kindly offered me a lift on his way home.'

'Nice to meet you, Toby, come on in.' Mam spun around. 'Dad, this is Toby.'

My father held out his hand. Min didn't give Dad a chance to say the typical Somerset greeting "'ow be on, then", but turned to me.

'And this is my brother. James.'

I saw the weed give a slight start when he saw me – I had the satisfaction of being in uniform, and towering over him, and of course my colour would have given him a bit of a shock.

'How do you do, James?' he said in his posh accent, holding out his lily-white fingers.

'How do you do, Tobe?' I replied. I knew that was the correct response to that silly question. Not "Yeah, I'm very well, thanks, how about you." And I couldn't resist calling him Tobe, knowing it would annoy Min. I took his white hand in my brown one and gave it a jolly good shake.

'Would you like a cup of tea?' Mam asked, her standard greeting to any visitor, as she ran her hands down her hips, smoothing out her best skirt.

'Er, no, thank you, that's very kind, but I'd better be on my way. The parents are expecting me, it's my mother's birthday.'

The parents! Hah!

He drew back the cuff of his left sleeve and glanced at his watch. A very expensive looking gold one. He looked at Min. 'I could pick you up about this time tomorrow, Minerva.'

Minerva! I nearly choked.

'That would be lovely, Toby, thank you.' Min beamed at him.

I gritted my teeth.

'Minerva?' Dad sounded a bit puzzled.

'Such a beautiful name,' Toby enthused. 'You did so well to choose it, a Roman Goddess!'

Dad swallowed.

'So nice to meet Minerva's family.' The wanker smiled at us all. 'See you tomorrow.' And he moved towards the front door.

I watched him stride down the path, jump down the steps and out to his car which was parked behind mine. When he took off with an engine roar I was filled with envy. My old rust box of a Morris Minor of which I'd been so proud looked like it belonged in a scrap yard.

Feeling a bit cast down, I turned back inside where Mam and Dad were fawning over Min.

'What's this Minerva business, Min?' I knew I was shouting, but I couldn't help it.

She shrugged. 'Oh, when I first went to Cambridge someone asked me what Min was short for, was it Minerva, so I said, yes.' She looked me in the eye. 'Minnie is such a childish name, don't you think?' She raised her chin defiantly.

That "don't you think" was said in such a posh way, I could think of no reply. But I was hurt. She knew I'd named her after Minnie the Minx comic character, but I'd only been five years old at the time. And she could have used her middle name of Julie.

I turned away. 'Better go, I'm off to Devonport to start a two-month deployment to the Caribbean and North Atlantic.' No-one seemed interested, Mam busy asking for details about the wanker.

Dad saw me to the door. He winked. 'She'll get over it,' he whispered. 'Have a safe trip.'

My car sounded the same as this Toby's when I took off. The exhaust was rusty and full of holes. I roared back to base.

Chapter Ten - Wedding Plans

I didn't hear from Min for a while, but I didn't write to her either. I was pissed off with her snooty behaviour. Then I chided myself. At least she'd brought Toby in to meet Mam and Dad, a lot of girls would have been ashamed to invite a man like him into a small semi-detached council house. I wondered if he'd continued to see Min after that. But I wasn't going to ask. Anyway, I was too busy on board. While we were in the North Atlantic, the Ark Royal was detached from its exercise with the US Navy and ordered towards British Honduras, together with HMS Bacchante as escort. This was in 1972.

I hadn't been great at geography at school, but I discovered that there'd been a bit of a tussle between England and Guatemala for years over this small country in South America. Eventually some kind of treaty had been agreed resulting in British Honduras.

However, the United Kingdom now responded to intelligence suggesting an imminent Guatemalan invasion, and announced it was sending the aircraft carrier HMS Ark Royal and her air wing (Phantom FG.1s and Blackburn Buccaneers) alongside eight thousand troops to Belize to conduct amphibious exercises.

This was exciting stuff and we were dispatched, *with haste* from the North Atlantic to *show presence* over British Honduras, in the face of Guatemalan threats to invade. Steaming hard at twenty-seven knots, and eventually off Bermuda, two Buccaneers were launched along with two more buddy tanker versions to make one of the longest journeys of its type, five hours and fifty minutes! In case you don't know, a buddy system is where an aircraft is refuelled in mid-air. That would have been exciting to watch but it didn't happen near the Ark, and even if it had I wouldn't have seen it, as I was working under the flight deck, in the hangars. Anyway, the Buccaneers showed up over Belize avoiding Cuban airspace, and made the Guatemalan government, with its P-51D Mustangs and limited ground forces withdraw for a few years.

A great cheer went up when the Buccaneers landed back on Ark. I felt proud to be a part of this exercise.

I started to write to Min to tell her, but changed my mind and wrote to Alison instead. I'd been a bit slack with my letters to Alison, she didn't appear to be that interested in what I wrote, and all her letters were about wedding plans and bridesmaids and her wedding dress. In her last letter she'd asked if I was a Catholic and if not, had I been baptized as a Christian. Apparently if I wasn't a Catholic she would have to get permission from the Bishop to marry me. I felt like replying that I was an atheist, with the hope that she might call the whole thing off. But I had to be honest. Mam had a photo on the sideboard of me in a christening gown when I must have been still a baby. Mam and Dad went to christenings, weddings and funerals. That was the extent of their religion.

✳✳✳

As soon as I returned to base, I called to see Mam and Dad. I must confess I was curious to know more about the posh boy.

Dad had been retired a couple of years by then, and they were both sat by the fire with the radio on, listening to some kind of serial, *The Archers* maybe, and didn't hear me come in through the back door. 'Hello,' I said.

'What a lovely surprise, Jim!' Mam jumped up and smoothed her apron. Dad nodded.

'I'll put the kettle on.' Mam bustled out to the kitchen.

They were pleased to see me and wanted to know what I'd been doing, some of the details about Honduras had been on the news, but Bloody Sunday in Northern Ireland had taken precedence.

I went over to the fire and warmed myself. There was no heater in the old Morris.

'Good to see you back, Son,' Dad said. You couldn't call him talkative.

When Mam came back with the tea tray, I sat at the table idly stirring my tea.

'So, did that Toby chap come for Min last time she was here?' I enquired casually.

Mam beamed. 'Yes, such a polite young lad. Wasn't he, Dad?' She turned to Dad, who nodded. 'Yes, he brought us a cake – said it was left over from his mum's birthday party. It was lovely, wasn't it, Dad?'

Patronising jerk, I thought – bringing leftovers – probably thought we were too poor to eat cake. 'So is Min still seeing him?'

'Don't know,' Mum replied, a slight frown on her face. 'We don't get many letters from her.'

I felt a bit guilty – I should have written to them while I was away.

Mam took up her knitting. 'Last letter we had she said she was busy studying for her Masters. What does that mean, Jim?'

I had to confess that I had no idea.

Mam's needles clacked. She started a new row. 'Min said she'd be too busy to come at Easter.'

'You need to get a phone, then we both can ring you for a chat.'

Dad looked thoughtful. 'Too expensive, and who would we ring?'

'Anyway, in an emergency we can always go next door and use the Proctor's phone.' Mam interrupted. 'Now, tell us the latest on the wedding plans.'

'Oh, nothing much, Alison is organizing everything, she's getting her dress and the bridesmaid's dresses made.'

'How many bridesmaids – you'll have to get presents for each of them, you know.' Mam's eyes lit up. 'I can help you choose – something like a little necklace, or bracelet.'

My heart sank, I'd been saving up for a new car – well a better second hand one, that is, and for the airfare to Australia.

Dad must have seen my expression. He shuffled on his chair. 'As we won't be able to afford to go to the wedding, we thought we could give you a bit towards the airfare.'

Mam nodded. 'Yes, we talked it over, well, it won't be a lot, we have to save up for when Minnie gets married and now that Dad's retired, we only have the pension.

'You're the best parents,' I managed to croak, blowing my nose, then the rest of Mam's words sunk in. I straightened up. 'Is Min getting married?' I demanded.

'Not that we know of, but she's bound to soon, beautiful girl like that.' Mam stood. 'Another cuppa?' She picked up the tea pot and looked at us.

I drove back to base in a thoughtful mood. Going to Australia to get married preyed on my mind. I'd never met any of Alison's family. I'd given her a photo of me in uniform, which she would surely have shown to them, but with my beard there wasn't much of my face to see.

And I really knew very little about her. She'd sent me a few photos – some of her parents and her brother. The house where they lived looked big with a large garden. What would she think of Mam and Dad's?

Chapter Eleven

S unday, 14th May – Mothering Sunday, or Mother's Day as they call it now. As usual I went around to see Mam with some flowers and a nice card. I noticed another card on the sideboard, obviously from Min.

'Happy Mother's Day, Mam.' I gave her a kiss on her cheek, and a bit of a hug. We're not the most demonstrative of families.

'The flowers are beautiful, thank you, love.' She opened the card. 'It's lovely, Jim.' She put it on the side board next to Min's, then fumbled up the sleeve of her cardigan for her hanky and blew her nose. 'I'll put the kettle on.'

She gave a little cough as she made her way to the kitchen and gave Dad a look. He lowered the Sunday paper he was reading and mumbled something about the Black September gang and a hijacking.

I nodded, pre-occupied with thinking about my birth mother. This happened every Mothers' day. It might be a good time to try and contact her, now that I was getting married. Who knew, she might want to come to the wedding.

Dad cleared his throat. 'Was thinking, Jim.'

I looked up, for Dad to voluntarily start a conversation was unusual. 'And?'

'Well, when you bring your new wife back to England, where will you live?'

I stared at him. I hadn't thought that far ahead.

'Mam and I were thinking you might like to come and stay here until you find somewhere.'

My mind whirled, I didn't know what to say, but was saved when Mam came in with the tea tray, put it on the table, went back to the kitchen and returned with the flowers in a vase.

'They're lovely, Jim,' she repeated, carefully placing them in the centre of the table. 'Brightens up the room.' She studied the flowers. 'Did Dad mention about coming here to live?'

I nodded. 'That's thoughtful of you both. Um ... I'll talk to Alison about it. We may be able to get married quarters.' The notion had just occurred to me.

'It would be nice to have her to stay, get to know her.' She rearranged a flower in the vase. 'And it might be a bit lonely for Alison in married quarters when you're away.'

I could think of nothing to say. I nodded at the cards on the sideboard. 'Heard from Min lately?'

'Yes, she put a nice long letter in with her card. She's very busy with her part-time job and studying, so she won't be coming down for a while.'

'Did she mention that Toby bloke?'

Mam hesitated. 'No, she just wrote about this Masters stuff, the subjects she was studying and her job coaching students ... another cup of tea?'

'No, thanks, I'd better get back to base and write to Alison.'

'I'll pack you up some cake to take back with you.'

When Mam had disappeared into the kitchen, Dad cleared his throat.

I looked at him expectantly. The throat clearing was usually a prelude to Dad speaking.

'You don't have to get married, you know,' he said softly. 'You can break it off.'

I blinked. 'I couldn't do that,' I stammered. 'She's got it all organized.'

'Marry in haste, repent at leisure.' Dad coughed and raised his newspaper as Mam came back into the room carrying a brown paper bag.

'Here you go, love.'

***

I felt unsettled driving back to Yeovilton. It wasn't like Dad to speak in that way. Maybe he wasn't keen on Alison and me coming to live with them for a while.

And taking Alison there! Okay, the upstairs now had electric light, but I couldn't imagine Alison having a bath in the old bath with the gas hot water geyser that seemed like it was going to explode every time it was lit. I couldn't picture her in amongst the mangle, washtub and collection of boots, shoes and dirty clothes waiting to be washed.

Later that evening I went for a drink with the lads.

'You're a bit glum, tonight, Jim,' one of them remarked. 'Getting wedding nerves? Cold feet?'

I laughed, a fake smile on my face. 'Not at all! Can't wait.'

'She's a bit of all right, you lucky bugger,' someone said.

I'd shown them photos of Alison, one in a swimming costume on a beach in Fremantle.

'Yeah,' was all I said.

***

The very next day I had a letter from Alison, saying the date was fixed, the church, priest and venue booked. Saturday 21st October, and asking me to send a certified copy of my birth certificate and a letter of freedom. I had no idea what a letter of freedom was. But there was another problem. I'd never told Alison I was adopted, and now I'd have to get a copy of my adoption paper in lieu of a birth certificate. This whole business was getting harder and harder. And, she was asking about the honeymoon – she'd love to go to Tasmania.

My heart sank. *Shit, shit, shit.* More expense! All right, her parents were paying for the wedding, but I had to pay for my return airfare and her one-way ticket back to England.

At least I didn't need to buy a wedding ring. Mam had given me Nan's when I told them I was getting married.

'Nan always wanted you to have it when you married,' she'd said. 'She hoped you'd be as happy as she and Gramps were.' Tears came to her eyes, so I mumbled something about being sure Alison would be proud to wear it.

Now I was pleased – one less thing to worry about, and I'd already told Alison I wouldn't wear a ring, it was too dangerous. Several men had lost fingers when jumping down from an aircraft and the ring had caught. She'd been horrified and agreed.

I took the bull by the horns, so to speak. Sat down and wrote to her. Told her that I couldn't afford a honeymoon to Tasmania or anywhere else for that matter, I had a reasonable salary, but not only were the airfares expensive but we would need somewhere for us to live after our wedding. And we'd have to live with Mam and Dad, in their small, two-bedroom house in the meantime. I thought that might make her think. I guess a part of me hoped she'd call it all off. We'd been apart for so long only the photograph I had of her reminded me what she looked like.

Well, she didn't. A few weeks later I got a letter from her, saying it was okay, we could have a honeymoon later, and she'd be able to get a job to help. And for me to arrive a few days before the wedding to get over the jet lag.

I didn't know much about jet lag, so on my next weekend off, I drove to the travel agent in Yeovil and booked my flight to arrive three days before the wedding and our return flights a week after the wedding. It cost a fortune. I was glad to have the money Mam and Dad had contributed, then I put it out of my head. It was still four months to October. Too early to start looking for somewhere to live.

My thoughts turned to my birth mother. After booking the flights, I headed up to Mam and Dad's

'Got the tickets to Australia,' I announced as I came through the back door into the living room. Dad was listening to a football match on the radio. I looked around, 'Where's Mam?'

'Oh, she went round to see old Elsie Whatshername down the road.' He smiled. 'I think she likes to go out when I'm listening to a match.'

I nodded. 'Who's playing?' I settled down to join him, hardly paying any attention to the match, my mind on my mission. At half-time, I said, 'Dad, while Mam isn't here, I wanted to ask you about my real mother.' Seeing the blank look on his face, I hurriedly continued. 'You see, I thought it might be a good idea to try and contact her before I got married ... um, in case my new in-laws ask.' It was the best excuse I could think of. I didn't want to say that maybe she'd be able to come to Australia for the wedding, and I might even have half-brothers or sisters. I didn't want to upset Mam.

'I wondered if you knew anything that would help me find her.'

Dad frowned and turned off the radio.

I jumped up. 'Don't turn off the radio, Dad, we can listen to the rest of the match.'

'No, Son, this is more important and we need to sort it out before your Mam comes back.' He pointed his walking stick at the sideboard – he'd had problems with one of his hips for a while now. 'Look in the sideboard, bottom left, right at the back, the big old biscuit tin, bring it out.'

I did as he said and brought out the tin, a faded Christmas scene decorated the top, the edges showing a bit of rust and put it on the table.

Dad stood and shuffled to the table. He hung his stick over the back of a chair and opened the tin. It bulged with papers.

'Should be right at the bottom in an envelope,' he muttered. He carefully lifted the top documents out and laid them on the table. 'Must put them all back in order, or your Mam will know someone's been looking.' He smiled ruefully.

'Here we go,' He took a fat brown envelope from the bottom with "Certificates" written on it in Mam's handwriting.

I held my breath as he sorted through the papers. I'd had to use my Adoption Certificate in order to get my passport and to join the Navy back when I was fifteen. But at the time I hadn't thought much about what it meant. Dad took the certificate out and I saw that it had a piece of paper pinned to it. That hadn't been there when Mam gave it to me when I went to get my passport.

'When we adopted you, we had to go to the registrar and hand over your original birth certificate. They issued this adoption certificate with our names as your official parents.'

He paused and I could see his eyes moisten. He swallowed and handed me the piece of paper.

'But your mam was smart. Before going to the registrar, she copied out the details of your original birth certificate.'

'I'll get some paper and copy it.'

'Good idea,' Dad said, 'then we can put it all back and Mam will never know – well, unless you decide to tell her.'

I went to the sideboard where writing paper and envelopes were kept and copied down the entries. There wasn't much detail, only my mother's name, Jean Higgins, with an address at Yeovil Marsh. A blank for my father's name. My heart was in my mouth.

'I think the father's name wasn't put on the certificate unless the mother was married to the father.' Dad patted my hand.

'Thanks, Dad.' I folded the copy I'd made and put it in my pocket, pinned the original back on the adoption certificate, and replaced everything as it was. Watched by Dad.

'Put the kettle on, Son. Mam'll be back soon.' He returned to his chair and turned on the radio. 'We can listen to the rest of match.'

Not a moment too soon. The back door opened and Mam came in. She smiled when she saw me.

'Thought you'd be here, saw your car outside.'

'Yep, came to tell you, I've got the air tickets for the wedding. And thank you both for paying towards them.'

She beamed, hung her coat on a hook behind the living room door and placed her black felt hat on top. 'See you've got the kettle on. I'm dying for a decent cuppa; poor old Elsie Jennings can't make a proper cup of tea for toffee – it's like dishwater.'

***

My mind whirled as I drove back to base. How to track down Jean Higgins? She'd probably moved from Yeovil Marsh, it was only a very small hamlet, I didn't think it even had a shop. And it was now twenty-seven years since I'd been adopted. However, someone there might remember her and know where she'd gone. I glanced at the note I'd written; it should be easy to find her address.

As soon as I could make a turn, I sped back to the road leading to Yeovil Marsh. I passed the church and drove about two miles, until I found the turn off. I went slowly along, looking for her number. There were very few houses. Eventually I came to what I assumed to be the place. I stared at it in dismay. It looked unlived in. I stopped the car and opened the rickety gate and walked up to the front door and knocked on it. No sign of life. I looked over at the adjoining house and saw an elderly man watching me with interest. Seeing me looking at him, he lifted a hand.

'Looking for the 'iggins's are you?'

'Yes.'

'They left a few years ago. Old man 'iggins passed away and the place was a tied cottage, so Missus 'iggins 'ad to leave.'

'Do you know where she went? Was a Jean Higgins with them?'

'Don't recall a Jean. But I only bin yer twenty yers.'

'Thanks.' I waved to the old bloke and managed to turn the car in the narrow road. As I approached the church, I had a sudden idea. Maybe there were church records. I screeched to a stop, startling an elderly man who looked up from sweeping the leaves from the porch. He smiled as I walked down the path.

'Can I help you?'

'Um, I'm trying to track down a woman who used to live here, Jean Higgins. Thought I might get some information from the church records.'

'Dunno about that, vicar keeps the records. You'd have to go and see him, but not at the moment, saw him driving out about ten minutes ago. But you could have a look at the graves. Might see if she'd passed away.' He waved his arm towards the graves around the church.

'Thanks, I will.' I wasn't so keen on this idea, if she'd died then I'd never know who my father was, or if I had any brothers or sisters. Another thought struck me. *Maybe she died having me! And that's why I'd had to be adopted!*

I mooched around the graveyard, the grass was still wet from the recent rain, and a lot of the gravestones were covered in moss and hard to decipher. I soon came across more recent graves and looked at each of them. No Jean Higgins.

The old bloke had finished sweeping the porch and came towards me as I walked back to my car.

He waved his broom at me. He must have seen by my face that I'd not found a grave, for he called out, 'Young man, you could always try Births, Deaths and Marriages.'

'Where are they?'

He came closer and scratched his chin. 'Last I 'eard they were in Zomerset House.'

'Where's that then, Taunton?' Taunton is the county town of Somerset – well it used to be, don't know about now. For some reason the powers that be keep changing the county boundaries. Bath used to be in Somerset. Now it's in Avon! Go figure! As they say.

'Nah, I think it's in London.'

Great help. 'Thanks, I'll look into it.'

I nodded at him and made my way back to my car. And the surname, Higgins, was quite common. As I was getting into the car, the old bloke came hobbling up.

'Could always try the Registry Office in Yeovil. Just thought of it.' He smiled and waved his broom again, nearly hitting the car.

I smiled back. 'Will do, thanks.'

***

I didn't have time to think much more about it, and it would have to wait until I could get a weekday off, and when I did eventually get a Monday off, Mam wanted me to go with her to choose bridesmaids' presents. She would ask to know why I was going to the Registry Office. Researching my birth mother would be the last thing I wanted to tell her, but now I had a valid reason.

'I think a little gold cross on a chain would be nice,' Mam was saying as I took her arm to guide her across the road to the jeweller in the High Street. 'How many bridesmaids did you say?'

'Three and a Matron of Honour, whatever that is,' I muttered, my heart sinking at the thought of the cost of four gold chains and crosses.

'Didn't you say Alison is a Catholic?'

'Yes.'

'Well then, her bridesmaids will probably be Catholics too, so they'll love a cross and chain.'

'And, Mam, I must go to the Registry Office to get a certified copy of my adoption papers.'

She stopped and stared at me. 'Why?'

We drew near to the Cadena Café. 'Apparently, it's a legal re-quirement. Now, why don't you have a nice cup of tea and a cream bun while I pop along to the Registry Office, and I'll meet you back here and then we can go looking for crosses?'

She hesitated. 'I suppose it's best you go before they close for lunch.'

I took her into the café, found her an empty table, and hared off to the registry.

The woman behind the counter was very helpful. 'It will take a while to find the record and copy it and get it certified,' she said, as she took my money. 'If you'd like to wait. Or come back in an hour or so.'

'I can come back, but also I'd like to know if I can find any details about my birth mother, her name was Jean Higgins.'

She drew herself up and looked grave. 'I'm sorry, I can't give you any details. If you want to get a copy of her birth certificate, you'll have to provide a date and place of birth.'

Neither of which I knew. I turned away from the counter. 'Thanks,' I mumbled, 'I'll come back in an hour or so.'

I went back to the Cadena. Mam was pouring out a cup of tea when she saw me.

'Oh, Jim, you weren't long. I've only just got my order.'

'It's okay, Mam, I'll sit here and wait. You take your time. I'm not hungry.'

'So, everything's organized now?' she said, cutting the bun and offering me a piece.

I shook my head and studied the rear of a waitress who was bent over taking an order at the next table.

'What else?'

'I have to get a letter of freedom from every parish I've lived in to say I wasn't married in that parish.'

Mam burst out laughing, a spray of sugar icing landing on the starched table cloth. 'Sorry, love, that sounds ...' her words were muffled as she wiped her mouth with her napkin.

She gave a little cough and cleared her throat. 'That should be easy. You've only lived in one parish, maybe two if you count Yeovilton.' Her eyes danced with laughter.

'It's not funny, Mam.'

'Don't you have a Padre or someone at the base? Ask him.'

Of course! Why hadn't I thought of that?

'You're a genius, Mam!'

'Like Min's genie?'

That had been a long-standing joke in the family. I smiled as I remembered little Min's face as she'd leaned over my maths homework. She'd been so cute. My smile faded. She'd changed.

'Okay, Mam. If you're finished, we can go gold hunting.'

***

I'd had a gut full for that day, and didn't feel like the usual Saturday night drinks with the boys at the canteen bar. Well, that is, I felt like a pint, but not amongst a crowd.

However, I didn't feel like staying in either. I drove to The Bull in Ilchester. Now that I no longer had a girl-friend locally, the foursomes had stopped, and it was just a few of us un-attached – or long-distance attached, like me – who sometimes met up. I could usually find Paul and John there. Paul was older than me and divorced. John's wife had died a few years before, leaving him with a little girl to bring up. She went to stay with her grandmother every so often, allowing John to get out a bit.

I sat in a quiet, less smoky corner of the lounge – smoking in pubs was allowed in those days – nursing a pint and hoping Paul and John wouldn't turn up, but of course they did. I wasn't very good company, and they soon noticed it.

'What's up Jim, lost your tongue?' Paul asked, as he lit a cigarette.

I shrugged. 'Nah, just a bit down with all this wedding stuff.'

'You don't have to do anything, isn't she doing it all from her end?'

I sighed, 'Yeah, but I have to send her a certified copy of my adoption paper, instead of a birth cert, and she doesn't know I'm adopted. Didn't even think of mentioning it. See, I never took her to meet my parents so she wouldn't have noticed that they're both white ...'

They stared at me. 'Well, you know how it is, trains and so on from London, and she was working ...'

'But you've met her parents, haven't you? When you first met her, in Australia?' John asked.

I swirled my pint. 'No.'

Paul shook his head. 'I can't see what difference it would make you being adopted.'

'It's you she's marrying, not your parents,' John chipped in.

'Yeah, and I have to sign something to say any children we have will be brought up as Catholics.'

The lads both frowned. 'Is that a problem?' John muttered.

I shrugged. 'Not really, I'm not religious. Don't care either way.' I sipped my pint. 'Then I found out my real mother's name. I've been trying to find her.'

'Goodness, that's pretty major.' John said sympathetically.

Paul leaned forward eagerly, 'And have you?'

'No, I've drawn a blank. Found she was called Jean Higgins and lived in Yeovil Marsh when I was born. I don't know how to get more information. I called in at the church there, but dunno what they could tell me anyway.'

Paul clicked his fingers, 'Put an ad in the Personal section of the Western Gazette.'

I stared at him. 'Aren't they for people looking for a girl or boy-friend?

'Some of them, but there's a lot with people looking for missing persons.'

'Good idea, you could put something like "Information needed for a Jean Higgins who used to live in Yeovil Marsh. Something to her advantage. Reward".' John smiled.

'Reward? I don't have money for a reward! And how would it be to her advantage?'

'Simple! They would think she's been left money in somebody's will and the reward would be finding her long lost son!'

The boys sat back, satisfied looks on their faces.

I raised my glass, suddenly feeling more optimistic. 'Cheers! You're both good mates.' I grinned. 'Next one's on me!'

***

I sent in my ad. Here's how it worked in those days, I wrote my ad on notepaper, and posted it to the paper, together with a postal order payment and enclosing a stamped, self-addressed envelope. The ad would appear with a Box number. Respondents would send in a reply in an envelope marked with my box number. These would be collected and posted back to me. Much more discreet than the present-day Facebook and dating apps.

I eagerly waited for the following week's edition of The Western Gazette, and there it was, my ad.

After much cogitating I started a letter to Alison.

Darling Alison,

I'm enclosing a certified copy of my adoption certificate, which I have to use in place of a birth certificate. I should have told you before that I'd been adopted when I was a baby, but I simply didn't think of it.

My adoptive parents are the most wonderful people, I'm so lucky to have them. They can't wait to meet you.

I also include a letter from the Padre here stating that I haven't been married before. I hope that helps.

I carried on with a lot of lovey-dovey stuff that I thought she'd like. I didn't mention about looking for my birth mother.

***

Two weeks later I got the self-addressed envelope that I'd sent in to the Gazette, I'd almost given up looking out for it. I managed to wait until I got back to the four-bed dormitory where I slept with others in my squad, before tearing it open. Two envelopes fell out. The first was addressed in block capitals.

My fingers shook as I took out and smoothed the folded piece of notepaper.

Dear Sir

I have information about Jean Higgins. What is the reward?

Send details and your name and address to F. Myers, 8 Stoney Lane, Martock

Signed, F.Myers

Hmm. On to the next one.

Dear PO Box

I knew Jean Higgins years ago when she lived in Yeovil Marsh. She was going out with my best friend, Ernest Smith. We were in a POW camp together. They got married soon after we came back from the war. She was a lovely girl. Ernie couldn't stop talking about her. I was his best man at their wedding.

They moved to Bristol, or maybe Bath, after their wedding. Good luck, sorry I can't be more helpful. I don't expect a reward, just like to help.

Yours faithfully

Bertie Osborne.

I sat on my bed, feeling a bit deflated. Don't know why I'd had such great expectations from the advertisement.

Of course, the lads were all agog next time we met at the Bull.

'Get any results?' Paul asked, taking a drag from his cigarette.

'Yeah,' I produced the two envelopes. They took one each.

'Don't like the sound of that F. Myers. What does the other say,' Paul said, leaning over to peer at the letter John held.

'This is more hopeful, Jim.' John smiled at me. 'You can check the telephone directory for Bristol now. Look for E. Smith.'

'Yeah, right. Can you guess how many E. Smiths there are in the Bristol phone book?'

John looked a bit crestfallen.

Paul lit a cigarette and took a drag, blowing smoke out the side of his mouth to avoid blowing it over us. 'We could help. Take a section and ring each one. Ask if a Jean Smith lives there.'

Why hadn't I thought of that? I stood and smiled at them. 'You're great mates, thanks. I'll get the phone book from the bar, and another round.'

In fact, there weren't that many E Smiths - about thirty or so. We sat with the phone book opened on the table. 'I can work my way through, a few at a time at the phone box at the base,' I said. 'Not fair on you two, taking your time and money.' I thought they seemed relieved. 'But thanks for offering.'

I had a sudden thought. 'What do I say if they say "Yes, Jean Smith lives here"?'

We all looked around for inspiration. 'It might be her answering the phone,' Paul volunteered. 'You can't just come out and say, "I think you might be my mother", she'd probably have a heart attack.'

'No,' Paul said, 'You just say, thanks and hang up. Then write to her, now you have the address, asking if you could meet somewhere private about an event that happened in ... um, when were you born?'

'January 1945.'

'Yeah, well, about an event that happened in January, 1945.'

'Good idea.' Paul blew a perfect smoke ring. 'Then if her husband opens the letter, she can pretend she knows nothing about it.'

I had a sudden thought. I don't know why it hadn't occurred to me before. 'If this Ernie Smith was my father, why didn't she keep me, and put his name on the birth certificate?'

They both stared at me. John cleared his throat. 'Um, maybe her boyfriend wasn't your father but some other bloke's and she, well ...'

'Well, what?'

'You know, um.' John looked embarrassed.

'Maybe you didn't look like her boyfriend, Jim.' It was Paul. 'You know ... you weren't white.'

I stared at my pint. How stupid I was not to have thought of that ...

'Anyway, Jim, things may have changed. Keep looking, her husband may have died and she'd love to meet you.'

I nodded at John. 'Thanks.'

***

I did as they suggested. It took me a week, spending an hour in the phone box each evening ploughing through the phone book, dodging in and out of the box as a queue formed outside, until I struck gold, and a woman answered. 'Sorry to bother you, I was wondering if a Jean Smith lives at this address?'

'Yes, that's me.'

I panicked. 'Oh, sorry, my money's run out.' And I hung up, my heart thumping. I was quite proud of my quick response. I made a note of the address and phone number.

I'd had a long letter from Alison that day, rambling on about her dress, the reception and finally, that the letter from the Padre was okay, and about me being adopted, well, she didn't know what to think. Why had I been adopted? Had my parents been killed in the war, had I tried to find out about them and so on. And the weather had been awful and hoped it would be good in October, and would I be wearing my uniform for the ceremony?

I definitely wanted to be in uniform. It always made me feel more confident and in control.

She went on to say that her father knew someone high up in the Royal Australian Navy, and he would put a word in for me to get a transfer from the UK. Now the dates were settled he'd arrange a meeting to discuss things while I was over there. I didn't pay much attention being far too pre-occupied thinking about my birth mother. I wasn't that dark, so she must have been fair skinned ... my thoughts skittered on.

Chapter Twelve

Dear Mrs Smith,

I wonder if we could meet somewhere private concerning an event which occurred in January 1945.

Perhaps Temple Meads station café in the main concourse?

If that would be convenient for you, please could you let me know a suitable time, preferably a Saturday. I enclose a SAE.

Yours sincerely

James Jones

I knew she wouldn't know my adopted surname as mothers were not allowed to see the names or addresses of the people adopting their baby. I hoped my name, James, wouldn't be a clue. Mam and Dad had told me that my real mother had called me that.

I envisaged our meeting. I would be sat at a table in the railway station cafe, cup of coffee in front of me, trying to ignore the train departures being announced over the Tannoy and anxiously scanning all the women and then a voice would say, 'James! I've waited for years to find you! I'd know you anywhere, you're the image of your father!' And we'd hug and she'd tell me all about my father, and how he had been killed in the war and she married this Smith bloke. And she would be pretty with blonde curly hair ...

I started to get all emotional, thinking that I might have half brothers or sisters. Then she would invite me to meet them.

A week later I received a two-line reply:

I know nothing about any events occurring in January 1945.
Please do not contact me again or I will have to inform the
police.

That was all. I was gutted. She'd erased me from her life. But maybe she wasn't my mother! I hadn't carried on ringing the other E. Smiths in the phone book.

However, I knew in my heart she was. Surely, she would have wanted to meet me and find out about me? What I'd done in my life, had I been well cared for by my adoptive parents?

It was with a heavy heart that I met the lads for our Saturday drinks at the Bull. They were already there, a pint of my favourite beer on the table for me.

'Any news?' Paul asked, lighting a cigarette off the butt of his current one.

I nodded.

'Not good by the look of you.' That was John.

'Doesn't want to know me,' I replied pulling her letter out of my wallet.

The boys sighed. 'Bitch,' said Paul, reading it. 'Sorry, she's your mother, shouldn't say that.'

'She might not be,' John said. 'Try the others in the phone book.'

I took a gulp of my beer and shook my head. 'Nah, that's it, as far as I'm concerned. Spent enough time on it.'

John nodded. 'It's possible she was engaged at the time of your conception and didn't want her boyfriend to know – he might have been fighting, or a prisoner of war ...'

'Hmm, could be.' I didn't want to hear any more speculation. 'Subject closed. Now, what have you two been up to?'

I'd wasted so much time trying to find my real mother – it was now October and soon I'd be flying out to Australia to get married.

Chapter Thirteen

I carefully packed my uniform and dress shirt ready for the wedding. That was something the training at Ganges had drilled into us – how to look after our clothes.

The night before my flight, the lads took me out for a stag party. I tried not to drink too much, afraid I'd oversleep and miss my flight, but fair play to John, he kept an eye on me and got me up and in his car and drove me to Castle Cary to catch the train next morning. Luckily the train terminated at Paddington Station, as I fell asleep as soon as I found a carriage and an empty seat by the window and only woke when another passenger shook my arm. I had to change trains for Heathrow. My first time flying.

Alison was right about the jet-lag. I got off the plane in Perth in a daze. Admittedly, I'd had to work right up to the last minute, then call to see Mam and Dad and get the train to Heathrow for the flight, so I was pretty tired to start with. The stag party had been the last straw. I couldn't get comfortable on the plane, I'm tall and broad and the seats were not made for long legs. A very fat man sat on one side of me – I know, we're not allowed to use that word these days, but he was, and he seemed to ooze over the arm rest – and on the other side a woman who talked at me all the time. In the end I pretended to be asleep.

Alison and her parents were at the airport to meet me.

I staggered through customs, and came out in to the arrivals area. It had been so long since I'd seen Alison, that I didn't spot her at first in the crowd. Then I heard her screaming and saw her waving and running towards me. Before I knew what was happening, she'd thrown her arms around me and suddenly feeling so relieved to see her, I picked her up and held her up in the air. One moment to look at her then we were kissing.

A polite cough made us stop.

'Oh! Mum, Dad, this is Jimmy!'

I noticed the shocked expressions on their faces, but her father recovered quickly and held out his hand. 'Pleased to meet you, Jimmy.'

I released Alison and took his hand. I realized I must have looked pretty dishevelled and not exactly the man her parents could have wished their only daughter to be marrying.

Coming out into the sunshine I looked up at the sky. Amazed once more at how high it seemed.

I swung my case into the boot of the car and got in the back beside Alison. Her dad drove and her mum sat in the front passenger seat. She swivelled around in her seat to face me. 'Did you have a good flight, Jim?'

'Yes, thank you, er Mrs Sefton.'

'Please call me Janet,' she said, 'and Alison's father is Brian.'

Brian nodded.

'Thank you, Janet.'

Alison squeezed my hand. I turned to her – couldn't wait to get her into bed.

The next few days were a blur. I seemed to keep falling asleep in the day and then be awake half the night.

On one of the rare occasions when we were alone, I asked Alison about something which had been bothering me.

'Had you told your mum and dad that I was coloured before I arrived?' I asked.

'No, why?'

'I thought they looked shocked when they first saw me at the airport.'

She shrugged. 'I didn't bother telling them, in case they tried to talk me out of marrying you.'

'Why would they have done that?'

'They weren't keen on me marrying a Pom and going to live in England.'

I nodded. I could see their point – their only daughter.

'So, that's when I told them you'd be transferring to the Australian Fleet Air Arm, and Dad said he'd set up a meeting. Remember I wrote to you about it.'

That gave me a jolt. What with trying to find my birth mother, I'd totally forgotten she'd mentioned that. I had no intention of moving to Australia. I'd heard all about the White Australia Policy and discrimination against coloured people.[1] I'd had an earful of advice from well-meaning friends when I told them I was going to marry an Australian.

And another thing, who would look after Mam and Dad? Especially after all they'd done for me. And I'd formed good friendships over the years with my squad and felt respected, but this was no time to tell Alison.

'So, what happened about the meeting your dad had set up?'

She looked a bit embarrassed then shrugged. 'Dunno.'

I said no more. Obviously once our Brian had seen me, he would have cancelled the meeting.

***

Alison's and my bedrooms were separated by her parents', so there was no hope of sneaking into her room during the night.

It was a big house, there were two bathrooms, one adjoining her parent's bedroom. I thought of Mam and Dad's house and the old bath in the room off the kitchen ... it was cold in the winter. And it would be winter when we got back to England. Alison, having lived in London for a year or so would know what the weather was like – and the plumbing. At least I hoped so.

I was just about back to normal for the wedding day. I was very nervous. Alison's brother, Pete was my best man. Weird really, I'd only met him the day before the wedding, at the rehearsal. Rehearsal! I'd never heard of such a thing before, but he seemed a nice enough bloke. 'Brave man,' he whispered to me, 'Getting married.'

I gave the bridesmaids, who were young cousins of Alisons and the maid of honour, her best friend, their gifts when they all turned up for the rehearsal. They loved the little gold cross and chains. Mam had been right. I'd packed Nan's wedding ring in the pocket of my uniform jacket, so there was no chance of mislaying it.

I think they were all relieved when they saw me in my uniform waiting at the altar and looking fairly respectable. The sight of Alison coming down the aisle on her father's arm, all floaty stuff and veil, made my heart flip. She looked so beautiful.

I was sad that Mam and Dad and Min weren't there. Mam especially, she loved a good cry at a wedding.

The photographer took ages, making us take different poses, but when I saw them later, they did look good.

The reception was amazing, Brian had pulled out all the stops to make the occasion memorable. There must have been about a hundred guests, champagne flowing and a four-course meal.

Alison told me afterwards that I looked so handsome and smart, everyone thought so. Our honeymoon was brief – we got the train to Perth and stayed a few nights there before flying back to England. We arrived at Heathrow totally jet lagged and exhausted. Then the train to Yeovil Junction, and back to Mam and Dad's.

Alison had brought a lot of things with her so we got a taxi. She'd also packed two big trunks of stuff to be sent by sea – luckily, they would take three or four months to arrive as heaven only knew where we would put them.

It was after four o'clock when we arrived, and raining. Mam and Dad had the front door open, and I could see Mam dressed in her best clothes. She came out with an umbrella, holding it over Alison.

'Hello, love, welcome to Yeovil, sorry it's raining, come on in, I've got the kettle on, you must be gasping for a cup of tea. Jim will bring everything in.'

As I staggered up the path it suddenly hit me. I was now responsible for this woman. My wife ... I barely knew her. Well, I knew her bare ... but you know what I mean. A weight settled in my stomach.

I put the first two cases inside the front door and went to pay the taxi driver and get the remaining luggage. Back inside, I saw that Alison had a bewildered look on her face. Dad stood by the table leaning on his walking stick.

'Hello Mrs Jones, I'm Tom, Mr. Jones, the elder.'

I knew Dad was trying to make a joke to put Alison at ease, but she blinked a few times and held out her hand, 'Nice to meet you, er, Mr Jones.'

'None of the Mister, call me Tom. And Mam here is Ellen.' He indicated Mam, who bustled in with a tea tray laden with the best cups and saucers and plates of cakes. My heart went out to her. She must have been preparing this all morning.

'I've made up the bed for you in Min's room,' she said and turned to Alison, 'But I expect you'd like to wash your hands first.'

'Thank you, I'd love a shower and change my clothes if I may, it seems ages since I had one.'

Mam blinked. Dad shuffled back to his seat by the fire.

'Um, I forgot to mention it, Alison, but we don't have a shower here. Just a bath ...'

She smiled. God bless her. 'That's okay, I'd forgotten about the English plumbing. I'll just have a quick wash to freshen up.'

Mam beamed. 'This way love, there's hot water in the kettle, I'll fetch you a clean towel.'

Alison followed her into the kitchen. I heard Mam filling the washing bowl in the sink, then say, 'Soap's there, and here's a clean towel. Oh, and the toilet is out there.'

'Mam, you're the best,' I said, giving her a hug, when she returned, closing the kitchen door behind her.

'Now, about dinner tonight, what would Alison like?' Mam looked anxious. 'I didn't know what to get so I made steak and kidney pudding, it's all ready to heat up, but I can pop down to the butcher and get something else if she wouldn't like that.'

'Mam,' I said gently, 'Steak and kidney pudding's my favourite, so I'm sure Alison will love it, but ...'

'But what?'

'Well, we're both very jet-lagged, our bodies think it's the middle of the night, so we'll probably not feel like eating much, and we seemed to be eating all the time in the plane.' I knew Mam wouldn't understand about jet-lag.

Mam frowned. 'So, what should I do?'

'We'll ask Alison. Now you just sit down, and I'll pour the tea. Mmm, these cakes look yummy.' I poured tea for us all and took a piece of cake, even though I didn't feel like eating. I regretted not having tried to find a flat or somewhere to rent, instead of burdening Mam and Dad.

Alison emerged from the kitchen. 'I feel much better now,' she smiled. 'Thank you, er, Ellen.'

I smiled at her. It would all work out.

As you can imagine, the rest of the day was a bit awkward. I carried our luggage up to the bedroom that used to be Min's and before that was Nan and Gramps. The old double bed still remained, but with a new eiderdown. I resolved that first thing in the morning I'd look for a place to live.

That night, snuggled up to Alison with the two hot water bottles Mam had put in the bed, I kissed my new wife. 'Love you, Alison. I'm sorry this is not what you expected, but we'll soon find our own place.' Then, as her hand went down into my pyjamas, I whispered, 'Yes, but we must be very quiet.'

***

Fair play to Alison, she accepted the way things were, and Mam and Dad were delighted.

'She's lovely, Jim,' Mam said the next day, when I came down, indicating for me to sit at the table, and placing two boiled eggs and a plate of toast in front of me.

They had the range going so it was nice and warm. They didn't usually start the fire until dusk, coal was expensive. Dad must have lit it especially for Alison. Now, he nodded at me. 'You did well, Son.'

I sliced the top off one of the eggs and grinned to myself – Mam had cut some of the toast into fingers for me, soldiers. 'Thanks, Mam. Yes, she's lovely. I hope she settles down here. Big change from Australia.'

Mam set a cup of tea on the table beside me, gave a cup to Dad, then sat next to me with her own, watching me eat.

'What's happening with Min?' I asked – Alison was still asleep; she said she'd been awake most of the night. I was annoyed with Min. I hadn't seen her for ages. She'd sent a telegram, which had been read out at the wedding speeches, congratulating us, but I'd heard nothing since. 'Will she be coming home for Christmas?'

Mam clapped a hand to her mouth. 'Oh, Jim, I forgot to tell you, she came down last week to say she's been offered a scholarship to get a Ph. D. at a University in America and she's flying out next week and won't have time to come and see us before she leaves. What's a Ph. D, Jim?'

I'd checked out this stuff after Min had said she was studying for her Masters. 'It means you'll have to call her Dr Jones, if she gets it.' I know I sounded sour, but I couldn't help it.

'Doctor? Like our Dr. Barclay?'

'No, a Doctor of Philosophy.'

Mam looked puzzled.

'But it's a great achievement,' I hastened to add. 'She'll be living in America now, I suppose.' I was irritated that she hadn't bothered to wait and meet Alison.

'Oh, and she brought a wedding present for you. It's over there, in the corner.' She pointed to a small box behind her easy chair.

'I'll wait for Alison to open it. I have to go back to work tomorrow, Mam, but today I'm going to look for a place for us to live to give you back your own space.'

'Oh, but Jim, we love having you here!'

I got up from the table and gave her a hug. 'I know, Mam, and we appreciate it, but I think it best if we make our own way.'

Mam gave a big sigh.

I picked up the local newspaper and scanned the places to rent.

***

I spent the day walking around looking at the very few places available or soon to be available. I'd arranged with Paul to use my car to come and collect me the following day to go back to work, so I had no car. Not only was I exhausted with trailing around, not to mention the jet lag, but I was also panicking when nothing seemed suitable. However, I struck lucky with the last one on my list. On the ground floor of a semi-detached house, it was partly furnished, clean and had a living room, a bedroom and a kitchen. In one corner of the kitchen stood a cast iron bath with a board over it, serving as a low table when not being used as a bath. The usual gas geyser was on the wall over the bath. The toilet was off the kitchen.

We moved in a week later, and not before time. Alison was getting very restless. Her home-sickness was palpable. In the evenings she and I would perch on that old leather sofa which Mam had polished to icy slipperiness. I could see Dad itched to read the paper or listen to the radio, and Mam tried to make conversation with her fingers hovering over her knitting bag. We'd gone to the cinema one night, but I was at a loss to think of anything else to pass the long winter evenings. I suppose we could have met John and Paul for a drink, but it would have meant coming back late and disturbing Mam and Dad.

'There's nothing to do here,' Alison had grumbled, after a few days. 'Your mum thought I'd like to go to the library with her, and get a book to read, but I'm not much of a reader. And then, every second person we met she had to stop and introduce me. "This is my daughter-in-law, Alison," she'd say, "Jim's wife, all the way from Australia!" And they'd give me an odd look. I could see them thinking, "why did he have to go all the way to Australia for a wife. Why not a nice Yeovil girl?"' Her shoulders drooped.

'I'm sure they weren't thinking that, probably thinking well it was worth going to Australia for such a beautiful girl.' But privately, I imagined they were thinking that no respectable Yeovil girl would marry a coloured man.

'Sorry Jim. This weather's getting me down, and we went to the grocers and the fruit and veggies are pathetic!'

I gave her a hug. 'When we get our own place, we can grow our own stuff, maybe get a greenhouse so we can have tomatoes and salads.'

She shrugged. 'Maybe. I'm not much of a gardener.'

Neither was I, but I could learn.

We'd no sooner moved in when I was posted on the Ark Royal again, this time to Barcelona and then Corsica. I felt bad leaving Alison, who was dismayed at this news.

'What'll I do while you're away?'

'You can always get the train to London and meet up with your friends,' I said.

'They went back to Oz ages ago,' she said, shrugging a shoulder dismissively.

'You'll have the car while I'm away, you could explore the area.'

She just stared at me, then picked up the local paper. 'Let's go to the movies.'

'The lads wanted to meet up for a drink at the Bull,' I replied. 'I think you'll like them.' She brightened up at this.

The evening was a success, Alison seemed to come to life, laughing and joking with John and Paul. Eventually, I looked at my watch. 'We'd better make a move, early start tomorrow.'

Alison pouted. 'So soon? Do they have dancing here?'

John and Paul looked at each other.

'No, love, but there'll be dancing at the Christmas Party, you'll like that.' I tried to console her.

'Christmas! That's ages away.'

'Only another few weeks.'

Paul opened his mouth and started to say 'We could ...' but then he saw my face and stopped.

John nudged Paul. 'We'd better get back too, and let this lucky blighter take his beautiful wife home.'

Alison seemed more cheerful on the way home. 'Your friends are nice, Jim.'

***

I didn't hear from Alison while overseas, it was only for four weeks, Barcelona, Corsica and Gibraltar. When I got back to Devonport, I posted a letter to Alison giving her my ETA for being back in Yeovilton so she could meet me with the car. She was sat in the passenger seat when I met her in the car park. Throwing my gear in the back, I jumped into the driver's seat and embraced her. 'Missed you, darling,' I murmured. 'Can't wait to get home. How've you been?'

She shrugged and looked out the side window. 'Bored mindless.'

I was a bit taken aback at this. 'Never mind, I'll keep you busy for the next few days.' I winked at her but she kept looking out the side window, not meeting my eyes.

'And it will be Christmas soon. I thought it would be nice to invite Mam and Dad for Christmas Dinner. I can pick them up and take them home again afterwards.'

'Okay.'

'So, what have you been doing while I've been away?' I was desperate to get some response from my normally bright and cheerful wife.

'Nothing. There's nothing to do here and even if there was, there's no-one to do it with.'

She said no more, and I spent the rest of the way home in silence, thinking about what she'd said. In Fremantle she'd had her job in a department store, could swim at any of the lovely beaches, meet up with her friends, and most of the time the weather was good.

Here, it was getting dark at three in the afternoon, and raining.

***

Back home, I tried to cheer Alison up, but it was hard going.

'What about Carole?' I asked. Carole and Richard were the couple who lived in the flat above us.

'She's nice, but she's at work all day and then she and Richard go out at the weekends. They don't want a third person trailing along.'

I could see her point. 'Cheer up love, your trunks should be here soon, with all your stuff.'

She just shrugged. 'I'll put the kettle on and make a nice cup of tea,' she parodied Mam's accent. 'It's the answer to all English women's problems, isn't it?' She sneered.

I was taken aback. This wasn't the Alison I'd married. I didn't know quite what to do. 'Is it your time of the month?' It was the only thing I could think of.

She glared at me.

I hurried back to the car to get my gear – a load of dirty washing. I was about to take it out, then had second thoughts and stuffed it all back in my kitbag – I'd take it to the launderette in the morning.

'We can go to the Bull, have dinner there, if you like.'

***

As I had two days off before going back to work, we went shopping and bought a Christmas tree and decorations and on my return to work, I left Alison in a more cheerful mood when she dropped me off at the base. 'Call around to Mam and Dad and invite them for Christmas Day,' I said as I kissed her goodbye. 'Then you could go and order a turkey from the butcher. Mam usually makes Christmas puddings and cakes, she's sure to give us one of each, so no need to make them.'

'I wasn't actually going to.' She grimaced, waved and drove off.

I was surprised that evening when we got home to find the front window curtains open and the Christmas tree in the window with fairy lights blinking on and off. 'It looks lovely, darling,' I exclaimed.

'Took me most of the day,' she said. 'Oh, and your mum and dad were pleased when I asked them to come for Christmas dinner. And you were right, about the cake and pudding; she has them all ready for us.'

Christmas Day turned out all right apart from a few mishaps. Together we managed to stuff the turkey, put streaky bacon over the breast and light the gas oven. I lifted the heavy roasting tin and tried to manoeuvre it into the oven only to find the turkey wouldn't fit. Alison was getting a bit distraught by that stage, so I ended up hacking the legs off the bird and putting it in sideways. 'We can cook the legs tomorrow,' I said, 'Actually that's better than eating leftover turkey for the next week.' When I saw the dismay on her face, I took her arm. 'Come on, sit down for a bit and have a Christmas drink.'

By the time I returned with Mam and Dad, I could see Alison had had quite a few Christmas drinks in my absence. Mam and Dad were delighted by her enthusiastic welcome. I carried in Mam's shopping basket, laden with pudding, cake and what looked like presents.

'Happy Christmas! Come on in out of the cold! Give me your coats, I'll put them in our bedroom,' Alison cried out as she gave them each a hug.

Mam looked around the living room and smiled. 'It's lovely! And so warm and cozy.'

I followed her glance. I must say it did look nice. The furnishings were sparse – a dining room table and four chairs – old but solid, with a sideboard to match and two easy chairs in front of the electric log-effect fire. The curtains were drawn back and although the Christmas tree in the window had started to shed a few needles, it looked pretty with its shiny baubles reflecting the fairy lights. Alison had pinned a ribbon over the fireplace and hung our few Christmas cards on it.

We'd just received our wedding photos from the photographer in Australia and some were displayed on the sideboard beside red candles in little containers of holly.

'Alison's done a great job,' I said, putting an arm around her and pulling her close. I indicated the easy chairs, 'Sit down, Mam, Dad, I'll get you drinks.'

Mam took an envelope from her handbag. 'Oh, before I forget, Minnie sent you a Christmas card, she didn't know your address so put it in with ours.' She handed it to Alison.

I felt a twinge of guilt, I hadn't thought to send one to Min, but I noticed Mam eyeing the wedding photos, so, before she could speak, I grabbed a package from under the tree. 'This is our present to you and Dad,' I said, handing it to Mam. It was a wedding album we'd had made just for them. This seemed an opportune moment for Alison to show them and explain who everyone was.

It was nice to see Alison kneeling on the rug between Mam and Dad with the open album on Mam's lap, Mam exclaiming at each photo.

'Whiskey, Dad?' I winked at him.

'Just a small one for me please.'

'Mam, what would you like to drink? A white wine?'

'Just a cup of tea, please.'

I didn't ask Alison; I felt she'd had enough for the moment.

Apart from the gravy being a bit lumpy and the brussels sprouts a bit undercooked – for Mam and Dad's taste – Dad had a problem with his teeth – everything went well.

When I returned from driving Mam and Dad home, I poured myself a shot of whiskey – I hadn't had much to drink during the day as I'd had to drive. Alison was asleep in one of the easy chairs. I sat in the other and felt a glow of satisfaction. Everything was good in my life. I loved my job, and my beautiful wife seemed to be settling down in England. Then I remembered that I'd neglected to ask Mam how was Minnie.

Alison suddenly opened her eyes and sat up. 'I must ring Mum and Dad!'

Shit! I'd forgotten that she'd mentioned ringing them about nine at night as it would be Christmas morning in Australia. Now we'd have to go out in the cold and find a phone box ...

---

1. In 1973 the Whitlam Labor government definitively renounced the White Australia policy

Chapter Fourteen

The Christmas period and the New Year went well, I thought. I'd managed to get in touch with old friends who were married and we met up with them a couple of times. Alison always seemed to spark up on those occasions and I was optimistic that she would soon make friends with the wives.

However, when I told Alison that I would be going on exercises on HMS Bulwark in the Caribbean Sea in January, she pouted. The weather wasn't too bad for January, but it was still damp and bleak outside.

'How often are you going to be away, Jim? What am I supposed to do all day on my own when you're not here?'

I avoided her first question. 'Maybe go and visit Mam, help her out a bit, shopping and so on ...'

She scoffed and threw herself down on the bed – I was getting dressed for work.

'And how long will you be away this time?'

I wasn't sure, you never knew on these exercises what might crop up.

I tugged at my tie. 'A month, maybe.'

'A month!'

'Might be less ... Come on, Alison, I'll be late. If you want the car, you'll have to drive me.'

***

When I'd told Alison we would be going to the Caribbean, she stared at me, folded her arms and snorted.

'So, you'll be swanning around in tropical sunshine while I'm stuck here in the freezing cold with nowhere to go, nothing to do and no friends!'

'It won't be like that! I'll be on board most of the time.' I was getting rattled. 'Do you realise that Bulwark carries sixteen Wessex helicopters? I work in the hangars below deck, and hardly ever get up and see daylight! It's not easy, you know, crammed in with a load of other men, sleeping in a narrow bunk bed ...'

'All right, all right, I get the picture,' She snarled, pouted and turned aside.

'Alison,' I said, catching her arm. 'I love you, and I'm working hard to earn a living and make a life for us. I know it's not easy, being cooped up here, but it'll be Spring soon and the weather will be nicer; your trunks will arrive and as soon as we can save enough, we can buy our own place and start a family. Come on, love, give me a cuddle.'

She sniffed and nestled into my arms. I thought I heard her mumbling something about no point having a baby with me being away half the year.

***

Crossing the Atlantic was no joke, it took ten days, and due to heavy storms, the Bulwark suffered a bit of damage. Our first stop was at Charleston in South Carolina. I don't know about swanning around in tropical sunshine; the day after we arrived at Charleston, there was the worst snow storm in eighty years which lasted a week! I made sure to write and inform Alison of this, and tried to cheer her up with the story about how in 1718, Charleston had been besieged by the pirate Blackbeard.

After Charleston we had exercises in the Caribbean with visits to Puerto Rica. The weather was nicer but I didn't tell Alison.

Arriving home, I discovered her trunks had arrived. These were two large metal trunks which she'd been gradually packing for weeks before the wedding, and that her parents sent just after we left.

I stared in dismay at the mess in our living room. One trunk occupied the bay window, and the other the middle of the room. Both were open and items of clothing, shoes and handbags were strewn around the floor, together with unopened wedding presents.

'So, your stuff came?'

She nodded and smiled. 'So good to have my own things here, Jim.'

'But where will we put it all?' There was only a small wardrobe in the bedroom which had to serve for both of us.

'I thought you could put one in the bedroom, and we could store a lot of things in it, like some of your clothes and shoes, and the other one,' she pointed to the one in the bay window. 'We could leave here and cover with a table cloth and make a feature of it. We can store a lot of the wedding presents that we don't need at the moment.'

Looking around at the crystal champagne glasses and other presents that I couldn't foresee us ever using, I shook my head in disbelief. It was already cramped in the bedroom. My reasoning was ignored. One of the trunks ended up on my side of the bed, which gave me barely enough room to get out of bed and sidle past, invariably stubbing a toe or scraping my shins on the sharp corners.

Things settled down for a while until just before Easter, when Alison decided it would be nice to get away for a few days over the Easter break.

'We can get bed and breakfast, Jim, your mum told me about it. Just drive along and stop when you see a B & B sign.'

My heart sank. 'I'm afraid that won't be possible just at the moment,' I said carefully.

She frowned. 'Why?'

'I'm being sent to HMS Bulwark again ...'

'What! Over Easter?'

'Sorry, darling.' I moved to kiss her but she wasn't having any.

'Where to this time?'

'Can't say. You know we all have to sign the official secrets act and must never discuss anything about our work or whereabouts. Even with our nearest and dearest.' This was true, but if she knew we'd be going to Malta and Istanbul, as well as other places in the Mediterranean, she'd get all huffy.

She got all huffy anyway.

***

I received a letter when we were based in Gibraltar. She wrote that she had news but would wait to see me before telling me. Of course, I was all agog. The only news I could think of was that she was pregnant. I'd assumed she was still on the pill, but apparently it wasn't always fool proof. My feelings were mixed. Initially, I felt proud and overjoyed that I'd fathered a child, but then the doubts crept in. The rental terms on the flat stipulated no children. Where the hell would we live? As soon as I got back, I'd have to see the Fleet Air Arm Welfare Officer, or whatever they were called and see if we could get a house somewhere.

And all the expenses, pram, cot ... and our lives would be limited. We wouldn't be able to pop out to the cinema, or the pub ... I panicked.

I thought of Mam and Dad. They would be ecstatic, their first grandchild. That made me smile. Then I started to panic again. I was too young to be a father. No, I was twenty-eight. My head whirled. Eventually I relaxed. It will all work out, plenty of men had children when they were much younger than me, look at John. He worshipped his little girl ...

Work was so hectic that I didn't have much time to think and before I knew it, I was back in Yeovilton with Alison picking me up. I was a bit coy when we met.

'So, what's the big news then, sweetheart?' I quickly scanned her figure but could see no change, no little bulge around her middle.

She flung her arms around me. 'Jim! I've got a job! Wanted it to be a surprise, I'm working as a bar maid at the Bull, Paul put in a word for me. Four nights a week and Saturday afternoons.'

My mouth opened and closed. I was like the goldfish Min won at the fair one year. She brought it home in a little plastic bag and Mam gave her a jam jar to keep it in. Its mouth opened and closed as it swam around and around in the jar, until we found it floating upside down the next morning. Min had been heart-broken. Why did that image haunt me now?

'Oh, that's great,' I managed to croak, swallowing the words which I had been preparing – *Oh that's wonderful news! I'll be a daddy!* And such like drivel.

'So, I'm working tonight, sorry, love. I'll drop you home, get changed and come back to work.'

So much for the welcome home I'd been expecting. Alison stopped at our gate, kissed me then drove off. Inside the house, I went to the bedroom to drop my kitbag. The bed was unmade

and clothes littered the room. I'd forgotten that Alison wasn't
the tidiest of people. Dirty dishes were piled up in the kitchen
sink. I sighed, filled the kettle with water and put it on to boil to
wash up. I spent the evening on my own, no car and rustling up
a meal for myself.

***

The following evening, I went with her to the Bull and met up
with John and Paul – I guessed they'd be there. They were both
ground staff so were on the base most of the time. We sat and
watched Alison. At first, I felt proud to see my pretty wife serving
up the drinks but as the evening wore on, it seemed she was
getting flirty with the men who came up to the bar. John must
have seen my face and the bit of a scowl I had on me, because
he caught my arm when Paul went up to get us another round,
and said quietly, 'She's not really flirting, Jim. That's just an act
she's putting on to make people feel someone likes them and
cares for them.'

'Hmm,' I muttered. 'I hope so. A lot of the young blokes are
hanging around the bar.'

'I thought you said that Alison had worked in a pub in London?'
I nodded.

'She can handle it, Jim. See how she looks in your direction
every so often and gives you a wink.'

I sighed. 'I guess so. Paul's taking a long time with our drinks.'

John cleared his throat and started to say something about
Paul, just as he returned with our beer.

Carefully setting the three glasses on the table, Paul raised his
eyes, 'Was talking to the owner, Jim. He reckons your Alison has
brought in more customers than any other barmaid.'

Somehow that was no consolation, and anyway on the few occasions I'd been to the pub in London where Alison had worked, she hadn't been my wife.

***

Alison did seem much happier now she was working at the Bull. No more talk of hating it here, the food, the people who were so reserved and insular, the weather, nothing to do etc. etc. It made it easier for me to leave her when away at sea or training.

Even though we were saving for a deposit on a house, we decided to get a phone installed. It would mean Alison might be able to get extra shifts, if any of the other barmaids were unavailable. I worried that she would rack up some hefty bills ringing her mum and dad, but she said it was cheaper for them to ring her, so she'd write and tell them our number and the best times to ring.

Later in the year her mum and dad announced they were thinking of visiting us the following northern summer. That made us sit up. After the initial flurry of excitement, we decided now was the time to buy a house. We'd saved enough for a deposit, but there were few properties available in our price range. Eventually we found a small cottage in a village near enough to Yeovilton for both of us to get to work.

It was in a poor state, which was why we got it so cheap – the kitchen and bathroom were very basic, and Alison said there was no way she'd put up with another explosive gas geyser over the bath – we simply had to have an electric hot water system – and a shower. We hadn't much money for tradesmen and although I tried, I wasn't much good at that kind of do-it-yourself work. Electrical work, radio and electronics yes, but plumbing and carpentry, no. But we were anxious to get it liveable by Christmas, as our lease on the place we were renting ended on the 31st December.

I brought Mam and Dad to see the cottage and they were enthusiastic.

'I can make you new curtains, Alison,' Mam said, as she looked around. She caught hold of one of the bedroom curtains and it fell apart in her hands. 'Oh!' she murmured, then turned to Alison. 'These are rotten.'

A small frown appeared on Alison's forehead.

'Mam was a skilled glove maker, she's wonderful at sewing,' I said, smiling at her.

Mam looked pleased. 'I can measure up the windows and calculate what you need, Alison dear. And we could choose the material together.'

Alison nodded. 'That would be great, Ellen. I was never very good at sewing.'

In the living room, some of the old, faded wallpaper had started to peel off.

'Hope that's not a sign of rising damp,' Dad muttered.

My heart sank. I'd been hoping they'd be enthusiastic about the place. I hadn't given a thought to things like rising damp, in fact, I had no idea what it actually was.

Dad must have noticed my dismay, as he quickly changed tack. 'A lot of these old buildings had no damp proof course, but the foundations were on old-fashioned rock rubble. Reckon this place is okay ...'

'It's lovely, Jim!' Mam butted in. 'You and Alison will be very happy living here.' She looked coy. 'And it'll be a great family home, lots of room for children!'

I tried my best, pulled up the tatty ancient linoleum and managed to strip the old wallpaper in the living room — some of it was peeling off, anyway, but my efforts at hanging the new paper that Alison had chosen was a disaster. Not only did it end up with bubbles but I pasted one length upside down. I didn't notice it until about to hang the next piece. That was the last straw. Alison doubled up laughing, but I wasn't amused. The last thing I wanted after working all day was to spend the evenings and weekends painting and decorating.

The place was still a mess when we moved in, the week before Christmas. We'd bought the minimum second-hand furniture – a double bed with an okay mattress, dining room table and four chairs. That was it. Alison's trunks pushed against a wall served as a settee with some cushions Mam had made on top.

I'd found someone to sand, polish and seal the floorboards, so they looked nice. It was worth the money.

Mam had suggested we go to them for Christmas dinner, which was a relief, our kitchen being only half finished. I'd managed to get a new gas stove and get it connected, but the kitchen sink was the old stone one like Mam's. Believe it or not, those sinks are now the height of fashion! I was waiting for the New Year sales to buy a new one.

It was good to go to Mam and Dad's for Christmas Day – good to be in a neat and tidy house, and Mam's cooking.

The living room was warm and cosy and I could see Mam had made a special effort to make everything look nice. She came in from the kitchen with the turkey on the big serving dish.

I jumped up 'What can I do to help, Mam?' I threw Alison a look that I hoped would make her get up and help Mam in the kitchen, but she just sat at the table fiddling with a napkin.

Mam put the dish on the table. 'Jim, would you carve, please?'

I tried to make conversation and include Alison. 'This must be a bit different from Christmas in Australia,' I said, smiling at her as I sliced the turkey.

'Oh, how is that?' Mam looked up from bringing in dishes of vegetables and roast potatoes.

Alison stared. 'We usually have seafood on the beach.'

Dad looked surprised. 'Seafood? You mean fish and chips?'

I hastily intervened. 'Tell us more, love.'

Alison put down her napkin, picked up a knife and stared at it. 'We have a barbecue on the beach, prawns and Balmain bugs, maybe steak, garlic bread, salads ...' her voice trailed off and I could see her eyes filling with tears. I took her hand and squeezed it.

'Bugs?' Dad murmured, a puzzled look on his face.

'You must miss your family,' Mam said.

'Talking of family,' I quickly broke in, trying to deflect Alison from thinking of her parents. 'What's the news on Min? I guess she must miss home. I haven't seen her for ages. She seems to only come over from America to visit you when I'm at sea.' That fact had only just occurred to me.

Dad was still mumbling about eating bugs, but thankfully Mam caught on and started to tell us about Min, and how she was going great in her job and was now a doctor. 'And anyway, Jim, you're away so often, it's not so strange that you miss her visits.'

'Eat up love,' I whispered to Alison at the same time as I was trying to focus on what Mam said. Luckily, I'd brought some nice wine and I refilled Alison's glass.

'I haven't seen her for ages, not since before we were married,' I now said to Mam. 'Did you take her to meet Alison when she was here?'

Mam's mouth opened and closed. She looked a bit uncomfortable and shuffled on her seat. 'Min got the train down.'

'Alison could have driven over to meet her.' I frowned.

Alison looked up; her brows drawn. 'I didn't know your sister was here, when was that?'

Mam looked a bit sheepish. 'Oh, a couple of months ago, Jim was away, and Min was only here for a day or two, she didn't have time, and we knew you'd be working, Alison, and wouldn't have time to drive over here.'

Alison pouted. 'I'd have made the time. I only have a brother; I'd love to have a sister.'

I thought to myself that Alison and Min would have little in common, but that wasn't the point. I made up my mind to contact Min and tell her Alison would love to meet her next time she came to see Mam and Dad.

The day dragged on. Alison picked at her food and only spoke if someone asked her a question. I tried to jolly things along, told a few of the more repeatable jokes I'd heard on my last assignment. They went down like lead balloons. Mam looked somewhat bemused, Dad only heard half of it and Alison just stared sullenly into space without a flicker of a smile.

Eventually we all sat back patting our bellies and complimenting Mam – except for Alison who'd hardly eaten anything. I rose and started clearing the table. Alison made a move to help, but I told her to sit by the fire and talk to Dad. She dutifully sat in Mam's easy chair and I heard her asking Dad how was his bad leg. I don't think Dad heard her properly but I left them to it and began washing up.

As soon as I deemed it was polite to leave, I looked out the living room window. 'Getting dark.' I pointed to the gloom outside. 'Looks like it might snow. We'd better make a move. And Alison must ring her parents.' I knew it would be far too early to ring

Australia but Mam and Dad wouldn't know that and it was a good excuse.

It may have been my imagination, but it seemed everyone was relieved. I fetched our coats from the lobby by the back door and helped Alison on with hers.

'Thank you for the lovely meal, Ellen,' she said, embracing Mam, 'And Happy Christmas, Tom.' She patted Dad's arm. 'Don't get up now,' she added as he made an effort to get out of his chair.

Goodbyes said and we were in the car driving home. Still the old Morris with no heater. Alison sat hugging her coat, saying nothing. I felt like challenging her about her behaviour but I didn't want to start a row, especially on Christmas Day. Or maybe I was too cowardly.

***

One Saturday afternoon soon after we'd moved in, I needed a break, so we drove to the Bull as Alison was working and I thought I'd have a quiet pint and maybe a game of darts, if the boys were there, as the Saturday afternoon shift was a short one for Alison.

Paul and John were at the bar. They were interested in hearing about the cottage and when I mentioned the amount of work that needed to be done, especially before Alison's parents' visit, Paul said he'd be happy to lend a hand. I fancied I saw a flicker of doubt cross John's face, but thought nothing of it at the time, and welcomed Paul's offer.

He turned up the following Saturday morning and went around sticking a screwdriver into window frames and announcing there seemed to be a bit of dry rot in some places. When he saw our faces, he smiled and reassured us. 'A couple of bits, which I can replace for you.'

He roared laughing when he saw my wallpaper efforts – I didn't think it looked too bad, I'd stuck a pin in the bubbles and flattened most of them out, and had torn off the upside-down length, but the pattern was obviously slightly mismatched.

So, when he said he could come over at weekends and help in return for a few beers, I was relieved, particularly as I'd just been told I had another posting coming up.

'Thanks, so much, Paul, but we must pay you for your time.'

'Nah, think nothing of it, Jim. It's good for me to be doing something at the weekends, particularly since Anne and I split up.' He grimaced.

He'd been going out with a new girl for a few months but it hadn't worked out. The few times he'd brought her to the Bull, I thought she seemed nice. Poor old Paul, he didn't have much luck in the romance department. I looked over to where Alison was working and thought how lucky I was.

Chapter Fifteen

I t was early February 1976 when I kissed Alison goodbye and set off on the Ark to the Western Atlantic. We had 824 Squadron with Naval Air Service Sea King choppers embarked. I wasn't sure how long I'd be away, but I had the feeling it would be a few months. It was still winter and I'd left plenty of firewood and filled the coal bunker before I left. We'd installed an all-night fire so Alison would be able to come back from work at night and the place would be warm.

As usual, she wasn't happy at being left.

'It's not fair, Jim. I'm so lonely when you're away. It's not like I've got friends and family here.' Before I could open my mouth, she continued, 'I know your mum and dad are only twenty min-utes-drive away, but I never know what to talk about with them.'

I nodded sympathetically. 'Paul said he'd try and come over at the weekends and do a bit more on the house.'

'Why can't you be like John and Paul and get work as ground staff, instead of being posted so often,' she grumbled. 'And it's dangerous, I've heard them talking at the Bull about accidents.'

I pulled her close, ignoring her comments about accidents, 'Don't worry love. I'll be fine. And your mum and dad will be here in June, not long to wait.'

She sniffed.

***

It was mid-July when I returned. It had been a gruelling trip. By then I'd been promoted to an aircrew man, and not only do they have to be the ears and eyes of the pilot, but they have to load and fire weapons, chart the weather, look for submarines, do air sea rescue and a million other things. I love my work, but it's difficult to explain exactly what's involved, especially as we were bound by secrecy. Alison seemed to find it hard to understand that I was tired. She was at the car park at the base when I arrived, sitting in the passenger seat as usual, but in a grumpy mood. I threw my gear in the back, got in the driver's seat and leaned towards her to give her a kiss. She turned her head to look out the window.

'Mum and Dad have been here a month already and you haven't been here. I think that's a poor show.'

I could see her pouting. 'Well, I'm here now and looking forward to seeing them.'

'They're in Scotland for a few days, wanted me to join them, but I said I had to wait for you.' Her tone implied that my return had deprived her of a visit to Scotland, where she'd never been.

'Sorry, darling, I would have loved to be here but it's my job and I had no choice.'

She sniffed, and turned back to look out the window. 'And they only have a few days left before they go back to Freo. How do you think I felt, stuck here on my own, trying to find things for them to do in this god forsaken backwater?'

I was annoyed at her description of our village. 'I thought they'd rented a car at the airport and drove down.'

'Yes, they did, but it only took a week for them to see everything around here.'

I thought she may not have suggested all the interesting places like Chesil Beach and the Clifton Suspension Bridge.

'And before you start, yes, I did take them to Chesil Beach. It's just a load of pebbles! No sand! Nothing like a proper beach, not like Freo! And don't start me on Cheddar Caves.'

Her arms were folded and she breathed heavily.

I changed the subject. 'Did you take them to meet Mam and Dad?'

'Yes.'

'And?'

She shrugged, 'You know your mum and dad.'

I said no more. We'd arrived back at the cottage.

Once inside, I dropped my bags in the hall and went through to the living room, then stopped short. 'Wow!' The room looked amazing, new – expertly hung – wallpaper, book cases built in either side of the fireplace, pretty curtains graced the window with matching cushions on the settee. I noticed all my text books on the shelves and our wedding photos,

'It's lovely, darling! You've done a magnificent job! Your mum and dad must have been impressed.' I took her in my arms and tried to kiss her.

Slightly mollified she muttered, 'Most of it thanks to Paul, and your Mum.'

'I must buy him a case of beer.' I tried again to kiss her, but she pulled away.

'Have to work this evening. I've got to get changed.' I followed her down to our bedroom.

'Oh, I put mum and dad in our room, we're in the spare room.'

'Okay,' I nodded, opening the door. We'd only had enough money to buy a second-hand double bed for the other bedroom, and had put a clothes rail in an alcove and Alison's two trunks under it.

'Haven't had time to make the bed and tidy up,' Alison muttered, fishing around on the bed for her barmaid clothes. 'There's some left-over stew on the stove if you want to heat it up.'

'Okay.' I walked over to her as she pulled off her dress, and slid my hands up under it, but she pushed me away.

'I'll be late, Jim.'

She dressed and gave me a quick kiss. 'Sorry, Jim.'

I didn't mind too much as I just felt like chilling out in front of the TV. Yes, we had a TV then, only a very small black and white one, and not much on it worth watching. I'd probably fall asleep in front of it.

Later that evening I went out in the garden for some fresh air to try and stay awake for when Alison got home. The next-door neighbour, Ted, was mowing his lawn, one of those push mowers – at least they were quiet. I breathed in the smell of the freshly mown grass. When Ted saw me, he stopped, came over to the fence, took off his cap and used it to wipe his brow, exposing a white scalp above his sunburned face.

'Been away, have you?'

'Yes, Ted, long posting, it's good to be back.' I loved the way Ted always stated the bloody obvious!

'Seed your in-laws was visiting.'

I nodded. 'Yes, from Australia.'

'And your mate. Doing a lot of work.'

'Yes, he's been great.'

Ted gave me a hard look. 'Better get back to me mowing.'

I had a sudden thought. 'Our lawn looks good. Did my father-in-law mow it?'

Ted looked a slightly embarrassed. 'I popped over and gave it a bit of a go. Your missus said her parents were coming – and what with you being away, defending our country, like …' he looked at his feet.

'Thanks, Ted, I appreciate that.' I made a note to get a case of beer for him. 'What beer do you drink?'

His face brightened. 'I like a Worthington.'

***

It was good to meet up with Alison's parents again. They were very impressed with the cottage.

'It's so quaint, Jim,' Janet said, after greeting me with a hug. 'It's just like we imagined an English village would be.'

'And we loved Scotland,' Brian chipped in. 'Of course, we couldn't understand a word anyone said, until we'd a had a few whiskeys!'

'We did the distillery tour.' Janet rolled her eyes. 'But it's lovely to see you again Jim, and to find our Alison looking so happy and blooming!'

I glanced at Alison. It appeared she was putting a brave face on things. Smiling and nodding. She did look good.

'Have you been to the Fleet Air Arm Museum at Yeovilton?' I asked Brian.

'Not yet, waiting for you to come and show us around.'

'The Concorde prototype is there.' I was proud of Britain's achievements with supersonic flight.

'Great! Maybe tomorrow?'

'Yes, I have a few days off.'

'I might spend the time with Alison.' Janet smiled ruefully. 'Not that interested in aircraft. I'd like to go into Glastonbury again and look around a bit more.'

I was pleased with this arrangement, as I thought it would be good for me to have some time with Brian.

***

The next day, Brian and I set off in their hire car. Alison was going to take her mum into Glastonbury in ours.

I parked in the museum car park and was about to get out when Brian put a hand on my arm.

'Hold on, Jim. I just wanted to have a word now we're on our own.'

I paused and sat back, a knot of tension forming in my stomach.

'You see, Jim, Janet really misses Alison, and although Alison seems happy here, I think she secretly would like to be back in Australia.'

I knew this was true, and I could sense the way the conversation was going, but I remained silent.

'I've been doing a bit of research, and being a Leading Aircrew man involves a lot of responsibility – obviously the British Fleet Air Arm think highly of you.'

I gripped the steering wheel.

'I must admit that when we first met, well, I was a bit taken aback ...' he touched my arm again. 'Jim, you must understand, we knew nothing about you and Alison is our only daughter, and I didn't know much about the Fleet Air Arm. We were worried about this marriage.'

I frowned.

'But now we've met your parents – who are lovely, by the way – and seen a bit more of you, well, we were thinking it would be great if you could transfer to the Australian Fleet Air Arm ...'

I loosened my grip on the steering wheel and unwound the window. I needed some air. After a few seconds thought, I turned to him.

'Brian. I know Alison would love to go back to Australia, but realistically my life is here. And I believe my wife should be here – at my side.'

That may sound a bit old-fashioned in these days of Women's Lib, but that's how things were in those days.

Brian gave a half smile and a bit of a shrug. 'The thing is, Jim, you're not exactly always here for her to be at your side.'

I brushed his comment aside. 'Well, Brian, I'm well respected, love my job, happy with our little cottage in the country and love my wife. Hopefully when we start a family, Alison will settle down. We may be able to afford for her to visit you fairly frequently.'

Brian sighed. 'I've got connections ...'

'Look, Brian,' I said, turning to him. 'I'm coloured. I know the white Australia policy no longer applies in Australia, but I'm not prepared to face any kind of discrimination, and if it came to light that I had received some sort of favouritism, well, that would be the end.' I spread my hands in a kind of entreaty. 'You see there's a unique bond between us air crew men. We have to trust each other, work together as a team. It doesn't happen overnight. I can't see that working if there was any kind of special treatment for me.'

Brian pursed his lips, then patted my knee. 'Got ya, mate! Yes, I see the problem. Just thought I'd ask anyway. Okay, let's visit this museum. Looking forward to seeing Concorde.'

***

After her parents left, Alison became very quiet and hardly responded to me. She had to get up early in order to drop me off at work if she needed the car, which was most days. She'd pull on a dressing gown, get into the car and hardly speak. I suspected she went straight back to bed when she got home, and only get up to go to work at The Bull.

I ended up buying an old motor bike so I could get home as some days she'd forget to fetch me from work. I didn't know what to do. And I had another deployment coming up.

Looking back, I guess she was depressed, but it wasn't something recognized in those days. At least by me.

And things got worse between us. When she wasn't working, Alison seemed to spend her time lying on the old settee we'd bought, mindlessly watching some rubbish on the television.

One evening I got home from work and blew up. It had been a hard day and I was tired. I went through the kitchen to our bedroom and saw red. I marched into the living room and confronted her. She was slumped on the settee in front of the TV.

'Why can't you at least make the bed and wash the dishes?' I roared.

She flew into a temper and raged off to the bedroom, shouting that she was bored and lonely, especially when I was never there.

'But I'm here now and you make no effort. You only seem to be interested in going to the Bull!' I snapped,

'At least the patrons at the Bull appreciate me!'

I stormed into the bedroom. She lay sprawled on the bed, crying,

I felt bad then and went over to the bed, bent down and tried to take her in my arms. 'Oh, Alison, darling,' I murmured. 'I appreciate YOU, but you don't appreciate ME!' That probably wasn't exactly the right thing to say.

'I should have stayed in Australia and never married you,' she sobbed.

About to make a cutting retort, I took a deep breath and bit my lip. I managed to say, 'Come on darling, give me a cuddle. I didn't mean to hurt you. Look, as soon as I come back from this next assignment, how about we go away for a little holiday? I should have some leave coming up.'

We managed to patch things up, but I must confess I found her untidy ways hard to cope with. She grumbled at me, saying I was obsessive compulsive. I didn't know what she meant.

I thought about suggesting we started a family, but that would probably set her off saying what was the point when I was away so much, and with a baby she'd have to give up her job in The Bull, and would be trapped at home. No grandparents around to help. Mam and Dad didn't have a car, so Mam wouldn't be able to come and babysit, and anyway, Dad wasn't in the best of health.

It got to the point where I dreaded my return after being away for any length of time. She worked most nights now at the Bull. When I was home, I'd be working days and we hardly saw each other. Ships in the night, ha ha. Sex was a perfunctory affair. I suggested she give up work – I earnt enough now so that she didn't need to work – then she wouldn't be too tired for love-making.

But she scoffed. 'And what would I do all the weeks and months you're away? Sit here navel gazing? Waiting for my sailor boy to come home?' Now her hands were on her hips and she confronted me. 'And what were you doing on the occasions when YOU had shore leave? Visiting prostitutes? Wife in every port?'

I was aghast. 'Never,' I shouted. I felt like shaking her. I wanted to say that like most faithful married men on board, I spent myself in the shower, but she didn't give me the chance.

'And what am I supposed to do here on my own at night?' she continued. 'No-one to cuddle in bed, no-one to satisfy MY needs!' Her face was red and a tear trickled down her cheek.

'Oh, Alison darling.' I tried to take her in my arms, but she flounced away.

'I'd like to be shown some love and affection,' she muttered.

'So would I!'

'I've got to get ready for work.' She went into the bathroom and slammed the door.

I sighed and walked out into the garden. I really didn't know what to do. There was no way I'd give up my career and find work outside of the Fleet Air Arm. And the thought of moving to Australia filled me with apprehension.

The garden was a mess too. The lawn overgrown and the few flower beds had more weeds than flowers. I mooched around until I heard the front door slam. I raced around to the front garden. Alison was about to get into the car and I managed to catch her arm.

'I love you, darling, come on, give me a kiss.'

She tossed her head. 'I'll be late.' She jumped into the driver's seat, slammed the door and drove off.

I returned to the house wondering what to do. Our wedding anniversary was coming up and I tried to think of something nice we could do together. October wasn't the best of times to travel around England, but I thought a short holiday might heal our relationship. I decided to broach the subject the next day that I didn't have to work and Alison didn't have to start her shift until after lunch.

I went into the bedroom. She lay curled up in the bed, sound asleep. 'Alison, darling,' I said gently. touching her shoulder, 'I've made breakfast. Would you like me to bring you yours in bed?'

She turned over and yawned. The sight of her nightie slipping over her shoulder and revealing her breast turned me on. I took a deep breath and waited for her reply.

'I'll have it later.'

I sat on the bed beside her. 'I was thinking we could have a short holiday to celebrate our wedding anniversary.'

She turned her head and stared at me. 'A holiday? In the English winter? Are you mad?'

'We could go to Brighton, or the Isle of Wight, somewhere like that.'

'And sit on the pier under our umbrellas? With all the old fogeys? In our raincoats and gumboots?'

She never understood that gumboots are called Wellingtons ...

She sniffed, turned over and wrapped herself in the blankets.

I tried to stroke her shoulder, but she pulled the blankets tighter.

'Where would you like to go, Alison?'

'Australia.'

I sighed, and returned to the kitchen. The plates of bacon and eggs were congealing and the toast already cold. I ate mine, covered up the other plate and put it in the pantry. I'd probably have to eat it for my dinner, it was unlikely she would. So much for a relaxing Saturday with my wife, I thought as I started cleaning the house – making as much noise as possible, just to annoy her. Petty, I know, but I was fed up. I tinkered around with my old motor bike to take my mind off things, then later, after she'd got up, dressed and stormed off to work, I decided to go to the Bull, hoping to meet up with the lads for a game of darts.

I wasn't in the best of moods when I went quietly into the bar. It was crowded, smokey and noisy. I stood at the doorway looking around for the lads. Alison was behind the counter, laughing and joking. My guts churned. How could she be so happy and laughing here and miserable at home? I spotted John – he was usually there on a Saturday evening – and made my way over to him.

'Hello, stranger!' He greeted me, getting up. He patted the bench seat beside him. 'Get you a pint?'

'Thanks,' I said, reluctant to go to the bar and confront Alison. I squeezed into the corner bench seat.

Morosely I watched him push his way through the crowd at the bar.

He returned a few minutes later. 'Alison's in top form tonight.'

I grimaced. 'Yeah.'

John frowned. 'What's up, Jim. You seem a bit down.'

It was hard to hear him over the noise, I shrugged. 'Nothing. How's Maddy?' His little girl. I didn't feel like shouting out my marital problems and knew that John loved talking about his daughter. I finished my pint and pushed some money across to him. 'Get us another drink, please, John, I'm a bit squashed in here.'

He drained his glass. 'Righty ho.'

I stayed for another half hour, then excused myself. 'Better go and warm the bed for the little woman,' I tried to joke. I'd never felt more miserable. Going home on the bike, I was only glad that another deployment was coming up soon. I had other things on my mind too.

Min. She seemed to be avoiding me. It appeared she only visited Mam and Dad when I was at sea. I was beginning to feel it was deliberate. I was in a bad mood anyway, so as soon as I got indoors, I dialled her number. So far, I'd avoided ringing her – finding the code for America and getting the time zones right – but now I didn't care. I found the notebook where Mam had carefully copied down Min's number. The phone rang for ages, then Min's voice: 'I can't answer the phone just now. Please leave your name and number and I'll get back to you.'

'It's me. Jim,' I snarled, and slammed the phone down. That's something you can't do with a mobile phone today, but it felt satisfying then.

A drink! Drown my sorrows. I found a bottle of brandy in the pantry. Neither Alison nor I usually drank spirits. This bottle was left over from the last Christmas pudding. I poured myself a generous measure, turned on the television and sat brooding and getting drunk.

Chapter Sixteen

Next day Alison told me she'd found me laid out on the settee, snoring my head off, with an empty bottle of brandy on the coffee table and a broken wine glass on the floor. She couldn't rouse me, so left me there. I'd woken during the night, feeling cold and sick, fumbled my way to the bathroom and then to bed. I tried to cuddle into Alison and get warm but she pushed me away.

'Marital duties,' I remember mumbling – to my shame. I cringe now to think of it.

'Piss off. Go and sleep on the settee.'

I tried to remonstrate and say something like I was the head of the house but the words didn't come out right. I turned over and fell asleep. Next morning I woke with a brutal headache. 'Can you get me some aspirin,' I called to Alison. But she wasn't there.

The phone rang. I couldn't be bothered answering, but it kept ringing. Finally, I dragged myself out of bed and picked it up. 'Yes?' I growled. My head throbbed.

There was a pause. 'Jim! What's wrong? Are Mam and Dad okay?' It was Min. She sounded very shaky.

'Yeah. They're fine. So am I, thanks for asking.'

I think I must have roared this because she was silent for a few seconds, then said, 'What's up Jim? I just got home from work and got your message. I'm so worried.'

'Go back to work,' I shouted. 'Sorry to have disturbed you.' And slammed the phone down. Again.

I managed to find some painkillers and lay down for the rest of the day. I didn't know where Alison had gone and to be honest, I didn't care. I'd never had a bad hangover before. Luckily it was Sunday and I could stay in bed, as the next day I had to get ready for a new deployment.

Alison barely spoke to me as she drove me to work on the Monday.

'I love you, Alison,' I said as I got out of the car and retrieved my gear. I went around to the driver's door to say goodbye, but the window was up and she stared straight ahead. I opened the door and bent to kiss her. She put her cheek up to me.

'Have a good trip,' she muttered, pulling the door closed, and before I could say anything, drove off.

I stood staring after the car, then picked up my gear and walked towards the security entrance.

One of my squad, Pete was at the gate as I arrived. He must have seen me trying to kiss Alison goodbye and her reaction, for he looked at me sympathetically.

'My wife's always a bit cool for the week before I go on deployment,' he said, picking up his kit. 'I think she's trying to adjust to me being away.' He shouldered his bag. 'Think it happens a lot. And this is going to be a long one.'

I just mumbled something as we walked through the gates. He was probably trying to console me.

***

It *was* a long tour. We started in April 1978 We berthed in Malta at one stage and some of the wives were allowed to join their menfolk. I'd mentioned it to Alison, but she'd merely shrugged and said something about not knowing the other women and what was the point.

I was hurt, especially when we docked and some of my squad got time ashore to be with their wives. And Alison's letters were few and far between. I tried to keep up a regular correspondence, but there was nothing much I could tell her.

We arrived back at base early December. I looked forward to spending Christmas at home with Alison.

I wasn't too worried when Alison wasn't there to meet me. I'd written several times with our ETA so she should have been there, but maybe she'd forgotten. I walked out to the gate with Pete, and saw his wife waiting for him. No sign of Alison.

Pete noticed this, fair play to him, I knew he must be longing to get home, but he turned to me.

'Can we give you a lift, Jim? Looks like your wife has been delayed.'

I gratefully accepted.

'Nice place,' Pete said as he stopped at our gate. The car was parked in the driveway, so Alison must have slept in, or something.

'Yes.' I jumped out and got my bag from the boot. 'Thanks, Pete.' I slapped the side of the car; he waved and drove off.

As you can imagine, I was pretty annoyed by this time. I tried the front door handle and it was locked. I frowned, a slight worry creeping over me. Was Alison okay? I pushed open the letter box, felt for the string holding the spare key, pulled it out and unlocked the door.

I had a job pushing the door open. I wondered what was blocking it, mat wrinkled or something, then looked down and saw a pile of letters on the floor. Panicking, I dropped my kit bag and ran to the bedroom. No-one. No sign of her. I went to the kitchen and saw the letter propped up against the teapot on the kitchen table.

I grabbed it and read.

Dear Jim

I'm sorry to give you the news like this, but I didn't want to tell you while you were away, and upset you.

I'm going back to Australia. I can't take it anymore here.

I'm sorry Jim, but it just hasn't worked out, and it's better this way.

Alison.

Typical Alison, she hadn't put the date on the letter. I collapsed onto a kitchen chair, my thoughts all over the place. What did she mean, not working out? I thought we'd patched up our differences. I know we'd had a few disagreements lately, but nothing I thought would warrant her taking off and leaving me. I looked around the kitchen, got up and opened the fridge door. Except for some butter, a bit of cracked and discoloured cheese and a bottle of milk, it was empty. I shook the milk bottle. White jagged lumps sluggishly slopped around.

I went to the bedroom and flung open the wardrobe doors. Only my few jackets were there. Feverishly I pulled open the tallboy drawers. None of her clothes were there. Her trunks! Where were her trunks? Not in the spare bedroom. She'd gone. Lock, stock and barrel.

I found a bottle of brandy in the sideboard, still half full and took a swig. I frowned. Where had this come from? I thought I'd finished the last bottle. Then I remembered her parents had brought some from the duty free when they'd come. Brian liked a brandy nightcap. Gradually I calmed down. Then the anger grew in me again. How could she have done this? Just up and left? With never a word? I punched my right fist into my left palm, again and again ...

I finished the bottle of brandy and stumbled to the bathroom, peed and fell into bed. The unmade bed. Of course ...

***

Next day I felt like shit. I didn't wake up until midday and had no idea what to do. I made a cup of strong black coffee and took two pain killers. How could I tell Mam and Dad? Did Alison not love me anymore? Should I have agreed to try and transfer to the Australian Fleet Air Arm? Should I try and follow her? I looked at the telephone. Ring her parents? I looked at my watch. Two o'clock. What would that be in Australia? 3am? They wouldn't be happy being woken up in the middle of the night.

Like an automaton, I cleaned up the house, emptied my kit bag and started the washing machine. One of those old twin tubs, so it took a while. All the time my mind went over and over trying to figure out where I'd gone wrong. By the time I'd hung out the washing it was evening. I paced around feeling more and more lonely and unsettled and decided to go to the Bull. Probably be a good idea to try and eat something, even though I felt sick in my stomach.

***

Getting my pint, it seemed strange not seeing Alison behind the counter. The few men around the bar greeted me. I was sure it was with an undertone of sympathy. They'd all know Alison had left me and gone back to Australia.

I'd just settled in our usual corner seat when I saw John come in. He went to the bar and as he waited for his pint he saw me.

He nodded at me as he sat opposite and took a swig of his beer. 'How're things, Jim?'

Unexpected tears came to my eyes. 'She's left me,' I managed to croak, taking out a handkerchief and blowing my nose, blinking away those unwelcome tears.

'I know, she gave in her notice here. Word got around.'

I put my head in my hands. 'How can I get her back, John?'

'Don't think you can.'

That wasn't what I wanted to hear. I tried to gather my thoughts, looked up and around the bar. It was unusually quiet.

'Where's Paul? He's here most weekend nights.'

John shuffled on the bench seat. 'He's moved.'

'Oh? Where?'

John said nothing. He shrugged and looked around, not meeting my eyes. 'So how was your deployment? Long one this time,' he eventually said.

'Yeah, good. Pretty hectic.' I wasn't interested in talking about work. I finished my beer and stood up. 'Another for you?'

He nodded. 'Thanks.'

On my return from the bar, John slid beer mats across the table and started talking about his daughter. 'Thanks, Jim. Maddy wants me to take her to see the pantomime next month. She asked if she could bring her best friend ...'

I was annoyed. How could he be talking on and on about nothing, while I was in the depth of despair? I sat drinking and fiddling with a beer mat.

He eventually fell silent.

'What should I do, John?'

'Not much you can do, old sport.'

'Should I get compassionate leave and fly over and see her?'

'Don't think that's a good plan,' he mumbled.

'Why not?' I was getting a bit belligerent and the headache was coming back. Probably the beer hadn't been such a good idea after the brandy. And I'd still had nothing to eat.

John looked everywhere but at me. He finished his beer and stood up. 'Better get going.'

'Why not?' I said, my voice getting louder.

'Shh.' He sat back down, and leaned across the table. 'Didn't want to be the one to tell you, Jim,' he whispered.

'Tell me WHAT?'

John took a deep breath, leaned back towards me and whispered, 'She's pregnant.'

I nearly jumped off my seat. 'Pregnant! Why didn't she tell me? That's great news!'

'Settle down, Jim. Don't shout.' He grimaced and stared at his drink.

I had a sudden thought. 'Wait a minute ... I left in April, it's now December. When did she leave? She would have had it by now!' I leaped up, 'I must go home and ring her parents.'

John caught my arm. 'Sit down, Jim. Um. The baby isn't yours.'

'Not mine!'

'It's Paul's'

A red haze veiled my eyes. Blood pounded in my ears. 'Paul's? I'll kill him.' I gasped as I sat forward and clenched my fists.

John pushed me back on the seat. 'Shut up! Do you want everyone to hear you?'

I was breathing heavily. 'Who else knows?'

'No one. Paul only told me. He thought she was on the pill, but apparently, she didn't bother taking it when you were away. They never meant it to happen. She didn't want to hurt you. Late one night after her shift finished your old car wouldn't start, so Paul gave her a lift home. And well, she asked him in and well ...'

'Where is he? Where's he gone?' I was stuttering with fury, saliva spitting out over the table.

'Don't know. Overseas, I think.'

'She could have got rid of it – had an abortion!' I'd never been so angry.

John sighed. 'Against her religion.'

'What religion?' I snarled. 'So, fornication is allowed in her religion?'

'Stop, Jim. She was lonely.' John looked around as the room went quiet. He took my arm. 'Let's get something to eat.'

I shrugged him off, drank the rest of my beer, slammed the glass down and made to go.

'Come back to my place, Jim.'

I ignored him, strode out of the pub, jumped into my car, stamped on the accelerator and stormed home. Luckily there was no traffic.

***

How could she? And Paul? I'd thought he was a mate. Visions of my wife and Paul in our bed went round and round in my head. I tossed and turned, eventually falling into a fitful sleep.

Next morning I sat at the kitchen table drinking a cup of black coffee and flipping through all the mail that had accumulated behind the front door Mostly bills. I'd deal with them later, first I'd better go and see Mam and Dad and tell them the bad news.

Mam and Dad were delighted to see me. As usual, I went in the back door and surprised them. 'Hello!' I called from the kitchen.

They were sat by the fire listening to something on the radio, Mum busy knitting.

'Oh, Jim!' Mam exclaimed. 'How lovely to see you after all this time away. We thought you'd be calling round. How's Alison, is she with you?'

I shook my head as Dad smiled and mumbled something.

Mam jumped up. 'You look a bit pasty, love, did you pick up a germ over there? I'll put the kettle on.' Anywhere outside of England was "over there" to Mam, and full of germs.

'No, I'm fine. But I don't have any good news. Alison has gone back to Australia. It seems she's left me.'

Mam halted on her way to the kitchen. 'Left you! Why?'

I shrugged. 'She never really settled down here, and she wasn't happy about me being away so much.' I pulled out a chair and sat at the table. No way would I ever tell them about Alison being pregnant.

'She'll come back, love, probably just needs a bit of time with her family.'

I grimaced. 'Unlikely.'

I looked at Dad who was frowning. He seemed to have aged a lot since I'd been away.

'Will you go over to her?' he said.

'No point.' I put my head in my hands. 'Anyway. It's over. End of story.'

Mam tutted and carried on about all newly married people had these little tiffs, she'd get over it and be back before I knew it. Just give her time and a bit of space ... blah, blah, blah. I felt like screaming at her *she's pregnant with another bloke's baby!* But I didn't. I clenched my teeth.

Mam patted my back. 'Don't you worry, love, it'll all work out.'

Dad grunted, 'Tell us about your trip, Jim.' For all the world as if I'd just been to Majorca for a week's holiday.

Chapter Seventeen

It was hard being in the house on my own, and I looked forward to being back at sea. At least on a deployment you didn't have time to think much about home.

I spent the weekends in the garden, and that seemed to help ease the ache in my guts. I met up with John most Saturdays for a game of darts. I knew I wasn't the only one at the base whose wives had left them. It was hard for a woman married to a naval man.

On the few occasions when I saw John, he tried to console me. 'This too will pass, Jim,' he said a few times.

I wanted to say something like, *yeah, by the time I'm sixty!'* but I didn't. Not when I reminded myself about his wife. Losing her to cancer at a young age and bringing up his daughter by himself.

For ages, every time I saw Mam and Dad, Mam would be all eager for news of Alison. "Have you heard from her, love?" She'd ask, putting the teapot on the table and arranging cups and saucers.

Eventually she gave up, until one day, ages later, off she went again. I really didn't need this. I'd been away on a training exercise and was tired. I'd planned to visit them in the morning and then go home and watch a match on TV.

'No Mam,' I sighed. 'I've heard nothing.' I tried to change the subject. 'How's Min these days?'

That did the trick. 'She's doing great, apparently. Got a promotion. She's now a Project ...' she turned to Dad. 'What did she say, Dad?'

'Project manager.'

'I haven't seen her since before I was married,' I said.

'But that's ages!'

'I know.'

'Well, she's in London at the moment, but can't make it down to see us, she's only there for two nights.'

I blinked and felt hot anger rising in me. Mam must have told her about Alison, but Min hadn't rung me or tried to contact me. I was fed up with the way she carried on, always avoiding me. I made a sudden decision.

'Where's she staying?'

Mam blinked. 'In London.'

'Yes, but where?'

'Oh, she said in her last letter. I'll find it.'

I waited impatiently while Mam found the letter, then her glasses.

'Look, just here,' Mam held out the letter. 'I can't see the name very clearly. I've got cataracts, so the optician said.'

I glanced at the letter and made a mental note of the hotel – a big posh one at Heathrow Airport.

I looked at my watch, and made a sudden decision. I drained my cup.

'Thanks, Mam, that cuppa was just what I needed. I'd better fly, got a lot to do today.'

'Oh, really, so soon?' Her smile faded.

'Sorry, Mam, Dad. But I should be able to call in next weekend.'

I jumped in the car and sped to the railway station. I'd learned the Paddington train table by heart, after all the trips I'd made to see Alison when she was working in London, and it probably hadn't changed much since then. I just had to change at Reading.

Once at Paddington station I knew I could get a train to Heathrow.

I settled in my seat and wondered what on earth I was doing. I was so angry with Min. We'd always been so close. I was going to confront her and sort this out once and for all.

At Heathrow I got a taxi to her hotel and went in. All very plush. I went to reception – it was five thirty by that time – and asked for Min.

'Is Dr Jones here?'

The receptionist – a suave looking callow youth – looked me up and down, then checked the register. He swivelled in his chair and studied a wall of pigeon holes.

'The key is here, so they're not in.'

'I'm Dr Jones's brother, perhaps I can wait in her room?'

He raised one eyebrow, and gave me a look which said, "Yeah, really?"

'I'm terribly sorry but we're not allowed to do that. Perhaps you'd like to wait in the reception area.'

He wasn't being unreasonable, a big black bearded man in jeans and a loose jacket probably didn't look like a petite white woman doctor's brother.

'Thanks.' I found a chair, one of those low backed affairs that only come up to your armpits, so your head has nowhere to rest, and sat and surveyed the area. I kept looking at my watch and wondering if Min was ever going to arrive.

All these affluent looking people were coming and checking in, some looked at me as if wondering why the porter hadn't thrown me out.

I actually didn't recognize her until she spoke at the reception and got her key.

I stood up and went towards her.

'Dr Jones, I presume?'

She spun round, and did a double take.

'Jim?' she frowned.

'Yes, it's me. Come to see you at last.' She looked amazing. The complete business woman. My heart thumped.

She went pale. 'What is it? Are Mam and Dad okay? Are they alright?' She clutched my arm.

'As far as I know, yes.'

Her frown deepened. 'You'd better come up to my room.'

She walked towards the lift and I followed her. In the lift the two other people edged away from me as if I had "germs".

The strange thing is that when I saw her, all the anger that had been building up in me dissipated. I just wanted to take her in my arms and hug her, like I used to do when she was little and upset about something.

Inside her room she kicked off her high heeled shoes, sank into one of the lounge chairs and turned to me.

'What is it, Jim? What's brought you here?'

I looked around, there were two chairs next to a kind of writing desk. I drew one out, sat on it and took a deep breath.

'Why have you been avoiding me, Min? I haven't seen you since the time that plonker gave you a lift. What was his name?'

'Toby.'

'Yes, our Tobe,' I said scathingly.

She bent her head and fumbled at the back of her neck and pulled out a few hair clips. Her hair came tumbling down around her shoulders. I took a sharp breath.

She blinked a few times, then stood. 'I'm tired, Jim, I need to go to the bathroom and take out my contacts.'

I was puzzled for a few moments before I realized she meant her contact lenses. While she was gone, I looked around the room. Very opulent, I'd only ever stayed in one hotel, in Perth on my honeymoon. That one had been very basic. I dwelt on the memory of those few nights with Alison ... then Min came back, now she had glasses on, and looked just like my old Min.

Thinking about the honeymoon had made me feel a bit nostalgic, but then my stomach rumbled.

'Are you hungry, Jim?'

I nodded. 'Yeah, haven't eaten since breakfast.'

'I'm too tired to go out. I'll order something from room service.'

'Okay.'

While she was ringing, I went to the bathroom and when I returned, she was lying on the bed indicating the chair by the writing desk.

'Sit down, Jim, my feet are killing me. Not easy standing in those shoes all day.'

I looked at the red shoes and the stiletto heels. 'Uh huh.' I'd never had a chance to ask her about her job. 'So, what do you actually do, Min?'

A little wrinkle appeared on her brow. 'There's a small bottle of wine in the bar fridge, could you pour me one, please, Jim? And get a drink for yourself.'

I did as she asked, getting a beer for myself. She started telling me about her work.

It was all a bit beyond me and I was getting somewhat restive when there was a knock on the door. She put her glass on the bedside table, slid off the bed and opened the door. Why didn't I answer it? Dunno. Just transfixed by Min, I suppose.

It was room service. A youngish man came in with a trolley, laid the table with cutlery and glasses, plates of food and two bottles of wine. One red and one white. He pulled out one of the chairs and smiled at Min, indicated the bottle of white wine and raised his eyebrows.

She smiled back and inclined her head. He filled her glass then looked at me. 'Yes, thanks,' I said.

He made a little bow as he folded a napkin over his arm and started to push the trolley away. I noticed Min gently pressing one of her hands into his. 'Thank you, that all looks lovely.'

He nodded and thanked her. I guessed she'd given him a tip.

'Come on Jim, tuck in.'

I was ravenous. 'Thanks, Min.'

She only picked at her food, but I noticed she soon emptied her wine glass, refilled it, then pushed her plate away.

'Don't you want anymore?'

'No, I'm full.'

I pulled her plate over. 'Can't waste it,' I mumbled spearing an asparagus stalk with my fork.

Min burst out laughing. 'Oh, Jim! You haven't changed a bit!'

I laid down my fork and studied her. 'But you have, Min. Why have you been avoiding me? You heard that Alison left me?'

'Mam said Alison had gone to Australia but that she'd be coming back soon.'

'That's Mam's wishful thinking. Alison's never coming back to me. It's nearly two years since she left.'

'What happened?'

I finished my beer and poured myself a glass of wine. Swirling it around I looked at her. 'She cheated on me. Got pregnant by another bloke while I was away on a long deployment.'

Her eyes widened in surprise. 'I'm sorry.'

'Yeah. Well, these things happen. Not easy to be a naval man's wife. Mam and Dad don't know about it. Our marriage was on the rocks anyway.' I paused and sipped the wine. 'I've not told anyone else.'

'Open the bottle of red, Jim and pour me a glass.'

I went to fill her glass, but she put out her hand to stop me. 'The other glasses, Jim.' She pointed to a big wine glass.

'Anyway. Why have you been avoiding me?'

She took a deep breath and seemed to be thinking. 'Jim. You were my hero. My beautiful big brother, who always solved my problems. I worshipped you. Then you suddenly dropped a bombshell on us that you were marrying a woman from Australia that none of us had even met and knew nothing about. Mam and Dad were a bit shaken. But I was devastated, Jim. Heartbroken.'

'Heartbroken?' I echoed.

'Yeah. You broke my heart, Jim. No man I've ever met came near what I felt about you. Yeah. Sounds stupid. A grown woman.'

She took a gulp of wine. I was a bit worried about the amount she was drinking.

I thought I heard her mutter, 'Still do.'

'So, is there a special man in your life at the moment, Min?' I asked casually. I had to know.

She smiled, that mischievous twinkle in her eyes. 'What do you think, Jim?'

I shrugged, then smiled back. 'Several, probably.'

She nodded, and changed the subject. 'So, what are you up to now, Jim.'

I'd finished all the food and filled a glass with some red wine. I wasn't a wine drinker, and would have preferred a beer, but I was feeling happy and relaxed.

'Been on deployment, and training, you know, technology is changing all the time.'

'Tell me about it.' She laughed, got up from the table, went to the bed, rearranged the pillows and lay down, still holding her glass of wine.

I started to tidy the table, and began stacking the plates when she burst out laughing.

'Jim! Stop that! The staff do all that. Come and sit down.'

I didn't like leaving a mess, but I took my glass of wine and sat on the easy chair.

We started chatting and it was just like old times, Min and me. I'd forgotten how we used to have fun together, laughing about stupid things.

'I've missed you, Min,' I mumbled at one stage. She got up and filled our glasses again. The bottles were empty, I noticed, plus the ones we'd got from the bar fridge.

'Where are you staying tonight, Jim?'

I stared at her. 'Um, never even thought that far. I was just so angry at you, I got the name of your hotel from Mam, jumped in the car, drove to the station, and well, here I am.'

She looked at her watch. 'It's ten-thirty.'

I struggled to my feet. 'I'd better get a taxi back to Heathrow station.'

'And end up at Paddington and wait for the early morning train, then change trains three times?'

'I can see if they have a free room here.'

She gave a sardonic laugh. 'Jim this place is criminally expensive. My company pays for it. No, you'd better stay here with me.'

I looked at the lounge chair and small settee. I didn't think I'd be able to sleep on either of them. She must have seen my face as she said softly, 'We can share this bed, Jim, it's big enough for three.'

My heart raced. I didn't know what to think. But I knew the first train from Paddington wasn't until four or five in the morning. 'You sure?'

She nodded. 'I've got to fly back tomorrow morning. Nine-thirty flight, so I must be up early.' She got off the bed and went to the bathroom. I heard the shower and sat thinking about all she'd said about being heartbroken, and wondered if she still loved me in that way.

She came out of the bathroom, all glowing and wearing nothing but a short cotton nightie. I gulped and felt desire rising in me. 'My turn.' I hurried to the bathroom, my thoughts in a whirl. I had nothing to change into so put the underpants I'd been wearing all day back on. What else could I do? I hadn't planned on staying the night, in fact I hadn't planned this trip at all.

I opened the door and called out, 'Have you got a spare toothbrush?'

'Look in my toiletry bag, should be one there that the airlines give you.'

I found a white bathrobe behind the door and put it on. It was a tight fit, but at least it covered the bulge in my underpants.

She was watching me as I came out. 'Can you bring me a glass of water, please, Jim?'

I nodded, found a glass, filled it, placed it on the bedside table and went to the other side of the bed. I climbed in, making sure to leave a big space between us, loosened the bathrobe, threw it over one of the lounge chairs, and turned to her. 'Goodnight Minnie.'

Next thing a tear rolled down her cheek. I frowned. 'What's wrong, Min.'

She sniffled, 'Oh, Jim.' Then she started crying in earnest.

Somehow, I couldn't help myself. I drew her close and started to kiss away those tears.

She mumbling something along the lines of being in love with me since the day I graduated from the Navy School. I groped on the bedside table for a tissue and gently wiped her eyes.

She gave a gurgle. 'Jim, next thing, you're going to hold a tissue to my nose and tell me to give a big blow! Like you did when I was a little girl with a cold!'

I smiled.

She sniffed and held out a hand for another tissue. 'I'm sorry, Jim, I can't help it. I know it sounds stupid; how could a young girl fall in love with her brother? And still be in love with him. But you're not my brother, Jim. You were my best friend.'

I couldn't take in what she was saying, too distracted by her silhouette through that skimpy nightie. I pulled her close and gently kissed her.

Well, you can guess what happened next ...

After a while she fell asleep in my arms.

I woke early next morning, and lay looking at her. My beautiful Min. I knew then that she was the one and only person with whom I wanted to spend the rest of my life. How stupid was I, not to have realised this until now. I must have been blind not to have seen years ago that she was the love of my life.

'Min, darling,' I whispered, kissing her forehead, then her lips with the intention of carrying on down her body.

Her eyes flew open. 'Jim!' She leapt out of bed. The sight of her naked body aroused me again.

'Come back to bed, it's early.'

'No! I have to get my flight.'

She disappeared into the bathroom. I followed her. She was in the shower. I stepped in with her.

'Min,' I groaned, putting my arms around her and pressing her into me. 'I want to spend the rest of my life with you.'

She touched my cheek. 'Darling, Jim. I want that too. But it's impossible. It would kill Mam and Dad. They must never know about this. It must never happen again.'

I hadn't thought about Mam and Dad.

'We can still be together.'

She shook her head, sending a shower over my chest; her hair was wet and curls clustered around her face.

'Jim. It wouldn't work. I'm in the US and you're in England and off on deployments or whatever. One of us would have to give up their career.'

I couldn't think straight. 'There must be a way.'

'Jim. I'm sorry. Last night was amazing, but it should never have happened. I have to get dressed now and pack.' She broke away from me, wrapped a towel around her body, a hand towel around her head and went into the bedroom.

I had a shower and came out. She was packing her case.

I fumbled around for my clothes and dressed.

'Min, we can work something out.'

She shook her head. 'Jim, I hardly slept last night worrying about this. Will you give up the navy and come to America?'

I frowned. 'What would I do there? Don't you have to have a green card or something to be able to work there? Why can't you come back to England?'

She paused from putting some folders into her brief case and looked up at me. 'And live where, and do what? And when would I see you? We couldn't live anywhere near Mam and Dad, so that would mean far from your work, and you're away on deployments so I'd rarely see you anyway.'

She snapped shut the brief case and looked around the room. She found those high heeled shoes and slipped them on.

'I'm ready, Jim,' she said, picking up a small carry-on bag. 'I've got a taxi booked. We can go to Heathrow together and you can get a train to Paddington. We can have coffee at the airport.'

I stared at her as I pulled on my jacket. 'Okay, Min.' What else could I say?

I waited at reception while she checked out, then followed her outside and into the waiting taxi. I desperately wanted to take her in my arms, but she was studiously looking out the window, avoiding my eyes.

At the airport, she checked in and made her way to the security entrance, I trailed after her. She looked at her watch then turned to me her eyes full of tears. 'No time for coffee. Bye, Jim.'

I hugged her and kissed her until she broke away and walked through the entrance without looking back. I stared after her until she disappeared around a corner.

Chapter Eighteen

Going back on the train my thoughts were all over the place. I'd thought I'd loved Alison at the time, but it was nothing compared to how I felt about Min. I was a complete idiot not to have realized it before. It was because Alison reminded me of Min that I'd thought I loved her. But like Min said, it would be impossible. Well, now it looked like I'd be single for the rest of my life, with an ocean separating us.

I wondered if Min would go back to her "several men". A tide of jealousy swept over me. I clenched my fists, then looked up to see a little old lady on the seat opposite staring at me. I relaxed my hands and smiled at her. She sniffed, blinked and looked down at the book she was reading.

I took a deep breath and tried to relax, forcing myself to think about the next deployment coming up.

***

I called to see Mam and Dad before I left. I was unsure if I should mention that I'd met Min in London as I didn't know if she'd told Mam about our meeting during their frequent phone calls.

'Talked to Min recently?' I asked casually, fiddling with the spoon in the sugar bowl.

'She rang last week,' Mam said, frowning at my fingers.

I put the spoon back in the sugar bowl. 'Oh, how is she?'

'She said she was all right. Why don't you ring her?'

I shrugged. 'Been busy, and the time differences, you know.'

Mam nodded, as Dad started to cough. Mam frowned. 'Dad's had a nasty cough for the past few days.'

I looked at Dad, he didn't look well, his skin a kind of pasty grey.

'Have you seen the doctor, Dad?'

Mam butted in. 'You know your dad, he won't go to the doctor, says he's fine.' She folded her arms. 'You tell him, Jim. Make him go.'

How did Mam think I could make Dad do anything? But I tried. 'Dad, I really think you should go, the doctor can give you something to ease your chest.'

He shook his head as another bout of coughing overtook him. 'I'm all right,' he managed to mutter. He spat into a bit of rag – Mam tore up old worn sheets into rags to use as handkerchiefs, if we had a cold – then opened the range and threw it into the flames.

'Got any jobs you'd like me to do before I go?' I asked Mam. I tried to help as much as I could, I'd told Mam to make a list – things that neither of them could manage anymore.

She rummaged in her apron pocket and brought out a crumpled piece of paper. Putting her reading glasses on, she frowned as she read from the list. 'The toilet keeps running ...'

***

When I called to see them after returning from an especially long deployment, I was shocked to see Dad.

I took Mam aside. 'Mam,' I whispered, 'what's wrong with Dad? He looks awful, and he's still in his dressing gown.'

She shrugged, and tears welled in her eyes. 'I know, Jim, but he won't go to the doctor. I've tried to persuade him. Maybe he'll listen to you. He barely picks at his food, and this morning he didn't even have the energy to get dressed.' She turned away and used her pinafore to wipe her eyes.

I went over to my father – he was sitting in his usual chair – and crouched beside him. 'Dad, I think you should see the doctor.' I took his hand, stunned at the sight of his skinny arm and sunken cheeks. I reckoned he must be in his late seventies, and had always been such a strong upright man. It was awful to see him like this.

'I'm going to call the doctor,' I told him.

He shook his head. 'No doctors, never been sick in my life. Not going to start now,' he said, breaking into a cough. 'He'll only take me to hospital,' he managed to gasp. 'Don't want to be prodded and poked for no reason.'

Mam sighed and shook her head.

Dad looked at me. 'I'm tired. Can you help me up to bed, Son?'

I helped him upright and realizing that he could barely stand, I picked him up and carried him up the stairs to the bedroom, amazed at how little he weighed.

'Bet when you used to carry me when I was a baby, you never thought I'd be carrying you,' I tried to joke, and Dad gave a weak grin but his eyes were closed.

I helped Mam get him into bed, then came down and rang the doctor.

'Doctor will be coming later this evening,' I told her when she came downstairs. 'Sit down now and I'll make you a cup of tea.'

When I got home, I checked my watch. Four in the afternoon, that meant it should be around eight in the morning in California. I knew it was eight hours behind London. I picked up the phone and rang Min.

'Yes?'

'It's Jim. Dad's pretty sick, I think you should come home. I don't think he'll ...' I choked up and couldn't continue.

'Oh, Jim! That's awful, I didn't realise he wasn't well.'

'Neither did I, but he's gone downhill a lot in the last few months. Think it best you come home as soon as possible.'

There was a pause. 'Jim. I can't.'

'You've got to, Min. Mam needs you.'

'Jim. I can't. I ... um, I've got to go into hospital next week.'

'Can't you postpone it? Why are you going into hospital?' I was suddenly gripped with fear. 'Is it cancer?' I whispered.

'No, thank goodness. Just a small procedure. I can't put it off.' Her voice sounded shaky.

'What'll I tell Mam?' I started to say, then changed my mind. 'You'd better ring Mam and explain why you can't get back. She might understand if it's female stuff. Bye, Min.' I felt like slamming the phone down, but I didn't.

I paced around feeling annoyed with Min, I'd only had a couple of brief notes from her since that night in Heathrow. It looked like she was firm in her resolve for us to only have minimal contact. But her coming home for Mam and Dad didn't mean I wouldn't be able to keep up a polite distance. It would be hard for Mam not to have Min's support.

Dad passed away two days later. I spent all my spare moments with him.

'Jim,' he whispered that last day.

'Yes, Dad?' I took his hand.

'You've been the best son I could ever have wished for.'

I thought I felt him give my hand a squeeze. 'Look after Mam for me, Jim.'

His eyes closed and after what seemed ages, I realised he'd passed away. A lump came into my throat. I sat with him for several minutes, then gently eased my hand from his and went to the landing at the top of the stairs.

'Mam.'

She came hurrying to the stairs.

'It's Dad. He's ...' I couldn't say the words.

She rushed up the stairs ...

***

I seemed to be in a daze organizing the funeral and comforting Mam. She was amazing, stayed strong right up until the last minute after the coffin was lowered into the ground and earth sprinkled on the top. I held her close as her tears flowed.

'Fifty years, it would have been, next month,' she sobbed. 'We've never had a day apart. What will I do, Jim?'

I had no words of comfort. I gently released her and led her back to my car. Silently, I cursed Min for not being here. Mam had been the youngest in her family, and she was the only one left. The neighbours had brought sandwiches and cakes to the house and although there had been a lot of mourners at the funeral – Dad had been well respected – not many came back.

I couldn't wait for them all to go, I could see Mam getting paler and shakier. Eventually I took the lead, stood and started shaking hands and thanking people for coming and they got the hint and Mam and I were left with the empty plates and cups and saucers.

I made Mam sit in Dad's chair and poured a glass of brandy which I'd brought just for this purpose. 'Here, Mam, drink this. I'm going to put a hot water bottle in your bed, then I think you need to sleep. I'll sort all this out.' I indicated the cluttered table.

Obediently, she took the glass and sipped it. 'Thank you, Jim.' Her eyes filled with tears again. 'You're the best son.'

'I'm thinking of moving back here for a while,' I said as I filled the hot water bottle. 'I can let my house and stay with you. It'll be easier. That's if it's all right with you.'

She took a deep breath; I could see the brandy had had an effect. 'Whatever you think, dear, I'll just go to the toilet and then to bed, I'm tired.'

***

The following few weeks were hard for Mam. I managed to take some leave to be with her and organize letting my cottage. But I worried about leaving her when I had to go on my next deployment. I mentioned it to Tony, one of the men in our squad.

'Why don't you get her a little dog?' He suggested. 'It would be company for her and give her life some structure and meaning.'

I stared at him. 'That's a brilliant idea! Thanks.'

'I'm not being entirely altruistic,' he laughed, 'Our old spaniel, who we thought had gone past it, had three pups quite out of the blue a couple of months ago. Not sure who the father was, but we managed to find homes for two of them, there's just a little bitch left. You're welcome to her if you want.'

That's how Lally came into our lives. I went straight around to Tony's after work. His children cried and protested when Tony said I would be taking her.

'She'll be going to live with a lady who'll love her and look after her,' I told them, as I held the warm, wriggling little puppy.

Tony's wife wrapped her in an old blanket and tucked her into a cardboard box. 'Just give her some warm milk, and a bit of whatever you have left after your dinner,' she told me. That was in the days before scientifically produced dog food.

I was a bit apprehensive when I stopped at Mam's, not sure how she would react to a puppy. Taking the box, I went indoors. Mam was sat by the unlit range, staring into space.

'Oh, Jim,' she said, making an effort to get out of her chair. 'I didn't realise the time. I'd better get the dinner on.'

'Um, Mam,' I said. 'One of my mate's dogs has had pups, and this little one was about to be put down, so I said, I'd take her. Is that okay?' I know it was a lie, but I was relying on Mam's motherly instinct. I took the little squirming bundle out of the box and put her in Mam's lap. Mam sank back into the chair.

'Oh,' she exclaimed, 'The little sweetie. What's her name?'

'I don't think she has one yet. What would you like to call her?'

'Lally.'

Strange name, I thought, but Mam seemed entranced.

'Better get the dinner on,' I said, going out to the kitchen, Mam was busy fussing around, hugging and patting Lally, talking to herself and arranging the cardboard box.

Mam didn't seem to mind when Lally squatted and made a little puddle on the floor. I hurried to fetch a rag and mop it up.

It was a relief as the weeks went by to see that Mam seemed happier and busy with Lally. I was thankful that in late February 1980 my departure on HMS Bulwark for a deployment in the western Atlantic went almost unnoticed.

But I was still angry with Min. At least she rang Mam every week and they had long chats but I felt it was Min's duty to at least come home for a visit.

Mam must have mentioned that I was away, because Min came and stayed for a few days, so Mam told me, when I managed to ring her.

'Min loved Lally,' Mam said.

'How is Min?' I asked. The line wasn't very good.

Mam rambled on, they went to see Dad's grave and Min was upset, but she looked well and was busy and was asking for you and I said you were great, I put her in your bed ... and so on, all jumbled and confused. But it sounded like Mam was much happier.

I was on and off deployments a lot, but on the second anniversary of Dad's passing I drove Mam to the cemetery to put flowers on his grave.

'I walk up here with Lally, most Sundays, if it's fine,' Mam told me.

I was impressed, it was a good distance from her house.

'It passes the time, and Lally likes the walk. We sit here,' she pointed to a bench, 'and I talk to Dad. Tell him about you on Bulwark and Min's work and how Lally is so good.'

I was gratified, I didn't think she'd registered the name of the aircraft carrier I was on. 'What's Min doing?'

'She's doing research on a new project, they're hoping to develop it in England, so there's a possibility she'll be working over here at some stage.'

'Oh! That will be nice for you.' Maybe Mam took in more than I gave her credit for.

'Well, it's early days.' She handed me a ceramic vase containing wilted flowers. 'Can you take it to the tap over there, Jim, and refill it, please. Put the dead flowers in the bin beside the tap.'

I obeyed, my mind occupied with thinking about the possibility of Min working in England.

I'd tried ringing her a few times using Mam's phone, and she'd answered but when she heard my voice, she immediately asked if Mam was okay, and when I said, yes, she just said: "Sorry, Jim. Can't talk. Busy." and hung up.

Maybe I was getting obsessed with thinking about Min and wanting to meet her again. She'd come back into my life and then just waltzed out of it again. I couldn't stop thinking about her. I made another spur of the moment decision. Well, it had worked before!

I had a week's leave coming up. I went to the travel agent in town and made arrangements to fly to California near where Min worked. The agent booked me on a flight to San Fransisco Airport and then she said I could get a bus and taxi to where Min lived.

I had to take a gamble on her being at home, but I arranged it so that I would be at her flat early on a Saturday morning. I didn't tell Mam.

One of the men in my squad, Jeff, had been to America a couple of times, so I had a chat with him, told him I wanted to pay a surprise visit to someone in California who lived in an apartment. Had he any tips ...

Jeff thought for a bit, then rubbed his chin. 'Well, the thing is with these apartments you have to press the buzzer with their number on it. Sometimes it will show their name, is it a male friend?'

'No. A woman.'

He thought for a bit more. 'Some of these posher apartments have a camera so they can see who's buzzing, so I suggest you buy a bunch of flowers and put it in front of your face, and when she answers, just say "flower delivery". When you get up to her door, do the same.'

I slapped Jeff's shoulder and grinned. 'Thanks, Jeff, come, I'll buy you a pint. That suggestion is pure gold!'

He laughed, 'Another time, Jim, wife's waiting for me.'

A week later a taxi dropped me at Min's address. A palatial looking building, in fact it seemed the whole area was very up market, with a nice park opposite. Taking a deep breath, I walked to the entrance and scanned the list of numbers until I saw hers. Holding the bouquet of flowers that I'd bought in front of my face. I pressed the buzzer.

After a few seconds a voice said 'Who is it?'

'Flower delivery,' I mumbled.

'Come up, second floor.'

The big plate glass entry doors glided open.

The marble staircase had a hand rail of black wrought iron. A large ceramic pot on each landing held some kind of flowery shrub. Maybe orchids, I'm not an expert on flowers. The rent must cost Min a fortune, or had she bought her apartment? I'd not slept much on the journey over, so this opulence increased my – not so much anger, more disgruntlement, if there is such a word. She should have contacted me and spent more time with Mam. Obviously, money was no object.

The door was slightly open when I reached it. I held the bouquet in front of my face, but far enough back so that she had to open the door to get it.

I put my foot in the doorway. 'Hi Min! Surprise!' I exclaimed.

There was a pause, then the door opened wide. 'Jim. What brings you here?' There was no tone of welcome, but rather a note of anxiety in her voice.

'I wanted to catchup with my, um,' I hesitated, as I folded her into my arms. 'My beautiful Min.' All my anger dissolved at the sight of her.

I stood back and studied her, the bunch of red roses still clutched in my hand. She was wearing a dressing gown, with her hair all over the place, and those glasses perched on her nose. She looked like she'd just woken up.

Then a small voice whined, 'Mom, I'm hungry'

I became aware of a young child on the floor in front of a big leather lounge, playing with some cars. *Mom?* I stared at Min, disbelief bubbling in me, angry that not only Alison but now it seemed Min had got pregnant by another man.

Min broke free of my embrace and turned to the child. 'Coming now, sweetie.'

She took the flowers from me. 'These are beautiful. Red roses.' She met my eyes. 'Come in Jim.'

Then I saw the wedding ring. It was like I'd been hit in the stomach at a boxing match. I felt like turning on my heel and leaving. She'd obviously found another bloke and my red roses suddenly seemed stupidly inappropriate.

I stared at the child. I've never had anything to do with young children, so I had no idea of how old it might be. I gestured towards it. 'So. You're married, and WHO IS THIS?'

'That's Tomas.' She paused. 'Tomas James Jones. Your son. And no. I'm not married.'

The room spun round and I groped my way to a large table in the center of the room and clutched it for support.

'My son?' I croaked.

Her lips twisted. 'Remember that night in Heathrow?'

How could I forget it? I nodded and stared at her.

A cloud passed over her face. 'That's why I couldn't come over when Dad was sick and for his funeral. I was about to give birth. In fact, Tomas was born the day Dad died. That's why I named him after Dad.'

My legs felt weak, 'I must sit down,' I mumbled, sinking onto a nearby chair.

'I'll make coffee, you've had a shock.'

The little fellow jumped up. 'This is my Daddy,' he said, pointing to a photo on a long sideboard. It was that photo of me in uniform, from years ago. And alongside it a range of photos of me from a baby upwards.

'Yes, darling, that's a photo of your Daddy, and now he's come to see you. This is your real Daddy.'

Tomas didn't seem fazed by this. He plopped down on the floor.

'Wanna play racing cars, Real Daddy?'

It was the last thing I felt like doing, but I managed to crouch down beside him.

'Wrum, wrum,' I said, feebly moving one of the cars.

He stared at me. 'That's not how you play.'

'Not now, Teej, Daddy's tired, he's come a long way to see us, and needs something to eat and drink. Maybe later.'

Relieved, I went back to the table. I couldn't take my eyes from Tomas. My son!

'Why didn't you tell me, Min?' I thumped the table with my fist. 'And what's with the wedding ring?'

She put a cup of coffee in front of me, then put her index finger to her lips. 'Hush, Jim.' Her eyes slid towards Tomas, who was staring at us with a worried expression.

She sat opposite me with her cup cradled in her hands. 'I didn't know how.' She took a sip of coffee. 'By the time I knew for certain, you'd gone on a deployment – according to Mam, and I was getting big by then. Dad got sick and I was near my time when you rang to tell me he probably didn't have long to live. But, Jim, I couldn't travel at that stage, and like I said. Teej was born the night that Dad died.'

I could see her eyes getting red, she sounded about to cry.

'Yeah, it must have been hard for you,' I muttered, and frowned. 'Teej?'

'Tomas James. T.J. Jones. Teej.'

'Oh. Right.'

She sighed. 'I couldn't go home after the birth as I was breast feeding, and couldn't leave him. I have a lovely woman who comes every day to look after him while I'm working. She stayed here when I managed to get some time off and visit Mam.'

'And you've kept it from Mam all this time ...'

'It was hard, Jim. But what else could I do? It would kill her to know you and I ...' Her voice trailed off and she rested her chin in her hands, her elbows on the table.

'You could have told me.'

'And then what? What would you have done?'

That floored me. 'I could have supported you,' I muttered.

'Been with me while I was in labour and also with Mam when Dad was dying?'

'Of course not, but in other ways. And you could bring Tomas to see Mam. She'd love him.'

'And tell her he was the result of a one-night stand with my brother?'

I flinched.

'And he's the image of you! Look at the photos of you as a baby and growing up. Mam had one taken every year of us and you know how they're all lined up on her sideboard.' She gave a sardonic laugh. 'Like me.'

I turned to look at the sideboard and the array of photos.

'Yes, I asked Mam to get copies of them for me. I wasn't interested in the ones of me. Just of you.'

I saw Tomas staring at us. He got to his feet and came over to Min.

'You all right Mom?' His little face was full of concern. He held out his arms to her and she swooped him up and cuddled him.

'Yes, darling,' she said into his hair. 'Your Daddy is so pleased to see you and I'm so pleased to see your Daddy. It's a lovely surprise, isn't it?'

Uncertainly, he nodded his head.

'It's a lovely surprise for me too,' I said, with an edge of sarcasm.

Min stood, putting Tomas back down. 'How about some breakfast? Who's hungry?'

'Me!' shouted Tomas, jumping up and down.

I sat and watched them. I was angry with Min, that she'd kept Tomas secret from me, but then the sight of him filled me with an overwhelming feeling of pride and joy. At this stage of my life, I never expected to become a father. I know that lots of men become fathers in their mid-thirties, but after meeting Min that time in Heathrow, I'd accepted that I couldn't remarry, even if I found a woman who was prepared to marry me, it wouldn't be fair to her. I loved Min, she was all I wanted in a woman, but we could never marry – at least according to Min. Now, even though I wanted to tell everyone I had this amazing child, apparently, I couldn't. I caught sight of the wedding ring again.

'What's with the ring?' I knew my tone was grumpy but I couldn't help it.

'Let's put these beautiful flowers in a vase, first, shall we?' She spoke to Tomas who nodded, then she turned to me. 'I wear it because it's easier. People just assume I have a husband.' She smiled her impish smile. 'And it keeps the men away.'

Well, that was something, I thought, walking over to the sideboard. There was one photo of me on what may have been my first birthday, lying on my stomach on a blanket, and next to it one of Tomas, in the same pose. The similarity was striking. Another one of me standing, all chubby and a serious look on my face. Beside it one of Tomas, also standing. The same features.

I did a quick calculation. If Tomas was born the day Dad died, that would make him just over two years old.

I turned to look at him, his skin was lighter than mine, more a coffee colour, but the brown eyes and dark curly hair were similar.

'A chip off the old block, eh?'

Min's voice broke through my thoughts. I nodded.

'Come and sit down, you need to eat something.'

I watched as she prepared breakfast. Tomas climbed up onto a chair and waited.

Min brought a boiled egg and fingers of buttered bread to him. She sliced the top off the egg and Tomas smiled at her. 'Thank you, Mommy.' He pointed to the bread. 'Soldiers,' he said to me.

'Your grandma used to make soldiers for your mam and me, when we were your age.'

'Grandma?' He looked puzzled.

'My mommy,' Min said.

I grimaced. The first of several things to explain when he was older.

'Where are you staying?' Min suddenly asked.

I blinked. 'I hadn't actually thought. Maybe you could suggest somewhere? Not too expensive.'

Min gave a sardonic laugh. 'Typical Jim! Sounds so familiar. This area is outrageously expensive.' She placed two boiled eggs in front of me and some toast.

I frowned at my hands. 'Thanks.'

'More coffee?'

'Yes, please.'

She turned back into the kitchen area. 'The thing is, Jim, this is only a two-bedroom apartment, and Teej has one.'

'I guess I could sleep on the couch.'

She laughed and came over with a fresh cup of coffee. Placing it on the table, she took my face in her hands and kissed me.

'Mammies and Daddies usually sleep together,' she whispered and smiled. 'Eat up, or do you want me to cut your toast into soldiers?'

My heart raced and relief flooded me. 'I think I can manage,' I replied, the taste of her lips still on my mouth.

'After breakfast, we usually go to the park across the road but you'd probably like a shower first, Jim; we'll wait for you.'

Min strapped Teej – I'd started calling him that – into the buggy and we got the lift down to the ground floor. I hadn't noticed the lift when I came in, the doors discreetly matched the timber panelling of the lobbies.

We looked the perfect family, Min pushing Teej in his buggy and me walking beside them. Brother and sister, father and mother.

***

Later that evening, sitting on the toilet seat in the bathroom, I watched Min bathing Teej. Plunging little boats in and out of the bath he splashed water everywhere.

'I'm a sailor, like you, Daddy.'

I raised my eyebrows at Min.

'I've been telling him about you, Jim, showing him your photo and telling him you were in big ships with aeroplanes which was why you couldn't visit us.'

'I could have, Min.'

She heaved a sigh. 'I know, Jim. I should have told you before, but there never seemed a right moment.'

'But the future, Min? A boy needs his father. I want to be part of his – and your – lives. We have to work something out.'

She was silent. Picking up a huge bath towel she turned to Teej. 'Come on big sailor boy! Pull out the plug and get the sausage roll treatment.'

Tomas giggled as he pulled out the plug and jumped up into the waiting towel. He squealed with laughter as Min rolled him around in the towel.

'Your turn tomorrow, Jim.'

I nodded. 'Okay.' I thought of our childhood baths. 'Remember the old tin bath in front of the range, Min? When we were kids.'

She laughed. 'Yes, I went first, then Mam topped up the bath with hot water and you went next. And you were so shy, trying to hide your willy!'

I grinned. 'Would you blame me?'

She rolled her eyes. 'Hmm. It's grown a bit since then!'

'Min! You're still Minnie the Minx!'

She laughed and dried our son through his muffled giggles.

'You can read his bedtime story to him,' she said. 'His favourite is "Dinosailors".'

I'd never heard of this book, it's about some dinosaurs who go sailing. Apparently, Tomas was into dinosaurs and of course, sailing.

Maybe my reading voice was boring because he soon fell asleep. I sat for a while, just taking in this amazing child. My own flesh and blood. I'd thought I'd never know how that felt. At dinner he had kept stealing glances at me, I guess trying to reconcile the photographs of me with this "real" daddy.

I heard Min calling me to come and have a drink. She was sat on the lounge with her feet tucked under her, holding out a glass of wine to me.

'Cheers, darling.'

I took the drink and stared at her. 'I never thought I'd hear you call me that.'

She smiled. I chinked my glass against hers then set it down on the coffee table. Taking her glass from her, I put it next to mine, and took her in my arms.

'I've been so happy, today,' she murmured. 'Just having you here with Teej and me, like a proper family.'

'Yes. It's been wonderful. But, Min, I was so angry with you when I came; angry that you seemed to have cut me out of your life, and angry that you hadn't been with Mam when she needed you. But the instant I saw you, well I was no longer angry, I just fell in love with you all over again. And then, of course, when you explained everything and I met Tomas – Teej – well, I understood.'

She nodded and pulled my head down towards her and kissed me. 'When do you have to go back, Jim?'

'I only planned to stay until Wednesday. Thought after I'd confronted you and cleared the air between us, that I'd see a bit of California while I was here. But now, well, I want to spend all my time with you and Teej.'

'I might be able to take Monday off, things are pretty hectic at work. Maria comes every weekday to mind Teej, but I can tell her to take the day off.'

'Maria?'

'She's lovely, she came to help me when I came out of hospital with Teej. She's a nurse – single mother with two school-aged children. I was so impressed with her that I offered her a better rate of pay than she'd get with nursing to stay and look after Teej when I went back to work. She works in the local hospital on a Saturday to keep up her nursing registration.'

I said nothing, thinking that Min must earn a huge salary to be able to pay this Maria, and have enough for this luxurious apartment. No way would I be able to afford this life style.

Min watched me. She always had the ability to know what I was thinking.

'So, Jim. What are we going to do?'

'Make love?' I regretted this facetious remark the minute I said it.

Min laughed. 'You know what I mean, Jim.'

I did. I sighed. 'There's no solution, Min. I couldn't leave Mam on her own, even if I could get a green card, or whatever it is, and work here, and what I would be able to earn would never match your salary.'

'I could support us both.'

'Min! there's no way I could countenance being a kept man!'

'I'd love it!' She laughed, that bewitching laugh that made me go weak at the knees.

'Seriously, Min! Anyway, I'm guessing you'd not be willing to give up your lifestyle here and move back to England.'

'Even if I did move back, I wouldn't be able to live with you, Jim. Not with Teej. Not without Mam knowing.'

'Maybe Mam wouldn't mind. She'd love Teej.'

Min shook her head. 'Jim! Even if she accepted Teej, she wouldn't be able to talk about him with her friends. How could she introduce him, "Oh, this is my grandson, he's the child of my son and daughter.

I could see her point.

'It's been so hard when I ring her not to mention Teej. He's my life. I've got nothing else to talk about. And I've had to ring her when he's asleep, so she doesn't hear a child's voice.'

She looked at her glass of wine. 'It's been hard, Jim.'

'Hmm.'

'But that was a master stroke of yours to get her Lally,' she smiled. 'She never stops talking about her.'

'It was a bloke I work with. His dog had pups and he thought it would help Mam. I can't take the credit for the idea.'

We were both silent for a while, thinking our own thoughts.

'When I'm not on a deployment and can get some time off work, I could come and stay here with you.' I spoke my thoughts out loud.

'How often would that be?'

'Realistically, um, one or two weeks a year.'

'There's talk of setting up a research team in the UK,' Min said. 'I'm in line to take that project on.'

I brightened. 'Where would it be located? I could see you at weekends when not on deployment.'

'Possibly Reading, or London; but wouldn't Mam wonder why you're not spending time with her? Aren't you living there now, and letting your cottage?'

'True,' I muttered. 'Oh, Min, why must it be so hard? We're not bad people, we're not blood relations, why can't we be together?'

God forgive me, but I couldn't help thinking that once Mam had passed away, things would be easier. She was seventy-four, and I hoped with all my heart she would live many more years, but, but ...

'At least things are out in the open with us now, Jim. You'll be able to ring and talk to Teej.'

And so we spent the next few days as if we were a happily married couple. I met Maria, and liked her immediately. Min introduced me as "Jim, Teej's father.". On Wednesday, Min drove me to the airport with Teej in the back in a child's seat. They both waved me goodbye. Min told me afterwards that they'd watched my plane — at least, she thought it was my plane — leave.

I was back in time to be deployed in September on Hermes — In the early 1980s, she'd been converted as a STOBAR[1] in order to better counter the threat from Soviet submarines. It resembled a ski jump at the bow, so she could operate the Sea Harrier fighters.

We were deployed on exercises in the North Atlantic and eastern USA. You can imagine my feelings being close to America, Min and Teej, and unable to see them. An ocean separated us. We returned in December in time for Christmas. I'd been away for his birthday in November, but had sent him a birthday card and a Winnie the Pooh book.

Whenever I could manage it, I'd ring Min and depending on the times speak to Teej. I couldn't ring from home with Mam there so it meant having to ring from the public phone box at work, and finding enough coins and getting a transatlantic connection was difficult. Plus, I wasn't very good on the phone — I never knew what to talk to him about, but I did ask him what he would like Father Christmas to bring him. He had no idea what I was talking about. Min later explained that he's called Santa Claus in America, and that Teej didn't really know much about the bearded fat man at this stage. He wasn't allowed to watch television, except for a very few suitable (to her) programs, but this year she would be taking him to see the Christmas lights. I asked her about a present that I could send but she was vague. Anyway, by this time it was too late to send a parcel in time for Christmas. I promised myself that the following year I'd be prepared ahead of time.

The rest of the winter of 1982 was the usual dreary season. During the long dark evenings I yearned for Min, picturing her and Teej snuggled up on the big couch with Min reading to him. I was very dejected at this time and it was hard keeping a cheerful face in front of Mam. Sometimes I just felt like bursting out and telling her she had a grandson, mine and Min's son. She was pretty broad minded – at least, I thought so. But I couldn't do it without Min's consent.

I still caught up with John at times and thought of asking him what a three-year-old would like as a present, but then I remembered that his little girl was big now, and I doubted he would know. He'd also met someone, a widow with two children and he seemed to spend most of our time together talking about her. I badly wanted to talk about Teej, but it was all too difficult to explain.

I'd been thinking about making a quick surprise trip to see Min and Teej after Easter when flights would be cheaper, Good Friday fell on the 9th April, that year 1982 so maybe the middle or the end of April. I was due some time off. However, it turned out it was lucky I hadn't booked a flight, because, on the 2nd April, Argentina landed on the uninhabited island of South Georgia and raised the Argentinian flag. Argentina maintained their sovereignty over the island due to its geographical position and claims from the Spanish colonial era.

When Britain didn't take immediate action, the Argentinians invaded the Falkland Islands, and overwhelmed the resident garrison.

I hope I'm not being boring by telling you about the Falklands War, but sometimes the details get forgotten as time goes by.

Well, the Argentinian Junta, led by Leopoldo Galtieri, hoped to strengthen their standing at home and thought that British cutbacks in Defence, plus political weakness made this seem like the ideal time to strike and regain their standing with the Argentinian people.

However, they didn't reckon with our Maggie Thatcher and Operation Corporate was immediately established.

I was so happy to be back on Hermes. Only for Operation Corporate, she would have been decommissioned. I know she wasn't generally popular, but I liked her.

We left on the 5th April carrying twelve Sea Harrier FRS1 attack aircraft and Sea King helicopters for 826 and 846 Squadrons. Over the next few weeks, this expanded to include sixteen Sea Harriers, ten Sea Kings, and ten Hawker Siddeley Harrier GR3s, plus fifteen hundred marines.

It was exciting, but scary, to be part of a team leading more than one hundred vessels to the South Atlantic. The Argentinians made it a high priority to try and sink our two aircraft carriers, Hermes and Invincible. They didn't hit the carriers but sadly, they did sink several escort ships. One of those escort ships, HMS Sheffield was hit, and from the flight deck we saw the terrible sight of her burning on the horizon.

On the 20th May, a Sea King helicopter of 846 Naval Air left us to fly to HMS Intrepid carrying SAS troops, when it dipped, hit the water, rolled over and sank. Twenty-one service personnel lost their lives and there were only nine survivors. There were other awful tragedies – The Atlantic Conveyor – a merchant ship – was initially requisitioned and adapted into an aircraft ferry in April. It ended up resembling a WWII merchant aircraft carrier equipped with Harrier jets and helicopters. However, on the 25th May she was destroyed by Exocets most probably aimed at Hermes and twelve men died. The next morning, the survivors were transferred to Hermes where they gathered on the flight deck for a multi-denominational burial service for their deceased mates..

Like everyone, I was relieved when the large Argentine garrison at Stanley surrendered and ended the conflict.

We arrived back at Portsmouth in July to a huge welcoming party, including fly pasts from RAF Harriers, Army Lynx helicopters and a naval Hunter training squadron. There were thousands of relatives and friends crowded on the dockside to welcome us home. I scanned the area in what I knew was a futile hope that Min and Teej might be there. Of course, they weren't but it made me come to a decision.

---

1. Short Take-Off, Barrier Arrested Recovery carrier

Chapter Nineteen

As soon as I got back to Yeovil and reassured Mam, that, yes, it was me and I was alive and well, I waited until she was busy in the kitchen then rang Min. I didn't care what the time was in California.

'Oh, you're safe,' she cried, when she heard my voice.

'Min. I've had enough of this charade. I want to marry you and I'm going to tell Mam about Teej.'

There was a moments silence.

'You can't do that, Jim.'

'What? Marry you or tell Mam?'

'Tell Mam.'

'Min, I'd like you to be here and we can tell her together. I'm sick of living this lie. I want to acknowledge Teej as my son. Tomorrow I'm going to the Registry Office here to find out if we can be legally married. In the meantime, get yourself and Teej on the next flight to Heathrow. I'll meet you at the airport.' I hung up.

Two minutes later the phone rang. Of course it would be Min.

'Who is it, Jim?' Mam called from the kitchen.

I lifted the receiver, and, so Min could hear, I called out to Mam, 'It's Min. She's coming over in a few days' time with some good news.' I quietly replaced the receiver.

Mam peered around the kitchen door, her face all flushed and her glasses steamed up from cooking.

'She's coming over? That's great, Jim.' She pushed her glasses down her nose and glanced at the phone with the receiver back on the cradle. 'Oh! She's gone?'

'Yes, she'll give us details later.'

Mam disappeared back into the kitchen. I lifted the receiver and dialled Min. She answered immediately.

'Jim, you can't do this to me.'

'I can and I will. I'll ring you tomorrow with wedding plans. Hopefully.' I paused. 'That's if you still love me, Min.'

'Oh, Jim! Of course I do.'

'Well then, organize time off and flights. Bye Min.' My heart thumped as I replaced the receiver. I only prayed that the Registry Office would approve of marriage between me and Min.

Mam waltzed into the room. 'What a wonderful day,' she exclaimed. 'You home safe and sound and Min coming too!' She started to lay the table. I was badly in need of a beer at this stage, but hadn't thought to buy any on my way home.

'Have I time to go to the off-licence and get some beers, Mam?'

She nodded. 'But don't be long, dinner's nearly ready.'

***

The next day I went to the Registry Office. Luckily there was no queue. The woman at the counter gaped at me, when I told her what I wanted to know.

'I was adopted as a baby,' I repeated, 'And I want to marry the daughter of the people who adopted me. She now lives in America.' What could be clearer, I thought.

She frowned. 'I'll have to ask the Registrar,' she managed to say. 'Please wait.'

She disappeared. I paced up and down the office for at least fifteen minutes until a door opened and the registrar himself came out.

He nodded at me. 'I understand that you want to marry the daughter of your adoptive parents.' He spoke slowly as if I was mentally retarded.

'Yes.'

'Hmm. Well, I'm sorry to have to inform you, but that's impossible. The law considers an adopted child equal in all respects to a child born to the parents of the adopted child. Therefore, any union between such a child and an adopted child would be considered incest.'

I stared at him, my hopes dissolving into a stone in my heart.

'Are you sure? Can I take this to a higher court?'

'I'd like to help,' he did sound genuinely sad, 'but that's the law.'

'Thanks.' I started to stumble out of the office.

'But.'

I paused and turned to him.

'If it's of any help, it might be different in America. I think the states have different laws.' He blinked behind his horn-rimmed spectacles. 'But that's probably not of much use to you.'

He was wrong. I went straight to the Post Office, changed a five-pound note for coins, headed to a phone cubicle and dialled Min's number.

'Can you find out which States in America allow marriage between adopted children,' I blurted. 'Not possible in England, but maybe in the US. Find out, Min. I'll fly over and we'll get married. It's important for Teej. Ring Mam's phone as soon as you find out. Can't talk now, in the Post Office, money running out.' There was a beep-beep and the line went dead.

I couldn't settle to anything, I had a few days leave and spent it doing odd jobs for Mam, then drove to the cottage and checked was everything okay with the tenant. Two days later Min rang.

'Yes?' I said when I picked up the receiver. In those days you didn't know who was ringing until they spoke.

'Jim? It's Min.'

'And?'

'It's illegal in California, but may be legal in New York. I'll have to do more research. It may be difficult because I'm domiciled in California.'

'But there is hope?'

'Yes.'

'So, you can come over with Teej and we can tell Mam we're getting married in America.'

Silence.

'Please, Min. It's important for Teej to know his grandmother.'

'Of course. I think I understand that now, Jim. You don't know your birth mother, and Teej needs the opportunity to meet his grandmother. I hadn't thought about it like that.'

'So, you'll bring him?'

'Yes.'

***

The morning of Min's flight, Mam was muttering away about Min having to sleep in my bed, and I could sleep on the settee, or was I going back to base. 'Stop, Mam,' I said. 'I've poured you a cup of tea. Now sit down, I've got to tell you something which will come as a shock.'

She clutched her chest and managed to gasp, 'Min has cancer – that's why she's coming over ...'

I reassured her. 'No, no, Min is fine.'

'You've got cancer?'

'No, Mam, both Min and I are fit and healthy.'

Once she'd got over that I took her hand. 'The thing is, Mam, Min and I are in love and are hoping to get married.'

She went pale. 'Is that legal?' she managed to whisper after a long pause.

I prevaricated somewhat. 'It's legal in America. Drink your tea, Mam.'

I gave her a few minutes to think it over.

'And, Mam, we have a son.'

Her mouth fell open, and I thought she was about to faint.

'Min has a baby?'

'Well, he's two now. He was born the day Dad died, which was why she couldn't come for the funeral.'

'And you're his father?'

'Yes.'

She shook her head as if trying to clear her thoughts.

'He's two years old and you didn't tell me?'

I hung my head. 'Sorry, Mam,' I muttered. 'I only found out a while ago. Min didn't know how to tell us.'

Mam was silent for so long that I thought she must have gone into a coma. To break the silence, I said, 'He's called Tomas James, but Min calls him TeeJay for short or Teej.'

'Thomas, like Dad?' she eventually whispered.

'Yes. He's gorgeous, Mam.'

She tottered to her feet, and started to fuss around. 'Where will he sleep? I might be able to borrow a cot.'

'Mam, we can all sleep in my bed.'

Her eyelids fluttered; she breathed heavily then sank back in her chair. I could see she was in shock.

'I'm sorry to dump all this on you now, Mam, but I thought it better to tell you before Min and Teej got here.

'Teej.'

'Yes, and he's all excited at meeting his grandmother. Min thought you'd like him to call you Nan.'

The colour crept back into her cheeks, then, a bit shakily, she stood. 'I'd better go to the shop; do you think he'll like ginger nut biscuits? They were Min's favourites.'

I stood and put my arms around her. 'I love you, Mam.' And we both started to cry.

Mam wiped her eyes. 'You'd better get going or you'll be late at the airport.'

***

Of course, I arrived too early at Heathrow to meet their flight. I paced around, had a cup of coffee, paced some more, kept looking at my watch, waited ages at the arrival gates and then there they were. Min trundling a suitcase with one hand and holding Teej's hand with the other. He had a large model car clasped to his chest.

My heart beat faster at the sight of Min. I pulled them both into a bear hug, until Teej squeaked, 'Real Daddy, you're squashing my car.'

Taking the suitcase, I led the way to the car park.

Min laughed. 'Jim, you've got a new car!'

'It's not new, I've had it a few years now. Come on, jump in.'

Back then there were no laws about seat belts and child seats. But I did have front seat belts, so Teej sat on Min's lap and I fastened the seat belt around them both.

I drove off, wondering how to broach the subject with Min. In the end I just came out with it during a pause in Teej's excited chatter.

'Min. This morning, I prepared Mam for this. I had to. I couldn't let us just rock up and say, "Mam, this is your grandson, and Min and I are getting married." She'd have had a heart attack.'

'Oh, my God! What did you say?'

I told her.

Min stared out the windscreen. 'Poor Mam,' she whispered. 'How did she take it?'

'Got to hand it to her. She's amazing. Took it in her stride, started fussing about a cot and ginger biscuits.'

Teej bounced up and down on Min's lap, pointing at the cars and exclaiming excitedly.

After a bit, Min said, 'I guess Mam would have been about seven or eight when the first World War started, so she's been through two world wars. Perhaps that's what's made her so resilient and stoic. Keep Calm and Carry On.'

'It's going to be difficult for her. I'm wondering how she'll tell the neighbours; they'll want to know all about her visitors. There'll still be a few around who remember you as a child.'

I had a sudden thought. 'Thank God the miserable old Great Aunts aren't around to crow over Teej. Do you remember them, Min?'

'How could I forget!'

'I recall them asking us what we would be when we grew up. You insisted you were going to marry me!'

She laughed, 'I remember. And I am.'

She stroked the back of my hand on the steering wheel, sending a thrill of desire through me.

'They were horrible old cows,' she said. 'They made Mam's life a misery.'

I had to concentrate on the road – there was a lot of traffic on the A303 – so nearly missed what Min said next.

'I've got some news,' she said. 'I didn't want to tell you about it until I was certain.'

'Hmm?'

'The powers that be at work have made the final arrangements about the new site in Reading, and they've asked me to manage it.'

I nearly caused an accident as I took my attention from the road to stare at her. 'Really?'

She smiled. 'Yes. I told them I'd think about it; it would be a big move.'

'You didn't!'

'Yes, and then they came back to me and said that of course all my removal expenses would be covered and they would be renting a house for me for a year to give me time to adjust.'

'Wonderful! Oh, Min! Things are working out after all.'

'Look, Teej, there's Stonehenge,' Min pointed to the megalithic structure, but Teej was more interested in a tractor holding up the traffic in front of us.

'It all happened quite quickly, but I was thinking maybe Mam would like to come and live with us and look after Teej while I'm at work.'

I thought I'd burst with joy. The thought of Min and Teej being only a couple of hours drive from Yeovil, and Mam being there would solve so many problems. I hated having to leave her on her own while I was on deployment.

At last, we arrived. I helped Min and Teej out, took his hand and led him up the steps to the path. 'I can manage, Real Daddy,' he muttered. Mam stood at the front door, a nervous smile on her face.

I stood back and watched as Min walked towards Mam, who'd bent down to Teej.

'Hello Tomas,' I heard her say.

He looked at her. 'Are you, my Nan?' he said, but his attention was diverted as Lally came rushing out the door

'Oooh!' He was in raptures. 'A doggie!'

Lally was all over him, wagging her tail like mad and covering his face with slobbery licks.

'He's kissing me!'

Mam took out a hanky and wiped Teej's face. 'She's a girl, and called Lally,'

I went to the car and took out Min's suitcase.

Inside, Mam had laid out the tea things, and a plate with a Battenburg cake on it and another plate with ginger nut biscuits. There was a bottle of orange juice and a small beaker.

Mam couldn't take her eyes off Teej, I could see her trying to restrain herself from the urge to cuddle him, but he was entranced by Lally and lay on the floor patting and stroking her.

'He's the spit of you, Jim,' she remarked, gazing at Teej.

After we'd all settled down, Min told Mam the news about Reading.

Her eyes lit up, 'So, you mean you'd like me to come and live with you and mind Tomas while you're at work?'

'Yes, if it wouldn't be too much for you, and once we've sorted ourselves out, I'll try and get him into a pre-school to give you a break.'

I thought her face would split in two with the enormous smile. 'I'd love to! How soon?'

'Next month, well, I guess about five weeks' time. I'll be flat out for a while, organizing and setting things up at work, but my company has already rented a big house for me in a nice area, apparently, and I can find someone to help with the housework.'

Mam bridled. 'I can do the housework.'

Min smiled, 'I know Mam, but you'll be busy with Teej.'

It had been a big day for Teej, and by seven o'clock I could see his eyes closing. 'Teej and I are pretty tired, Mam,' Min said, 'So if you don't mind, we'll have an early night.'

I'd already taken her case upstairs and made room for her stuff.

'Good idea,' I said. 'I'm going to sleep on the settee.' I'd decided this was the best way, the double bed in my room was too small for the three of us. Yes, that slippery old leather settee beckoned once again ...

***

Two months later and Min had organized everything. She left Teej with Maria for a week and flew over to organize the move; she'd found a "human resources manager" – what used to be called a "personnel manager" and an office manager as well as renting furniture for the house. She'd ended her lease on the apartment in California and managed to sell the furniture to the new tenant, and said we could choose new furniture together, once we'd moved in.

I hoped Mam would adjust to the new home. I decided to keep on her council house for the time being, just in case she wasn't happy being away from her friends in Yeovil, and it was a handy base for me too. When we left, as I locked the front door, I could see Mam getting a bit teary. I'd told her we'd only bring the minimum for now, until she'd been in Reading for a while and could then decide what she wanted to take. Perhaps not the settee ...

'Whatever you think is best, dear,' she'd replied, a bit sadly, I thought. It made me realise how much she depended on me and my opinion these days. She was into her mid-seventies now and I hoped the move wouldn't be too much for her.

I lifted Lally up onto Mam's lap. 'Hold tight to Lally now,' I told her.

The new house looked nice, set in a leafy suburb of Reading. Mam gazed at it open-mouthed as we pulled up in the driveway. I helped Mam and Lally out of the car. Min and Teej were at the front door as we stopped. Teej ran straight out past Mam.

'Lally,' he cried throwing his arms around her, as she enthusiastically licked his face.

'Welcome, Mam, Jim.' Min came running out, hugged Mam, and gave me a quick peck on the cheek.

'Come on in, Mam, you must be dying for a cup of tea.' She winked at me.

'I'll bring everything in.' Mam had three suitcases, plus Lally's bed, a bag of books, boxes of photos and other stuff she didn't want to leave behind. She stopped and gazed around the entry hall; in the kitchen, she just shook her head.

'Come upstairs to your bedroom, Mam. Jim, can you bring Mam's cases up please?'

Mam was even more awestruck when she saw the bathroom. 'I'd get lost in that bath,' she muttered

She loved her bedroom.

'Very posh,' I smiled. Mam nodded.

Mam settled in well – at least she told us she was very happy. I think it was a relief for her not to have to explain Teej to the neighbours. He'd only stayed one night that time we'd told her the truth. Now she was able to take Teej and Lally to a nearby park with a children's playground and be at ease with the other grannies with their grandchildren. When Teej started at a play school, as they were called in those days, if it was fine weather, Mam walked with him and waved goodbye at the gate. Having a dog and a grandchild seems to be a great way to make friends.

Min had installed a television in Mam's bedroom and a rocking chair, so she could relax in peace and quiet.

I was only there at weekends while not on deployment, and loved being with all my family.

Chapter Twenty

By this time, I'd turned forty. I'd been engaged in a few air sea rescues, which although mostly rewarding – when saving lives – could be traumatic when retrieving bodies. I'd been in the Fleet Air Arm for over twenty-five years, and although I loved it, I was tired. And I missed Min and Teej when I was on deployments.

In July 1986 I set off on HMS Illustrious on a mission to the Far East and Australia. I knew it would be a long assignment – five months, at least.

On the 4th October we were in Sydney Harbour for the 75th anniversary of the Royal Australian Navy. Hundreds of big and small ships passed Prince Philip, the Duke of Edinburgh, who was Admiral of the Fleet at the time. We lined the sides of Illustrious. We'd rehearsed doffing our caps and shouting Hurrah, when the call came up "Three Cheers for Prince Philip. Hip, Hip, Hurrah." He waved his cap in acknowledgement. Apparently, the Australian Prime Minister, Bob Hawke accompanied him but I couldn't make him out amongst all the dignitaries.

I must admit I felt a bit teary and had a lump in my throat at the sight of the fleet, and the helicopters flying overhead. I wondered if Min, Mam and Teej would watch it on television. I could picture Min telling Teej, "Look there's Daddy's ship," when she saw Illustrious.

Being back in Australia, I naturally remembered getting married to Alison in Fremantle. Apart from the divorce papers she'd sent me, I hadn't heard from her. Well, I hadn't contacted her either. I wondered now what her parents would have thought about her return and being pregnant with a man not her husband. Ah well. Not my problem.

It was December 1986 when we returned. I couldn't believe how much Teej had grown. He'd turned seven in November, and I'd missed his birthday, but at least I was home for Christmas.

Mam had already made the Christmas cake and pudding, with Teej's help.

I thought back to when I was seven and boxing with Dad. I bought Teej a pair of boxing gloves for Christmas.

Min and I were sitting by the fire in the lounge room on Christmas Eve. A big Christmas tree covered with tinsel, bells and blinking lights stood in the corner.

'No!' Min exclaimed when I showed the gloves to her after Teej had gone to bed with his pillow case stocking Mam had made for him. 'I don't want him learning martial arts.'

'Min,' I tried to explain patiently. 'He's part coloured. He needs to be able to defend himself.'

She stroked my arm – guaranteed to make me want to make love to her. 'Times have changed, Jim. There isn't the same feeling about coloured people these days. And anyway, Teej is only one-quarter ...' her voice trailed off when she saw my dark look.

'I've been thinking,' she remarked as I carefully wrapped the gloves in Christmas paper.

'Oh?'

'Have you still got the address of the woman you think is your mother?'

I'd told her how years ago I'd put the advertisement in the *Western Gazette* and the replies I'd got.

'Yes, Somewhere,' I muttered. I knew exactly where they were. I'm a very methodical person – what did Alison call me? Obsessive compulsive? Some kind of freak anyway.

'Could you find it for me?'

I sighed. 'I don't want to go down that route again, Min. Just leave it alone.'

'Why did you keep the replies to the ads, then, and the result of your phone calls?'

I shrugged. 'I've kept all of your letters.'

'That's different. I've kept all of yours.'

'Have you? That's nice. Why?' I tried to change the subject of my birth mother.

But she wasn't going to be side-tracked. 'So can you find them?'

'What? Your letters?'

'You know very well what I mean. The address of the woman you thought might be your mother.'

'You're like Lally with a bone,' I grumbled. I knew Min would keep on until I gave her the letters. 'I'll look for them now. You'll give me no peace until I do.' I abandoned my wrapping paper and stood up.

'Thank you sweetie.' She took my hand, turned it over, kissed the palm and winked.

***

On Christmas morning Teej came racing into our bedroom, dragging the huge Christmas stocking pillow case, and started pulling out the presents, tearing off the wrapping paper and leaving it scattered on our bed. He held up the boxing gloves.

'What are these?' he frowned, pulling them on.

'Boxing gloves,' I told him. I got out of bed, took out the pad and gave it to him to hold while I ducked around aiming blows with my bare fists.

'Now you put the gloves on while I hold the pad and you punch it.'

He lived in those gloves all day, only taking them off to eat. After he'd aimed a few blows at Min, I explained the Marquess of Queensbury rules of boxing. 'And you never, ever hit a woman, or anyone smaller and weaker than you.'

It was just after Christmas that Min broached the subject of marriage again. We were getting ready for bed. By the time I'd taken off my clothes, carefully folded and hung them in the wardrobe and was pulling on my pyjamas; Min was already in bed, looking seductive. Then she started.

'I know I told the miserable old Great Aunts I was going to marry you, Jim, but I've always been wedded to you in my mind.' She began.

I wondered what she was leading up to. 'What about those "other guys"?' I'd always been a bit jealous of Min's previous relationships.

'Not important,' she smiled.

'I couldn't care less about getting married either, except that us living together and having sexual congress,' I grimaced at her, 'is technically incest which is a criminal offence with severe jail terms. Can you image what it would do to Teej having both parents in prison, not to mention how it would affect Mam.'

She waved my objections aside. 'Anyway, I've done a bit more research, and I really want you to come with me to Bristol,' she carried on, as if I hadn't spoken.

My heart sank.

'Jean Smith is still living there, but her husband passed away last year, so I thought she might be more willing to talk to you without him around.'

I shook my head in disbelief. 'How did you find out all this, Min?'

'The Electoral Roll and the Births, Deaths and Marriages records.'

'You're amazing, Min.'

'I know.' She grinned. 'So, next Saturday, we're off to Bristol.'

I tried to think of reasons why we shouldn't go. 'Teej will want to come.'

'No. I've already told Mam we're catching up with a friend and would she mind Teej. She was delighted, there's some Disney movie on at the cinema and she wants to take him.'

'That's a fib, Min.'

She shrugged. 'If we can meet Jean Smith, it won't be.'

I slid into bed beside her. I had serious misgivings about this whole exercise, but I knew I'd get no peace until Min had ferreted out every bit of information about my adoption.

The following Saturday found us driving to Bristol. Min had the road map and was directing me. 'It's in Filton,' she said. 'Which kind of makes sense. If Ernest Smith was employed at the aircraft factory in Yeovil before the war, which he probably was, then he'd be more than likely to get a job with the British Aircraft factory in Filton ...'

I nodded, my spirits dropping with every mile we covered. We drew up at a row of terraced houses in a cul-de-sac.

'Come on, Jim. It's now or never.' She kissed my cheek. 'It'll be okay.'

I wasn't reassured. I hoped that at ten o'clock on a January Saturday morning Jean Smith would have gone shopping and we'd miss her and could just go back to Reading.

At the front door, Min paused. 'You stand here away from me.' She positioned me a few feet on her left, probably with the idea that I wouldn't be seen immediately.

She rang the bell. It was a few minutes before the door opened a few inches.

'Who is it?'

Min stepped forward. 'Hello, Mrs Smith. I'm Dr Minnie Jones, I wonder if you can help me.' The woman looked to be about fifty, with grey hair and a pleasant face.

The door opened a bit wider. Then I realized that Min was dressed in a casual business suit with her hair up in one of those French pleats, a kind of sausage roll bun, and instead of her contact lenses she wore a pair of horn-rimmed spectacles, sensible shoes and carried a bulky briefcase. She looked like one of those doctors who made house calls years ago when we were young.

As the woman opened the door further, I noticed Min had slipped one foot into the doorway.

The woman looked up and saw me. She did a kind of double take, the colour drained from her face and her hands flew to her mouth. 'Sammy!' She whispered.

I'd read about colour draining from someone's face, but never thought I'd actually witness it. I thought she was about to faint.

Min took her elbow, and steered her inside. 'Come, Mrs Smith, perhaps we could sit down somewhere. I'm sorry this has been a bit of a shock.' She indicated for me to follow.

My emotions were all over the place. This must be my mother, she'd had such a reaction when she saw me, but who was Sammy?

Subconsciously, I registered that the house was a typical English terraced house. Stairs led to the bedrooms, and straight ahead a kitchen. The woman stumbled to the room next to the kitchen, a comfortable dining room. A coal fire burned in the grate with easy chairs either side of the fireplace.

Min helped her sit in one of the easy chairs, then crouched beside her, holding one of her hands.

'I'm sorry, Mrs Smith. Take deep breaths.' She opened her brief case and took out a small flask and a stainless-steel beaker. Sitting back on her heels she half-filled the beaker and offered it to her.

'Have a few sips.'

Mrs Smith's hands shook as she took the beaker. Taking a gulp she spluttered. 'It's strong,' she gasped, before taking another sip.

Mrs Smith obviously thought Min was a medical doctor and this was some kind of medicine. I realized now that Min had dressed to give exactly that impression.

I hovered in the doorway, staring at this woman who might be my mother. She wore one of those pleated skirts a bit like a kilt, a white shirt and a knitted cardigan in a kind of purply-blue colour.

Min turned to me. 'Sit down, Jim.'

Like an automaton, I moved forward, pulled out one of the dining chairs and obeyed.

Min turned back to Mrs Smith.

'Can I get you a cup of tea, my dear?' Min's tone was solicitous and the woman looked up gratefully, nodded, and made an effort to get to her feet.

'Stay there. Jim can make it, if that's alright with you, Mrs Smith.'

'Jean,' she said. 'My name's Jean.' She looked uncertainly at me and took another sip of the brandy.

'Jim makes a good cup of tea; he's been well trained by his adoptive mother.'

Jean choked at this. 'Is he really my son?' she whispered. 'He's the image of Sammy.'

I thought she was going to cry so I got up from my chair, about to make my escape.

'How did you track me down?' she asked me through her sniffles.

I had to answer her. 'My adoptive mother had written down your name and address from my birth certificate before she handed it over to the registrar when applying for my adoption papers.'

Min interrupted. 'An adopted child can now get access to their original birth certificates.'

I didn't know this. 'So, then I put an ad in the *Western Gazette* and a had a reply from the man who'd been best man at your wedding.'

'Bertie Osborne – he was a very nice man; he'd been in the POW camp with Ernie.'

'Yes, he said you'd married his friend Ernie Smith and he thought you'd moved to Bristol, or maybe Bath. I went through the phone book, ringing every E Smith asking if a Jean Smith lived there. When you answered I panicked. But I had your address. And wrote to you.'

She fell silent for a few seconds until Min said 'How about that cup of tea, Jim?'

I was relieved to get out of the room and into the kitchen. It was very neat and tidy. I looked around, a kettle stood on the gas stove. I filled it and lit the gas – it had one of those push button ignitions. While I waited for the kettle to boil, I tried to gather my thoughts and emotions.

Above a small table, a shelf held plates and saucers; cups hung from a row of hooks below. Over the sink, a window with brightly coloured curtains overlooked a small garden. A tea pot and a cosy were on the draining board and the tea caddy on the window ledge.

I could hear Min and Jean murmuring together. I found a tray on top of the fridge and placed three cups and saucers on it. I peered inside the larder for a sugar bowl.

Min and Jean both looked up as I came in carrying the tray. I felt quite pleased with myself as I placed it on the dining room table and went back for a bottle of milk from the fridge.

Jean stared at me as she took the cup and saucer I offered her. I held out the bottle of milk. 'I have milk jugs.'

I helped her to milk and she shook her head at the sugar bowl.

Min sat in the other easy chair.

I couldn't really believe that at long last I'd found my birth mother. My stomach churned and my brain seemed foggy. I tried not to keep staring at her.

We sat silently drinking our tea. It seemed the brandy had relaxed Jean, who kept looking at me. Eventually she put her cup and saucer on a coffee table by her side and spoke.

'I suppose you'd like to know what happened,' she said in a low voice.

I nodded. 'Yes, if it's alright with you.'

'When I saw you, I knew you were Sammy's son, you look just like him. I'm sorry I had to give you up, but I had no choice. I couldn't have brought you up on my own and my mother arranged it all for me.' She paused and took a sip of tea. Her eyes filled with tears again. She brushed them away and took a deep breath. 'I told everyone I was going to help run a hospital, but when I got there, it was actually a mother and baby home. For unmarried mothers. I was treated like a scullery maid, washing dishes and scrubbing floors. I was informed that once the baby was born, it would be adopted, and I would have to go home as if nothing had happened and no-one would be any the wiser.' She tugged a handkerchief from her sleeve and wiped her eyes.

'Sammy was the love of my life, but he didn't come back after D-Day and later, when I saw the footage of the landings in the cinema, and the Americans being gunned down as they landed on the beaches, I knew he'd been killed.' She sniffed and blew her nose.

'When Ernie returned from the war, he was a mess mentally, he'd been in a POW camp and the war left him depressed and not wanting to live. At the time I felt much the same, I didn't care if I lived or died. In fact, I wanted to die. When Ernie asked me to marry him, I thought I might as well, I had nothing to live for and would have done anything to get away from my mother.' She looked at me. 'When I got your letter all those years ago, I was sure you must be my son, but I couldn't have Ernie know and I was terrified that if I met you and he found out it would tip him over the edge.' She took a deep breath. 'I'm sorry about what I wrote, but I was afraid of what Ernie might do ...'

'So, my father was called Samuel?' I asked.

'His name was James Samuels, but everyone called him Sammy. That's why I called you James.' She paused. 'Wait here. I must get something.'

She got up a bit shakily and we heard her going upstairs and opening and closing drawers in the room above us. I looked at Min, who smiled triumphantly and gave a thumbs up sign.

When Jean came back, she handed me a photograph. In her other hand she had a bunch of envelopes.

'He gave me that photo the last time I saw him.' Her voice shook as she held up the envelopes. 'These are his letters. I had them hidden, and only took them out after Ernie passed away.'

Min looked over my shoulder at the photo of the young man in army uniform. She gasped. 'You're the image of him Jim!'

She fumbled in her briefcase and brought out an old photo of me in uniform – I must have been about twenty-something at the time – and gave it to Jean, who studied it, and nodded.

'Do you happen to know his service number?' Min asked.

'Well, there's a number on the back of the photo, I didn't know what it was. Maybe that's it.'

Min turned over the photograph. I looked over her shoulder. Written under the number were the words:

To my beloved Jean – from your soon to be husband. All my love, Sammy.

I looked up at Jean. She was blinking away tears.

Min took out a notebook, wrote down the number and offered Jean another sip of brandy.

At last, I spoke. 'Do you have any other children, Jean?'

She shook her head. 'Sadly, no. Ernie did not want any. He said he didn't want to bring children into this world to suffer. His war time experiences really changed him.'

She had a faraway look in her eyes, which went all misty.

'Sammy was a wonderful man,' Jean eventually said. 'We were going to get married and go and live in America.'

Bloody war, I thought, remembering the men killed in the Falklands, some of the bodies we'd rescued during that time. Another thought struck me. If Sammy hadn't been killed, I would have been raised in America and never would have met Min. But maybe I would have met her there, even worked with her. My thoughts were chaotic.

Min stood, collected the cups and saucers and went to the kitchen. I heard her washing them.

Jean and I looked at each other.

I racked my brains to think of something to say. 'I'm so happy to have found you, Jean.'

She gave a watery smile. 'Me too.' She had a pretty smile. 'Tell me where you work and all about yourself. Were you happy growing up?'

'Yes, my adoptive parents were wonderful. My mother is still alive, but my father passed away several years ago.' Then I wondered if she would be hurt by my referring to Mam as my mother, and Dad as my father. But she only nodded. 'I'm so glad.'

Min came back into the room.

'Jean, this has been a huge shock for you. We might leave now and let you rest. We'd love to see more of you.'

Jean's brow wrinkled. 'So, um, who exactly are *you*?' She looked at Min.

'Ah. Now that's the sixty-four-dollar question! I'm the daughter of Jim's adoptive parents.'

'And you're a doctor.'

Min laughed. 'Yes, but not a medical doctor.'

Jean looked taken aback. Min went to her. 'I'm sorry if I misled you into thinking I was a medical doctor, Jean. I just wanted you to feel comfortable about me coming into your home. Will you forgive me?'

Jean smiled and stood. 'I've got no choice if I want to see my son again.' Her smile faded. 'My son,' she repeated softly.

I knew Min was right, we should go and let Jean get over the shock, I thought she was about to start crying again, when she said "my son".

Min held out the photo of me. 'Perhaps you'd like to keep this. I've got another copy, and maybe you could get a copy of Sammy's photo for us.'

'Yes. I will.' She followed us to the front door.

I stood awkwardly on the threshold, not knowing whether to give her a hug or a kiss. A handshake didn't seem right. Min resolved it with a hug, so I followed suit, bending over to wrap my arms around my birth mother.

In the car I drove around the corner and pulled over.

'What's wrong, Jim?'

'I feel a bit shaky; would you drive?'

'Of course.' She reached into her bag and retrieved the flask of brandy. 'Have a slug of this,' she said as we got out of the car and swapped sides.

'We didn't give her our phone number.' I suddenly realized as Min pressed the accelerator. 'Can you find your way?' I had a moment's panic.

She patted my knee. 'Yes. And I deliberately didn't mention giving her our contact details as I didn't want her ringing and then Mam answering the phone. Imagine her reaction if Jean said, "It's James's mother."'

I hadn't thought of that aspect. 'You think of everything, Min. But how will we tell Mam?'

'Yes, that's a tricky one. But I'm researching another avenue to enable us to marry, that might help her accept Jean.'

'Oh?'

'Don't laugh, but I wondered if an adopted child can be "unadopted".'

'WHAT?' My voice squeaked with astonishment. I took another slug of brandy.

'Well, I thought that if Mam unadopted you, then Jean could adopt you and we could legally marry.'

She nodded. 'Yeah, it sounds crazy, but how would the authorities find out? Anyway, I've done a bit of research,' she paused as she merged with some traffic on the A303. 'Apparently in New York state, marriage between an adopted child and a natural child of the parents is allowed as long as the siblings are not related by blood and the adoption took place after the age of eighteen.'

I mulled this over. 'So that rules us out. Anyway, we don't live in New York.'

'I know, but it might be the same in England. I have to do more research.'

I hated the thought that us living together was illegal. Not so much for us, but what the implications were for Teej. And Min was talking about having another child, company for Teej, she said. I could see her point. At the moment he was an only child, with no close relations, aunts, uncles, cousins. I rubbed my eyes. 'Dunno, Min, it all sounds too hard.'

Deep in my thoughts, I half watched Min. She was so serene; she took everything in her stride.

'Why is life so hard, Min?'

'Dunno, my love. Think how hard it must have been for Jean, losing the love of her life and having to give up his son.' She shuddered. 'I can't imagine what it would have felt like to have had to give up Teej and find out you'd been killed. I don't think I would have wanted to live.'

She patted my knee. 'We'll work something out.'

I hoped she was right, because I could see no light at the end of the tunnel. I had a recurring mental image of me behind bars in a male prison and Min in a woman's prison, locked up for twenty-five years, with Mam visiting us in turn once a month, holding a sobbing Teej's hand. Maybe only ten years with good behaviour ... But Mam wouldn't survive this – the shame would kill her and Teej would be nearly thirty when we got out and he probably would want nothing to do with us by then.

'But we did well today, Jim. We found your mother and now you know that your father wasn't a rapist but a brave war hero.'

'How do you know he was a hero?'

'Any person who died in a war saving the world from Naziism is a hero. And Jean is lovely. I liked her.'

I nodded. I still felt emotional and churned up. and thinking about my father having taken part in the D-Day landings[1] was a shock.

'Now that I have his name and the number on the back of that photo, I'm going to see if I can find out more about your father and Teej's grandfather.'

I hadn't thought about the fact that James Samuels was Teej's grandfather and Jean his grandmother.

'Why didn't you tell Jean she had a grandson?'

'Oh, Jim! Really. Think! That would have meant telling her about us, it was enough for her to take in meeting you today.'

She was right. As usual.

A bit later I said, 'And when are you going to tell Mam about Jean?'

'When the time is right.'

I left it at that, pleased that she didn't want me to do it. Anyway, I was scheduled for a deployment on HMS Gloucester, Armilla patrol, protecting civilian ships transiting the Strait of Hormuz. We didn't return until June. Min wrote to me every week. The last letter I had from her she said she had news but would wait until she saw me to tell me. I wished she hadn't written that, because of course, my mind was imagining all kinds of things – perhaps she'd found a way we could marry, maybe she'd found my father's service record – stuff like that.

When she heard me coming in, she flew out of the kitchen and flung her arms around me.

"Home is the sailor, home from the sea." She intoned in a deep sombre voice.

I picked her up and hugged her, 'Minx,' I murmured into her neck as Teej came running out behind her.

'Daddy!'

'Anyone would think I'd been gone years!' I smiled, as Mam came down the stairs.

Although I was bursting to hear Min's news, I didn't question her, in case it wasn't suitable for Mam and Teej to hear at that point.

'What's this news?' I asked, much later, as I sat in bed watching her engrossed in the business of removing her makeup.

She turned around, a smile splitting her cold cream covered face.

'Three things, first the big news.' She paused dramatically. 'I'm pregnant. Due early December.'

I blinked. I know she'd been talking about having another child, but I hadn't really registered it. I'd assumed she was on the pill. A twinge of annoyance went through me, but I knew I had to appear thrilled.

'Wonderful news, darling. And you're feeling okay?'

'Yes. No morning sickness this time!'

'That's good,' I murmured, the recurring nightmare vision of Mam visiting us in prison and dragging the sobbing Teej, reappeared, but this time she was also pushing a pram with a screaming baby in it. Did prisoners still wear those clothes with arrows pointing up or was that only in comics?

'Such a lot to tell you, darling. The other news is that I researched your father's war record but drew a blank. There was a big fire at the records office in 1973 and most of their records were destroyed.'

I nodded, not really taking this in, still pre-occupied with the news of the baby and prison uniforms.

'When you registered Teej's birth, what did you write on his birth certificate about the father?'

She paused, looking at my reflection in the mirror.

'I put your name, occupation: sailor, address: unknown.'

I thought about this for a bit, still watching as she finally finished with the face stuff and put on a skimpy nightie. 'What will you put this time?'

She shrugged. 'Depends where you are at the time.'

I didn't like this answer. I was beginning to get very anxious about this incest thing coming to light.

'It only needs someone from Yeovil who knew us when we were young meeting Mam, or one of us, to expose this whole mess.'

'But wait until you hear the rest of the news!' She climbed into bed and snuggled into me. 'Missed you, sailor boy.' And kissed me.

Oh God, I thought. She's expecting twins ... The nightmare vision returned but this time Mam was pushing a pram with screaming twins in it ...

She was beaming at me. 'I've done some research. Look.' She leaned out of the bed and pulled open the drawer in the bedside table. She held out several sheets of paper. 'Read this.'

Not really registering what she was saying, I took hold of it and read: *Adoption and Children Act*. There was a lot of it.

'Read section 74,' Min said, 'a bit further down.'

I managed to find it.

Section 74: Miscellaneous enactments

203.Section 74 provides that the general principle of section 67 (that an adopted person is to be treated as if he had been born as the child of the adopter or adopters) is not to apply for the purposes of marriages within prohibited degrees of relationship or to incest, and for these purposes an adopted person remains part of his natural family. The only exception is that an adopted person cannot marry his adoptive parent, as this falls within the restrictions set out in the table of kindred and affinity in Schedule 1 to the Marriage Act 1949. Otherwise, there are no restrictions on marriage within an adoptive family.[2]

I looked up. 'Otherwise, there are no restrictions on marriage within an adoptive family.' I read out loud. 'Does this mean what I think it means? Where did you find this Min?' I could barely think straight.

'I have my ways, Jim! One doesn't work in cutting edge computer research for nothing you know!'

I stared at the paper. 'Are you sure that means we can get married? I don't really understand it. Is it just wishful thinking on your part, Min?'

'Well, that's how I interpret it. We can get married, Jim!' Min was shaking with excitement, 'Read it again, the last line. No restrictions on marriage within an adoptive family!'

I looked up and grinned. 'So, we won't be living in sin anymore?'

'I think it means you'll just have to show your decree absolute divorce papers, and your original birth certificate and we're set to go!' A small frown appeared on her brow. 'You did get a decree absolute for your divorce, didn't you?'

'Think so,' I muttered, thinking that because I'm a pretty methodical person, it should be with all my other important papers. Then what she'd said hit me.

'Oh, Min! Must I get out of bed and down on one knee?' I laughed, climbed out of bed and got down on my knees. In a solemn voice, I said: 'Dr Minnie Jones. Will you do me the honour of becoming my lawful, wedded wife?'

She studied the nails on her left hand. 'Dunno. I'll think about it. Maybe I will if you're nice to me.'

'You'd better think fast.' I got to my feet and into bed beside her. 'That's my final offer.'

'Have you told Mam?' I managed to mutter through her embrace.'

'No, waiting to tell you first.'

***

'Mam, we've got lots of good news,' Min announced next morning at breakfast. It was a Saturday, so we were all together.

Mam looked up from buttering toast.

'We're expecting another baby!'

Mam gaped.

Min turned to seven-year-old Teej who was shovelling scrambled egg into his mouth. 'You're going to have a little brother or sister, Teej.'

He stared at her for a few moments. 'I'll have a brother, please. Sisters are hopeless, Michael Bailey has a sister and she just prances around in silly fairy costumes and won't play proper games.'

'We won't know if it'll be a brother until the baby arrives; it'll be a surprise.'

I watched Mam. It was hard to read her expression. Finally, she spoke.

'What's the other piece of good news, Min?'

Min looked at Teej. 'Have you finished breakfast, Teej?'

'Yes, thanks, Mom.'

'You may leave the table now; go and brush your teeth.'

He danced off muttering something about having a brother to play with.

Once he was out of earshot, Min turned to Mam, her eyes shining. 'Jim and I can get married!'

Mam gasped. 'At last!'

'Yes, a few hoops to jump through, but it should all go smoothly.'

'That's wonderful. I'll have to get a new outfit.'

'It'll probably be a simple registry office affair, Mam,' I chipped in.

Her face fell.

'But there's still more news, Mam. Oh, boy it's been so hard bottling it all up until Jim came home!'

Mam took a deep breath. 'Oh.'

'Yes! You see, Mam, Jim has been secretly worrying that his father had perhaps raped his mother and that was why he'd been given up for adoption.

Mam blinked at the word raped.

'I discovered that Jim's natural father was a US war hero, but all the records were burnt in a fire.'

I opened my mouth to say that wasn't exactly true but Min gave me a look and kicked my foot under the table.

Mam frowned. 'How did you find that out Min?'

'I did some research and managed to track down Jim's birth mother.'

I leaned across the table and took Mam's hand and squeezed it. 'You're still my mam.'

She stared at me as if she hadn't seen me before.

'So, I thought it would be a good idea to try and find his birth mother and get at the truth.'

'And?' Mam leaned forward.

'Well, I tracked down the mother, whose name is Jean Smith. She lives in Bristol. We went to see her, and she told us that she and Jim's natural father had met when he was over here during the war. They fell in love and they were going to get married, but he was killed in the D-Day landings, so when Jim was born, she had to give him up for adoption as she wasn't able to care for him. She later married another man, who died last year.'

Mam thought for a bit then nodded.

'She nearly fainted when she saw Jim,' Min continued, 'said he looked just like his father.'

'So, you and Jim went to see her without telling me,' Mam said slowly.

'We didn't know whether she would want to meet us,' Min replied. 'And we didn't want to upset you if she didn't. When I got more information, I was able to find out that Jim's natural father was a war hero, so I waited until I could tell you.'

Mam looked a bit bemused.

'And does she know about Teej?'

'Not yet. I wanted to tell you everything first.'

That seemed to mollify Mam.

'What's she like?'

I opened my mouth to say that she was tall and slim and looked elegant – at least to my eyes – but then I thought that Mam might be described as "homely", so I shut my mouth and stayed silent.

'She seems quite nice,' Min said. 'Ordinary.'

Mam sat and thought for a while. 'I'd like to meet her.'

I blinked, and even Min looked surprised.

'Yes.' Mam's voice grew stronger. 'To thank her for giving up Jim. We loved every minute of having him, and I can't imagine what life would have been like without him. Dad thought the world of him.'

I felt my face getting hot at this. I'd forgotten I was still holding Mam's hand, and now she gave it a squeeze, looked at me and I could see her blinking away tears. I didn't know what to say.

'Yeah,' Min interrupted, breaking the awkward moment. 'I always knew Jim was extra special, because he'd been chosen, and I was just a happy "accident".' She put on an exaggerated pout and made air quotation marks with her fingers.

Mam and I laughed.

'Anyway,' Min continued, 'I thought perhaps Jim could meet with Jean and they could get to know each other a bit better before we say anything more. That's if Jim and Jean agree.' She looked at me.

'Good idea,' I said, although I didn't know what I would say to her, I'm hopeless at making conversation.

'I could come too, Jim, if you felt it would be easier.' Min added.

She could read me like a book. I nodded. 'Okay, the next weekend we're both free.'

'And look, Mam, here's a photo of Jim's father in uniform.' She took the photo out of her handbag and handed it to Mam. 'Jean had some copies made and sent me them. His name was James Samuels, which was why she asked that the baby be called James.'

It was news to me that Jean had sent photos to Min, I thought she wasn't going to give Jean our details until Mam had been told.

Mam studied it for a while. 'He looks kind,' she said. 'Like Jim. And handsome too. Like Jim.'

I searched around for something to say, then came out with the truth. 'Well, what can I say, except you and Dad were the best parents a boy could ever have.'

'Now the compliments have been exchanged, someone other than this mutual admiration society had better clear the table and wash the dishes. This poor little domestic help I suppose.' Min smiled as she stood and started stacking plates.

***

Min and I duly returned to meet Jean. She seemed more relaxed this time. She must have been watching from the front room window, because as we walked up the path, she had the front door open.

'Come in.' She smiled, her eyes on me. It must have been a strange experience for her seeing almost the incarnation of her Sammy

We chatted for bit, then Min asked Jean if she worked.

'Yes, I work at a local estate agents, been there for a long time. But I'm going to retire next year.'

'Are you looking forward to retiring?' Min asked.

'Yes and no. I'm afraid I'll be bored at home all day. I don't have many friends, you see.' Then she added, hastily, 'Ernie didn't like people coming to the house.' She lowered her eyes and fiddled with her wedding ring. 'He had mental problems,' she whispered.

I glanced at Min, who nodded. 'It must have been very hard for you.'

We'd finished the coffee and biscuits that Jean had ready for us. Min leaned towards Jean and took her hand.

'Jean,' she said. 'We have some news for you, which may come as a shock.'

Jean's eyes widened.

'As you know, I'm the child of Jim's adoptive parents.'

She paused and I admired the way Min said it, rather than, I'm Jim's sister.

Jean nodded.

'Well, the thing is that Jim and I are in love. We have been for many years, but of course we understood that according to the law, we couldn't marry. Now it seems that it may be possible.'

Jean blinked and stared at Min.

'We're so happy, Jean.'

Jean looked a bit worried. 'I see,' she murmured.

I thought this meant she didn't really see.

'And the other big news is that we have a son. Your grandson.'

Jean gasped and sat back in her chair. She clapped a hand to her mouth. The colour drained from her face. Again. I was fascinated to see this, but collected my thoughts as Min took Jean's other hand and rubbed it.

'It takes a bit of getting used to the idea,' Min said.

That was an understatement, I thought. I felt sorry for Jean – I still couldn't think of her as my mother. I kept looking at her, wondering which of her features I'd inherited.

'My mother would really like to meet you, Jean,' Min continued. 'And, we'd like you to meet Teej. Oh, his name is Tomas James, but somehow, I started calling him TJ Jones which ended up as Teej.'

This seemed to confuse Jean even more.

'We didn't tell you before – we thought it would be too much to take in, after meeting Jim for the first time.'

'I, I don't know what to think,' Jean stuttered. 'I thought I'd never see my baby son again, and now I seem to have a grandson as well.' She shook her head and blinked a few times.

'Would you like me to make you another cup of coffee, Jean?' Min indicated her empty cup.

'No, thank you.'

'Maybe you need some of my special medicine?' Min smiled at her.

'That helped, the last time you were here. What was it?'

Min reached for her bag. 'Brandy.'

'Oh! I don't drink, so I had no idea.'

Min brought out the flask, and filled the little cup.

'Here,' she said handing it to Jean with a grin. 'Purely medicinal.'

Jean sipped it then rubbed her forehead. 'So, you would be my daughter-in-law ...'

'Exactly!' exclaimed Min her eyes widening with delight.

Jean drained the cup, coughed and smiled.

'Well, it seems I'm blessed,' she said, thoughtfully. 'Suddenly, not only do I have my son restored to me, but I have a beautiful daughter-in-law, and a grandson as well.'

Min got out a few photos of Teej, and before long the two women were oohing and aahing over them.

I got up and stacked the crockery on the tray and went to the kitchen.

Jean called out to me, 'Leave the dishes, Jim, I want to have you near.'

You can imagine how I felt. Like some kind of exhibit at the zoo.

I was relieved when after about an hour, Min stood up, 'Jean, it's been lovely catching up again. And like I said, my mum wants to meet you. I was wondering if you would like to come and stay one weekend; we have a spare room. And of course, you'd like to meet your grandson.'

Jean's eyes lit up. 'You live in Reading, I believe, so I could get the train.'

'Great! I can pick you up at the station. Hopefully, Jim won't be off on a deployment. He's in the Fleet Air Arm, Jean.' Min looked at me. 'Next weekend, Jim?'

I nodded. 'Should be okay.'

'We're very ordinary people, Jean. The house we live in looks big but it's not ours, the crowd I work for have let us have it for a year, then we must find somewhere else to live.'

In the car going home, Min said, 'What will Teej call this new grandmother, Jim?'

'Good question.' I laughed, 'Teej will wonder if there are any more grannies he hasn't met yet!'

'What about Granny Jean? Think she'd like that? After all we both call her Jean.'

'Sounds good.' I was silent for a bit, thinking. 'This Ernie must have been pretty difficult to live with.'

'Yes, and there was a stigma associated with mental health issues in those days.'

'Still is.'

We were quiet for the rest of the way. Min put the car radio on, and we listened to music, each thinking our own thoughts.

***

I was a bit apprehensive about Mam meeting Jean. 'She's quite shy, Mam, so don't go to any great lengths for her visit.' What I meant was, don't go putting on a show, but I didn't want to say that. I needn't have worried. Jean and Mam immediately bonded. I thought there might be a bit of, I don't know, jealousy or something about Teej, but it all went well.

Mam was all smiles when they met, instead of shaking hands, she gave Jean a hug – not a common thing in our family. 'Teej,' she said, catching his hand and pulling him forward, 'This is your other grandmother, Granny Jean.'

I saw Jean's eyes grow moist as she stared at Teej, 'Hello, Teej.'

'Hello, Granny Jean,' Teej replied politely, then stepped back hurriedly, afraid, I guess, of being swept into an embrace. He gave me a hunted look.

'Mam will show you your room, Jean,' I said. 'And Teej will take up your case.'

Teej grasped Jean's case and ran up the stairs.

Perhaps because they were both from the Yeovil area, and had a lot in common, and Mam is a very, I suppose the word is empathetic, person, she soon put Jean at ease. She showed her the spare bedroom, and I heard her say, 'It's all very posh, Jean, took me a while to get used to it.' And Jean laughing and saying, 'It's not what I was born to, Ellen!' and Mam laughing back.

Now that the incest thing hanging over us had been cleared, life was good.

Until ...

---

1. By the time the sun set on June 6, 1944, some 2,000 African Americans had landed in Normandy. They were engineers, stevedores, and gunners. They carried the wounded to safety and buried the dead. They drove ambulances, earth-movers and the trucks that would supply the front lines. Black quartermasters won praise from Gen. Dwight Eisenhower for salvaging their trucks sunk in deep water — and saving significant quantities of blood plasma and medical supplies that would save lives on Omaha Beach. Eisenhower praised the 320th Barrage Balloon Battalion for carrying out its mission "with courage and determination" and said the men exposed like sitting ducks on the sand "proved an important element of the air defense team." *NBC News*

2. Although this was not the law when Min and Jim were married it would have been mooted and Min with her research skills would have seen the initial stages of the bill:https://www.legislation.gov.uk/ukpga/2002/38/notes/division/4/1/4

Adoption and Children Act 2002 CHAPTER 4 – STATUS OF ADOPTED CHILDREN188. Chapter 4 provides for the status of adopted children, thereby making clear how they are to be treated in law. Section 66: Meaning of adoption in Chapter 4 Section 74: Miscellaneous enactments 203.

Section 74 provides that the general principle of section 67 (that an adopted person is to be treated as if he had been born as the child of the adopter or adopters) is not to apply for the purposes of marriages within prohibited degrees of relationship or to incest, and for these purposes an adopted person remains part of his natural family. The only exception is that an adopted person cannot marry his adoptive parent, as this falls within the restrictions set out in the table of kindred and affinity in Schedule 1 to the Marriage Act 1949. Otherwise there are no restrictions on marriage within an adoptive family.

Chapter Twenty-one

I got back after a few weeks away to find Min in a very quiet mood. Not like Min at all.

'What's wrong, Min?'

'Nothing.' She was doing the cold cream thing again in front of the dressing table mirror. I was in bed, watching her. She was very evidently pregnant now.

'Min. You've been so quiet the last few days. What is it?'

She finished her face stuff, came over to the bed and climbed in beside me. I took her in my arms. 'Tell me, Min,' I murmured.

It was early September, and the evenings still light until late, so I could see her clearly.

'I've got cancer, Jim.'

My arms stiffened around her. 'Don't joke, Min.'

'I'm not. A few months ago, I felt a lump in my left breast. I thought nothing of it, thought it was just the normal lumpy changes in your breasts with pregnancy, but mentioned it to the doctor when I went for my routine checkup last month. She sent me to a specialist and they did a biopsy and confirmed it.'

'Oh, Min!' My mind went blank. This couldn't be right. 'Get a second opinion, Min, I'll come with you, what did they say, what do you have to do?' My words came out all in a jumble.

'I didn't know how to tell you. They want me to have the breast removed and then have chemotherapy and radiation. I refused. It would harm the baby.'

I held her close. Her warm tears trickled down my cheek.

'But the breast removal, that would be okay, wouldn't it?'

'I'll think about it.'

'Oh, Min! Have you told Mam?'

'No.'

'Surely the doctors wouldn't suggest those treatments if they weren't safe for the baby?'

'Remember Thalidomide? I'm not taking a chance.'

'But it could save your life, Min!'

'And maybe harm the baby.'

'Is it too late to have an abor ...' My words faded away as I saw the look on her face. I regretted the words as soon as I'd said them.

She stared at me, shock registering on her face. 'How could you even think such a thing, Jim?'

It seemed there was no convincing Min. Eventually she agreed to removal of the affected breast after being assured by the doctors that she'd still be able to breastfeed with one breast, and that the anaesthetic wouldn't harm the baby.

It was late September by the time Min had the surgery. It was an emotional time for all of us, except Teej, who was simply told his mother had to go to hospital for a few days.

Mam had been devastated at the news of Min's cancer. To her generation the word cancer was never spoken. It was a death sentence.

There was no difficulty at the hospital with our relationship. When Min filled out the form and put my name as the next of kin it was simply assumed we were married. When I went to visit her one nurse who was with her at the time said, 'Oh, here's your husband come to see you, Mrs Jones.' Although Min had filled out her correct title of Doctor on the admittance form, because the name over her bed said Minnie Jones, and Min wore a wedding ring, she was called Mrs Jones.

By this time, Mam and Jean had got quite close, Mam had even gone to stay with Jean for two nights when they went to see *My Fair Lady* at the Bristol Hippodrome.

Jean was very excited at the thought of another grandchild, and it was funny to see the two expectant grannies comparing knitting patterns.

Min was keen to have our relationship formalized before the baby was born. I managed to get a copy of my original birth certificate, and my adoption certificate and Jean signed an affidavit to say she was my birth mother and my father was a James Samuels and we were set to go. I now regretted giving Alison Nan's wedding ring when I'd married her. And she hadn't left it behind when she'd bailed out. I asked Min if she wanted to get a new ring instead of the "fake" one she'd been wearing, but she said, no. At the time she'd bought it with me in mind and had grown to like it. She took it off and gave it to me before the wedding ...

We were married in Reading Registry Office on a Thursday with Mam and Jean as witnesses. Teej was at school so he wasn't aware of the occasion.

'You may now kiss the bride.' The official announced.

I gave Min a peck on the cheek, conscious both of my mothers were watching.

But Mam and Jean were too busy hugging each other to notice.

'What about our honeymoon?' I muttered as we went out.

'Living with you will be one long honeymoon,' Min grinned.

'Always Minnie the joker.' I smiled.

Chapter Twenty-two

Min went into labour the evening before Teej's eighth birthday.

'Good timing, Min,' I joked, on the way to the hospital. 'We'll be able to save money and have two birthday parties for the price of one.'

She grimaced as a contraction took hold. 'Better hurry, Jim,' she gasped. 'Think it won't be long now.'

She was right. At two o'clock in the morning I held a squalling baby girl in my arms.

***

'Happy Birthday, Teej darling.' Min opened her arms to him as he walked into the ward the next day. 'Sorry I wasn't at home to do your party, but look at your birthday present! A baby sister.'

Teej took a cursory look into the crib beside Min's bed. Mam was hovering behind him, anxiously trying to get a look.

'Would you like to hold her, Teej?'

'Not really.' He thrust the bunch of flowers I'd bought for him to bring, towards her. 'Here. They're for you.' He stepped back and looked with interest at the other women in the four-bedroom ward, one of whom was breast-feeding.

I fumbled in my jacket pocket for some coins. 'Here, get yourself a comic downstairs at the shop, Teej. Do you think you can find your way back?'

'Yeah. Thanks, Dad.'

I was beginning to wonder if he'd got lost when he appeared about half an hour later.

'We've been thinking about names for the baby, Teej,' I said. 'What would you like to call her.' I winked at Min, remembering how I had named her after a comic character.

He frowned and shrugged. 'Dunno. What about Miss Piggy?'

'Think of a few more names,' I encouraged.

He sniffed. 'Veruca Salt.'

'Like in the Willy Wonka book?' I said remembering he'd been reading Roald Dahl's books.

He nodded.

'But that's not such a good name for a girl, think of another, maybe from *The BFG*,' I prompted.

'Okay then, Sophie.'

'Sophie's nice,' Mam chimed in. 'Sophie Jones.'

Teej smirked as he turned away and I heard him mutter, 'Soppy Jones.'

Too late. Min smiled and nodded. 'Good choice, Teej. Sophie it is.'

Min and I had discussed names and agreed we'd ask Teej, but give her a second name in case she didn't like his choice when she got older. However, we hadn't settled on what it would be. Claire had been one of the names we'd both liked.

'Sophie Claire sounds nice,' I said.

Sophie Claire added her voice with few little mewls.

'We'd better go,' Mam said. 'Come on Teej, we can wait in the café for Dad.'

'I'm coming too, I must ring Jean and tell her the name of her new granddaughter.' I kissed Min. 'Love you, darling.'

'Can you give me Sophie, please. I must feed her.'

Gently, I picked up my daughter, I'd missed out on Teej's babyhood, but I wouldn't miss out on this one. I kissed the top of her head and placed her in Min's arms.

'My two beautiful girls ... I'll see you tomorrow, Min darling.'

Although I did the right thing, showing how pleased I was at having a baby daughter, at the same time I felt resentful. If Min hadn't been pregnant with this baby, she'd have had chemotherapy and radiation treatment and lived. Well, lived a lot longer anyway.

The next few months were hard. As Min grew weaker, Sophie grew stronger. The cancer had metastasized, but Min still stubbornly refused any treatment while she was breast feeding.

'I've done the research, Jim. For my type of breast cancer there is no cure. I don't want to go down the road of constant sickness from chemo and going for radiation therapy for a couple of years and suffering when I could spend the time enjoying my children, and being with you.' She smiled at me.

My heart was breaking. I'd found her and we were happy and now she was going to leave us.

'Anyway, there'll be no fear of us going to prison for incest now that we're married is there?' She laughed, that wonderful, gurgling laugh she'd always had.

I tried to smile. She was feeding Sophie at the time, who at the sound of Min's voice, paused and looked up at her mother. My heart skipped a beat. She was so like Min.

'I can remember holding you when you must have been about Sophie's age.' I was lying on the bed beside Min. I stroked Sophie's head. 'She's the image of you, that same little nose and eyes.'

'That's what Mam says.' Min looked down at the baby at her breast. 'But her eyes are going brown. Mine are blue. Blue is recessive.'

'Anyway, same shape.'

God forgive me, but the resentment sat in my heart like a stone.

*****

The company that Min worked for had been good, when she got to the point where she was just too exhausted to continue working, she resigned. They paid her a handsome leaving bonus and said they would continue paying the rent on the house where we lived for another year. But I'd found it hard commuting to Reading. It was over two hours' drive each way – and that was on days when the traffic was good.

It was about that time that the tenants in the cottage decided to move out. They'd been there for several years and had decided it was time to buy their own place.

We were in bed – Sophie asleep in her cot beside us – when I broached the subject with Min. 'Now that the tenants have moved out, and we have to start paying the rent on this place,' I said, 'And the rent isn't cheap, as you know.' I paused, wondering how to say what I was thinking. 'Um, how would you feel about moving to the cottage? It's close to Yeovilton and when ...' I didn't want to say the words.

'Hmm. Don't know, love. Teej would have to change schools, and there's only buses there. At least here in Reading there are trains. And ... well, my doctor's here.'

I bowed my head. 'Yes. I hadn't thought of that.'

She stroked my cheek with her good hand – the other was very feeble, the one on the side where her breast and lymph nodes had been removed. 'Darling, Jim, we must face the fact that maybe in a year or so, maybe less, I won't be here. We need to discuss what's best to do for the future – for Teej and Sophie.'

I knew she was right, but I couldn't face the thought of life without her – that Sophie would never know her mother. 'Oh, Min, I can't bear it.' Tears ran down my cheeks. Gently, she wiped them away.

'Jim, darling. We found each other, we have two amazing children. Children I thought I would never have. But we must talk about the future.'

My beautiful, clever Min. I blew my nose. 'So, what do you suggest,' I managed to croak.

'First of all, I want you to know that if you meet someone that you think would make a good mother for Teej and Sophie, and care for you, I'd be happy for you to remarry.

A strangled noise emerged from my throat.

'I just want you to know that I'd be okay with it,' she continued. 'Third time lucky, Jim.' And laughed.

'Don't joke, Min! Please!' I begged.

'Not joking. Serious. But also, Jim, Mam is getting older. She's tired.'

I felt guilty at this, in my heart I knew that, at eighty years old, Mam was finding it hard running the house and tending to Teej and Sophie now that Min was unable to do much. And she had the rheumatics, as she called it – aches and pains in her joints and fingers.

'It might be good if Jean were to move in at some stage – that is, if she'd like to. I think she must be a good fifteen years younger than Mam. But it would mean leaving her friends and her job in Bristol.'

I considered this. Jean seemed to be coming to stay more and more often at weekends – just to help out, she'd said and Mam welcomed her. At first, I was concerned that Mam might be jealous of Jean, but I needn't have worried. Mam had a heart of gold. "I had the gift of having you, Jim, for all those years that Jean missed out on. I'm happy for her to spend time with us. And she has no-one else.".

Min watched me digesting all this. She smiled. 'Okay Jim. So. I was thinking that if it's just you, Mam, Jean, Teej and Sophie you need to be somewhere close to good schools, transport, near where you work and where Mam isn't going to bump into someone from Yeovil who knew her when we were growing up.'

'You've really thought about this, Min.'

She grimaced. 'Not much else I can do at the moment.'

Min spent most of the day either in bed or lying on the settee downstairs.

'Your cottage is lovely, Jim, and handy for you for work, but not very convenient. Neither Mam nor Jean drive. Yes, there are shops, doctor, dentist and primary school, but transport is the real problem. And Teej will be starting secondary school in another year.'

Thankfully the Eleven Plus exam had been abolished and most secondary schools were now comprehensive.

'So, what do you suggest?'

'I've been doing a bit of research ...'

'Of course, Min.' I hugged her close.

'I've been looking at maps and there's a town, Bruton, that might just fit the bill.'

'Bruton ...' I mumbled, trying to recall the place. I vaguely remembered playing cricket against them at school.

'Well,' Min shifted in the bed, a slight frown creasing her brow. 'There are good schools in Bruton and there's a railway station. Jean would be able to get the train to Bristol, and it's not so far to drive to Yeovilton, about half an hour.'

'So, we're moving to Bruton are we?' I didn't think I'd ever been there. 'Maybe we could have a drive there at the week-end. Have a look around.'

'I'd like that.'

'So! It looks like you have it all sorted!' I managed to say. 'When do we move?'

'Oh, Jim. I can start looking at ads in the papers, see if anything looks suitable and ring the estate agents. That's if you're happy with that. Give me something to think about when I can't do much else.'

She took my hand. 'But, Jim ...'

'Hmm?'

'I don't want you to move until I'm gone.'

'What!'

'I've thought about it. You, Teej, Sophie and Mam, and hope-fully Jean, will make a new start. No one need know your situation. You'll be Jean's son. I will just be Mam's late daughter and your late wife. No other explanations needed. Please, Jim. I've thought it all through.'

I hated this talk about when she's gone. I didn't want to think about it. I shook my head.

'Jim. It makes sense. And here in Reading, I'm close to the hospital and my medical team. Think about it.'

She smiled. I nodded, leaned over and kissed her.

I spoke to my squad commander at work. Told him that my wife had cancer and the prognosis was not good. Said about the baby and not wanting to go on deployments. He was very understanding. Said he'd find out the options available to me.

I ended up as ground staff, working on the aircraft in the hangars. Still at Yeovilton. I missed the challenge and thrill of deployments, but my priority was Min. I could see her getting weaker, hardly eating anything and spending more and more time lying on the couch in the living room. I ended up moving our bed downstairs facing the window so she wouldn't feel so isolated. She could see the garden and passers-by. And watch Sophie, who had started to crawl, keeping Mam busy.

Jean had been excited when Min put the idea to her about moving to Bruton and joining the family.

'I'd love it,' she enthused, her eyes shining. Then her face fell. 'It's been awkward for me. The few friends I have, well, I haven't told them about Jim. I didn't want them to know about me having Jim adopted out, same for my sisters – not that I ever see them. They live in London. Just Christmas cards, that's all. I think my mother turned them against me.'

I could tell it was difficult for her to say this. It was different in those days. Having an illegitimate child brought shame on a family. I didn't feel so bad about the whole thing now I knew the facts, that Jean hated having me adopted, but I could understand that she hadn't been able to keep me at that stage of her life. I remembered how, years ago, when I was young, I'd pledged to find and look after my real mother.

I put an arm around her shoulders. 'Jean. What happened is in the past. The important thing is that I've found you, and you're now part of my life.'

I was getting used to her tearing up at any emotional point. 'I'll put the kettle on and make a nice cup of tea,' I said.

Shit! I was sounding just like Mam!

Min found three places she thought might be suitable in Bruton. She rang the agents and arranged that we'd visit them the following Saturday.

Jean got the train, and Min and I met her at the station.

Bruton looked like a nice place, all old stone buildings.

Min could barely walk at that stage. At the first house, she turned to me. 'You and Jean go in, Jim. I'll wait in the car. I'm not keen on it, now I see it. Busy road.'

'Okay.'

The agent came up all smiles, shook hands and started his patter. Seeing Min in the car, he looked in the passenger window, which Min had opened. 'Mrs Jones? Are you coming in?'

'I'll wait in the car; my husband and mother-in-law will look.'

He nodded and shepherded Jean and me up the path.

Ten minutes later and we were out. 'Thanks,' I said to the agent. 'We'll think about it.'

'On to the next one,' I said, holding the car door for Jean.

'What was it like?' Min asked as I slid into the driver's seat.

'So, so. What did you think, Jean?'

'I suppose you could make it nice with a bit of work.'

I recalled hanging wall paper in the cottage and frowned. 'Hmm.' I knew what "a bit of work" meant.

We stopped at the second house on our list and Min's face lit up. It was an old stone house with a pretty garden.

'I think I'd like to see this one please, Jim, if you could help me out.'

A different agent was waiting outside. His welcoming smile faded when he saw Min.

'Mrs Jones?'

'Yes. I've spoken to you on the phone. This is my husband, Jim and my mother-in-law, Jean.'

I helped Min up the path and into the house.

'You look upstairs, Jim. I'll wait here.'

'I can carry you, Min.'

She smiled at me. 'No, I'll stay here, but I love it Jim, just take a peek upstairs and see what you and Jean think.'

We took a cursory look at the third house, but it was unanimous. House number two.

The exchange went smoothly. I managed to sell the cottage for only a bit less than the house in Bruton and Min made up the difference with the money she'd saved from her leaving bonus.

***

Six months later Min passed away at home. She didn't want to die in hospital. Jean moved in and between us we managed her care. Her wonderful doctor and district nurse came every day and gave her pain relief.

It was agonising to watch her suffering and be unable to do anything. Thankfully her end was peaceful. I'd been spending all the time I could at her bedside, hardly sleeping. I must have functioned somehow, arranged the funeral and all the paperwork that goes with it. And gone to work. Probably work saved my sanity. You have to be totally focused in my kind of job.

Min had wanted to be buried in Bruton. It seemed strange at the time, but looking back, I can see her reasoning.

I can't remember much about the weeks following the funeral. I was frozen in my grief; I wasn't happy with Min being in Bruton and the rest of us in Reading. A few nights after her passing Teej came into my bedroom. I'd moved the bed back upstairs, and rearranged the furniture in the living room. It had been too confronting to come into the house and see the empty bed. He was crying. 'I dreamed that Mom had just gone to work and came home and was all okay, not sick anymore, and then I woke up.'

I hugged him close and tried to hold back my own grief.

The day after the funeral, I drove to Bruton with Teej. I thought it would help him to accept that his mother had died. Her grave was a mound of fresh earth, covered in wreaths. My wreath of red roses lay at the head. Teej's chin wobbled and he bit his lip. I blinked away my own tears, and thought that maybe bringing him had been a mistake. I don't know why, but it was the custom in those days not to let children attend funerals. It might have been so much easier for him with all the others around, and given him closure – as they say.

Now the two of us were there on our own. I held his hand tight. 'We must stay strong for Nan and Jean,' I said, trying to swallow the lump in my throat.

He sniffed and wiped his eyes.

Sophie was only eighteen months old, so didn't understand what had happened. It was hard for me, an adult, to accept that I'd never again see this woman who I'd known all her life, but even harder for ten-year old Teej. I tried to talk to him, but I had no words of comfort. He changed from being his normal lively self into a quiet, morose boy, spending most of his time in his bedroom, not wanting to go out with his friends.

I didn't know how to cope with him. And Mam was really shaken too. The strain of the last few years had taken its toll. Only for Jean, we wouldn't have managed. She quietly and competently ran the household.

About three months after Min's passing, she stopped me one morning as I was leaving for work.

'Jim, I think it's time we made the move to Bruton.'

We'd let the Bruton house on a short-term lease, and that was about to expire.

'The move might give Teej something new to think about,' she continued, 'And he'll be able to start in his new school in September with the other children, rather than part way through the year.' She patted my shoulder and turned back into the house. 'Think about it.'

It was probably a good idea. Like Min had said – a new beginning. And she had always been right.

***

With packing, moving and unpacking, the move jolted us out of our lethargy and depression. I'd been loath to tackle sorting out Min's stuff, but now I had to make decisions. I asked Jean if she would help Mam deal with Min's clothes. I couldn't face it. The rest of her things I put into packing boxes with the idea of sorting them once we'd moved and I was in a better frame of mind. All my letters to her over the years were in bundles tied with red ribbon. The tears threatened. I quickly sealed the box and marked it, *Min – personal.*

Teej started his new primary school and the change seemed good for him. His friends in Reading hadn't known how to relate to him after the funeral. They'd gradually stopped coming to the house when Teej said he was busy. The local boys in his Bruton school with whom he had gradually become friends, only knew he didn't have a mother. Teej mentioned that the parents of one of his new friends had divorced and his mother had moved away to live with another man, so it was just his dad, his sister and him living at their house.

The lead up to Christmas that year was dire. Jean was amazing, she organized everything, and was careful to get Mam's input. I think Mam had either forgotten or wasn't going to bother making any Christmas fare, but then I overheard Jean say to Mam, "I know your Christmas cakes and puddings are famous, Ellen. Perhaps this year you would show me how you make them". That jolted Mam into action.

'What would an eleven-year-old boy like to get for Christmas?' Jean asked me. 'Can you have a think?'

I asked around at work. It seemed a BMX bike was the most yearned for item and a Rubix cube. Teej hadn't given any hints like he usually did.

Jean asked Teej to help put up the tree and decorate it. "We must make it all Christmassy for Sophie". I heard her say. Sophie was walking and talking now and her hero was Teej. Initially he hadn't had much time for her, but early one morning, a few months after Min died, I heard Sophie whimpering in her cot. I dragged myself out of bed to see to her, but as I got to her bedroom door, I saw Teej beside her cot.

'It's okay, Soppy.' I heard him whisper. 'I know you miss Mom. Like me. Come and give me a cuddle.' Seeing him lift her out of the cot, I crept back to my room. When I peeped into his bedroom five minutes later, he had Sophie in bed with him, playing with her. I heard her gurgling and laughing. He didn't see me. 'You'd be proud of our son, Min,' I thought and managed not to cry.

Christmas came and went. It was hard for all of us. I don't know what we would have done without Jean. Early on Boxing Day morning, I took Lally for a walk, Mam wasn't feeling so good. When I returned, Jean was in the kitchen preparing breakfast.

'Just making a cup of tea for Ellen,' she said. 'She's not feeling so well, I think she might be getting the 'flu.'

'Oh, no!' I hung Lally's lead on the hook behind the kitchen door. Lally was getting on a bit by then, and only managed a slow totter around the park.

'Jean,' I said. 'I just want to thank you for all you've done. I don't think we would have got through the last few years without you. I'm proud to have you as my mother.'

She turned round, her face going pink. 'Oh, Jim, I'm so happy to have found you, and a family of my own!'

I thought she was going to cry, and I felt a bit teary too, but then Teej came in with Sophie in his arms.

'Soppy's hungry!' he announced.

***

Chapter Twenty-three – 1990

Yes. 1990 – a new year. A new decade. I hoped it would be the start of better times for us, but then Mam got pneumonia. The doctor said she needed to go in to hospital. Mam was adamant she wouldn't go.

'Your dad didn't believe in hospitals,' she wheezed. 'Only if you broke a leg or something.'

'Mam,' I said. 'It'll only be a day or two. Just to get you on the mend.'

'I'm alright! Just need a good night's sleep, if I can have something for this cough.'

'They'll give you something for that in the hospital,' I reassured her. 'And it'll be easier for Jean.'

That did it. 'Alright,' she said grudgingly.

I managed to visit her every night. After getting back from work, I'd drive straight to the hospital. One night a duty nurse saw me coming in. I knew it was after visiting hours, and thought she was going to stop me.

'Oh, Mr Jones, I'm glad I've caught you. We're worried about your mother. The doctor's been and he said to call you. But now you're here. You see, she's not improving and not eating.'

I went over to Mam's bed and took one of her hands. 'Mam,' I said softly. 'How are you, Mam?'

She opened her eyes and gave a small smile. 'I'm tired Jim. So tired.'

'I know, Mam. But we need you. Teej and Sophie need you. And Jean. And so do I.'

'Min needs me too.'

'Min's gone, Mam.'

'No. She's here and she needs me. She told me that you have Jean now. It's time Jim.'

I was terrified at her words. I know it was hard for her losing Min. "A parent expects to go before their child." she'd said to me at Min's funeral. Mam never got over losing Min.

'I'm alright, Jim. I'll just have a little sleep now. You go on home. Min's here.'

I looked up at the nurse. She nodded. 'I think it'll be another day or so.'

I squeezed Mam's hand and kissed her cheek. 'Love you, Mam. You're the best mother in the world.'

Sniffling, I bowed my head at the nurse and left.

I took Teej in to visit her the next day. Jean thought it more important for Teej and me to visit Mam rather than her. She stayed at home with Sophie.

Mam gave a weak smile when she saw Teej. 'Look after Sophie and Dad,' she whispered to him.

He nodded. 'Yes, Nan.'

On our way out, I said to him, 'I don't think Nan will live much longer Teej.'

His lower lip trembled, and he bit it. 'Hmm,' he mumbled.

Mam passed away in her sleep the following day. I was with her at the end. I kissed her forehead. 'Goodbye, Mam, best mother ever.' And I stumbled out to the car park and sat in the car until I felt composed enough to drive home.

Jean heard the car and was at the door when I parked. She took one look at my face and put her arms around me. 'She's gone?'

I nodded. 'Thank goodness Teej is at school,' I muttered.

After a few minutes, Jean gave a wobbly smile. 'Maybe we should have some of Min's special medicine, Jim.'

I hugged her. 'Good idea. Jean.' I blew my nose, took a deep breath and found glasses.

Sophie came trotting out from the living room followed by Lally. She held out her hands. 'Drinkie for me?'

Poor little Sophie. We'd all been so busy with looking after Min, grieving after she'd passed, then with the move and Nan getting sick, we hadn't had much time to think about Sophie. Poor little Sophie. I was now the only one left to tell her about her mother, how bright and funny she'd been, how clever and loyal. The stone of resentment still lodged in my gut. I stopped this train of thought as the waterworks were threatening again.

I picked her up and tried to cuddle her, but she struggled to get free. 'Want Nana!' she screamed.

How could I explain to her that Nana was no longer here?

I dreaded telling Teej, but he took it well. 'I think Mom will be happy to have Nan with her.'

I was proud of him. 'It's just you, me, Sophie and Granny Jean now,' I said.

'Yeah. And Lally. And we'll have to look after Granny Jean, 'cos she's old too.'

I hadn't thought about Jean. I knew she was about twenty years older than I was which would make her sixty-five. Still young by today's standards. But even so.

We buried Mam next to Min. Min had bought two adjoining plots in Bruton cemetery. She'd organized it all before she died, when we bought the house in Bruton. I hadn't thought much about it at the time, but like Teej said, it was nice Mam and Min were next to each other.

Lally never really got over losing Mam, and about six months after we buried Mam, Lally died in her sleep.

Remembering how we'd got Lally from my friend, at work and how she'd helped Mam get over losing Dad, I immediately went out and bought a puppy – a Labrador. The kids called her Poppy, and she worked her magic and somehow the whole household had a new focus. Sophie would crawl around after Poppy, and the dog seemed to know that little Sophie needed special attention as she would stop and let Sophie climb all over her, pulling her ears and tail.

Chapter Twenty-four – 1994

L ife went on. We managed somehow. Jean was amazing. The more I got to know her the more I was humbled and proud to be her son.

I was just home from work on that awful Friday afternoon that I now look back on with shame; Sophie must have been about eight and came rushing to meet me, followed by Poppy. I was tired, it had been a busy day, and I had a lot on my mind. I had to remember to get the car serviced and Teej, who was sixteen wanted me to drive him somewhere – I'd forgotten where.

'Look, Daddy!' She jumped up and down, waving an exercise book at me. 'I got a gold star for this project!'

'Lovely,' I said as Jean came into the hall. 'Now, let me take my coat off.'

Sophie's smile faded and she turned away. 'Okay, Daddy, I guess you're tired.'

'You did really well, Sophie,' Jean said to her. 'And Daddy's very delighted, aren't you, Daddy?' There was a note of rebuke in her tone. She frowned at me. 'Now, you start to lay the table for dinner, Sophie. I want a word with your father.'

This sounded ominous. I sighed as I hung up my coat. 'Has Teej been up to some mischief?'

'Not that I know of. Come into the lounge.' I followed her in, wondering what was coming.

She turned to face me. 'Jim. I know it's been hard for you missing Min, but you must stop treating Sophie like this.'

'Like what?' I frowned.

'As if you can't stand the sight of her.'

'What! What on earth do you mean?' I growled.

'Jim, it's like you can hardly bear to look at her.'

I was stunned. Her words hit me like a cold shower. I could think of nothing to say. Jean stood watching me.

'She absolutely adores you, Jim, but you always seem to push her away, which you don't do with Teej.'

I sat down suddenly on one of the lounge chairs, dropped my head in my hands and thought about her comments.

After a while she continued: 'I know it must be hard for you, she's so like Min ...'

I looked up at her. 'I knew Min from the day she was born,' I mumbled. 'Every movement Sophie makes, every expression on her face is Min at that age.'

She put a hand on my shoulder. 'I understand, Jim, but it's cruel to watch poor little Sophie trying so hard to please you. It breaks my heart.' She paused. 'Jim, she's not Min, please, please, try and see her for who she is.'

I felt incredibly low at that point. Jean wasn't a person to criticize and she was probably right.

I swallowed hard, and stood up. 'Thank you, Jean, it's not been easy for you either.' I put my arms around her. 'You're the best.'

Taking a deep breath, I went into the kitchen. Sophie had laid the table and was sitting down with an open book on her lap, staring into space, Poppy by her side. She had her hand on Poppy's head, idly rubbing her ears. She looked up as I entered the kitchen.

'Now, show me the project you've got the gold star for,' I said, trying to inject warmth into my voice.

She jumped up, beaming and scrambled to get the workbook.

'Come and sit on my lap and tell me all about it.'

She turned to me, a surprised look on her face. 'Really, Daddy?'

Feeling a complete cad, I looked up to see Jean give a nod of approval.

When Sophie had gone to bed I went out into the garden. 'I'm sorry, Min,' I spoke to the heavens. 'I didn't realise what I was doing.'

I tried very hard to alter my behaviour, and gradually I came to see that Sophie was not Min, she *was* her own person, with a bit of me in her too.

***

In June that year I was reading the daily paper, it was the 50th anniversary of the D-Day landings, and there were several articles about the events. I lowered the paper, my thoughts on my father who'd been killed in Operation Overlord.

'Tell me about Sammy,' I said to Jean, who sat opposite me, mending something. Sophie and Teej were in bed, Poppy had flopped down on the floor between us, snoring like a tractor as Teej put it. I'd never asked Jean much about my father, I don't know why, probably because I was so caught up in my grief for so long. Jean's lecture about my treatment of Sophie was the wake up call I'd needed.

Jean put down her mending – she was always busy with her hands – a far-away look in her eyes.

'I think it was love at first sight between us,' she said, then her eyes focused on me and she smiled. 'I know. It sounds so corny now to say it, but there was an instant attraction between us. I couldn't stop thinking about him. That first night when he walked me home, I just wanted to be with him all the time.' She sighed and took up her mending.

'And he felt the same way?' I prompted.

'Yes. He was kind and thoughtful, and he made me laugh. Told me about his family, how he was going to take me back to America and his people would love me ...' She paused. 'The coloured GIs were so polite and well mannered, more so than the white ones. A lot of people commented on it at the time ...'

'I think Min tried to track down his family from his service number,' I said, 'but she didn't have any success.'

'It was a long time ago,' Jean said. 'But it's strange, Jim, because you are so like him in your looks and gestures, but I think you're more like me in personality.'

I thought about this. Jean was a quiet, reserved kind of person, and I guess I'm a bit that way too. Min had been the bubbly, funny one in the family.

'And Teej looks just like you and Sammy, but he's so lively and bouncy and funny and like Min in his ways. And although little Sophie looks like Min, I think she takes after you in her personality.'

I nodded. She was right.

'Jim, I haven't mentioned this before, but I'm so grateful to you for bringing me into your life. I never thought I would have grandchildren and be able to spend time with them, seeing them grow up. Something I didn't have with you.'

I didn't know what to say.

'Bad things happen, and sometimes good things as well.' She looked at the hole in the elbow of one of Teej's jumpers that she was mending

'Cup of tea, Jean?'

She nodded. 'Please. Um, Jim?'

'Hmm?'

'Did you ever go to Ninesprings when you were young and lived in Yeovil?'

'Yes, of course.'

'Would you take me there?'

I was a bit surprised at this request. 'Whenever you like, Jean.'

'Next weekend?'

I nodded. I'd become very fond of Jean, but I still couldn't think of her as my mother and call her Mam, or Mum.

The following weekend, we drove to Yeovil. It was years since I'd been back. The last time had been moving the remaining bits of Mam's furniture and other stuff from the council house.

'It's a bit different than what I remember,' Jean said as she walked along the main path at Ninesprings. She led the way along a narrower path. Eventually she paused and stood for a while looking around and up at the beech trees.

'I think it was here.'

I followed her gaze. 'What?'

'The last time I was with Sammy.'

She turned abruptly. 'Right. Thank you, Jim. That's enough. We can go home now.'

I couldn't help wondering if this was where I'd been conceived. It looked the perfect secluded spot. I didn't want to think about it.

Chapter Twenty-five – 2010

My sixty-fifth birthday. Teej was working in London. He'd studied computer science at university, had a steady girl-friend, Rosie, and wasn't interested in further study. He and Rosie spent two years working in Australia, and I think they'd like to go there to live permanently, but I had the feeling that they didn't make that move because of eventually leaving me on my own. Jean was now eighty-five and Sophie wouldn't be at home much longer, having left school in November.

Teej and Sophie were funny. I think they thought I needed a woman in my life. Rosie's parents were divorced and Teej had obviously plotted with Rosie to try and get her mother, Sandra, and me together. Sophie, Jean and I had been invited to Sandra's for Christmas Eve drinks the year before last. Jean said she'd arranged to meet a friend so couldn't come. I knew that was a fib, and wished I could make the same excuse. Obviously, Sophie was in on the plot, because Sandra and I were left alone at one point while the young ones went off to some nightclub or other.

Sandra looked at me and smiled. She was nice, I liked her but there was no magic attraction between us.

'I smell a rat,' she said, taking a sip of her wine.

I laughed. 'Yes, I think our children are trying to make a match between us.'

'I don't know about you, Jim, but I'm a happy singleton, as they call us now, but it would be nice for us to be friends.'

I was delighted. 'I feel the same way,' I said, 'But maybe we can string them along and play their game.'

She looked at me with a twinkle in her eye – that sounds corny – but that's how it seemed. 'What a good plan! It would get Rosie off my back!'

'And Teej and Sophie off mine!'

And that was how Sandra became my – I suppose you would say quasi-girl-friend. It was handy for her to have someone to go to the cinema with, or to parties and the same for me. Friends stopped inviting me as "the spare man" to outings and Teej and Sophie were happy.

I wanted to tell them that I'd be fine on my own, I'd joined a local cricket club seniors' team, after Jean had told me I had to find a hobby. Then, when word got around that I worked with radar and electronics I had a few people ask me to help them with their computers. I'd made new friends and thought I'd be able to keep busy when I retired. I was about to look at a computer that Teej had left with me to fix for one of his mates, when Sophie bounced in.

'Happy birthday, Dad! Here.'

She dropped a small parcel in my lap.

'You're such a hard person to buy presents for, Dad.'

'Am I?'

'Granny Jean has made you enough jumpers to last five men fifty years, and you have enough socks and ties to start a shop. So, I hope you like this one.'

I smiled at her. 'But you found something.' I carefully opened the wrapping paper. It was a DVD of the BBC documentary series *Sailor*. It was about life on the Ark Royal.[1]

'Wow, thank you, dear, I loved watching that series, so you've found the perfect present.' I leaned over to give her a hug. 'Now, sit down and tell me what you've been up to, I haven't seen much of you since Christmas. Have you thought anymore about your future?'

She'd had a few part-time jobs in the lead up to Christmas. 'Are you planning on going to university like Teej?'

She grinned that Min smile. 'No, Dad. I'm going to join the Fleet Air Arm.'

I nearly fell off my chair. 'What!'

'Yeah. I've already filled out the application forms and I was waiting to see if I've been accepted before telling you, but as you've asked, well, I'm telling you now. Should hear this week.'

I didn't know what to make of this news. I thought about my early days at Ganges and Ariel and all the lads.

'It's awful Sophie, and with all those boys!' I had a vision of her in amongst those rough and ready youngsters. Testosterone-charged young men, all pawing at my baby girl. 'And it's dangerous!' I thought about climbing the mast. Surely, they wouldn't make girls do that!

'Oh, Dad!' She rolled her eyes, 'It's different these days, there are lots of women in the forces.'

'You're not doing this to please me, are you?'

'No, Dad. I've always been interested in aviation, and listening to you talking about your deployments.'

I frowned; I didn't think I'd talked about those times that much. 'Did I rabbit on and be a bore?'

Sophie laughed. 'No Dad, I liked listening to you talking with your old friends.'

I'd met up on several occasions with John and a few mates from my old squad and their families. 'Well, this is a turn up for the books! I wonder what would your mother think of this?'

Her face fell. 'Dad, you've never spoken much about Mum, but I'd like to know more about her. How did you meet, stuff like that. I asked Teej a few times, but you know Teej – he doesn't talk much about things like that.'

My guts twisted. Of course! She'd been too young to know about me being Min's adopted brother. Teej had been seven when Min and I married, and he'd never been told about me being adopted, there'd been no reason to talk about it. The same with mine and Min's wedding. There had been no reason to tell him about it. He just knew Mam had been Min's mother, and Granny Jean was my mother. He would remember Mam but Sophie had been too young.

'Your mother was amazing,' I said. Then stopped. 'It's a long story. But I've just had an idea.'

'Oh no! I know your ideas; they usually mean work!'

'I'll be retiring this year now I'm sixty-five.'

'Can't believe you're sixty-five, Dad!' She ruffled my grizzly grey hair. 'You're still that handsome man I see in the photos that Granny Jean has on her dressing table.' Jean had that old photo of me in uniform next to the one of Sammy.

'Flattery will get you everywhere.'

'Okay, tell me what your idea is.'

'Wait and see, I'm not exactly sure how to go about it.'

'Come on, Dad, give me a hint.'

'No. I must see if it works first.' I looked up at the sound of the door opening.

'Anyone like a cup of tea?' It was Jean.

'You sit down with Dad. I'll make it, Gran. He's just had a brain wave and needs to rest.' Giggling she ran out the door.

***

So, here I am writing it all down. That was my big idea. Mine and Min's story, Mam and Dad's, Jean and Sammy's. It's been more difficult than I thought it would be. And quite emotional at times. I used my letters to Min that she'd kept and hers to me to jog my memory. I remembered things Mam had told me about Dad and Nan and Gramp, and Jean filled in the gaps from her side.

I'm dedicating it to my beloved Min, who didn't live to see her children grow up to be the amazing people they've become.

I looked up as Jean came in with a cup of tea. She hadn't seen me growing up either ...

---

1. In 1976 BBC camera crews were invited on board Britain's best-loved warship, the aircraft carrier Ark Royal, to record what was intended to be her last voyage. As the Ark Royal sailed for America, the cameras captured a unique record of daily life on board for the officers and ratings, as well as the workings of an operational aircraft carrier with a full compliment of fighter and bomber aircraft and helicopters. Sailor remains by far the best series ever made about the Royal Navy as well as providing a historic record of the passing of one of Britain's greatest fighting ships

Acknowledgements

The author would like to thank the following:

Bob Graffham for answering in detail all my questions about the Fleet Air Arm, HMS Ganges, and the loan of the 1965 edition of the Naval Ratings Handbook.

Colin Lewis of The Fleet Air Arm Museum at Yeovilton for his time and patience and for checking my manuscript for Naval inaccuracies.

My Beta readers: Trish Behan, Barbara Spence, Stephanie Sutton-Gundry, and Pat Howell.

South Coast Writers Centre – Keira Fiction Writers Group for their helpful critiques.

Belinda Walsh for the stunning cover of this book, a wharf in Zumaia, Spain.

Resources

"Fleet Air Arm Boys" by Steve Bond
"Miracles" by Cassandra Eason
BBC Television Documentary "Sailor"
1965 Edition of the Naval Ratings Handbook

About the author

Lyn Behan grew up in the English West Country. She spent her working life as a systems analyst and computer programmer in Europe and Australia.

She now lives on the south coast of NSW with a variety of chooks and dogs.

If you enjoyed this book, you may also enjoy her other books:

***

The Men and the Medium - When radio inventor and spiritualist medium, Leslie Carter, meets the beautiful psychic medium, Lily Bancroft, he knows she's his soulmate and he could love only her. But Lily is focused on becoming a healer and spiritualist medium. Through two world wars and three marriages, she struggles to fulfil her dreams. Leslie stands by her as each of her marriages fail. Will his love ever be returned? Based on a true story.

***

Seeking Samuel Goldberg – In 1965, on the day of her beloved grandfather's funeral, Liesel discovers that she has Jewish heritage – a family secret held since the days of Nazi Germany – and learns of her grandfather's unfulfilled quest to find family members missing since the outbreak of World War Two. After an unfortunate love affair, Liesel takes on the task of locating her father's cousins, using the few clues her grandfather left. Her travels from Sydney to England and Germany bring her more that she could ever have expected.

***

Stolen Love, Fractured Lives – An incurable hereditary disease haunts the lives of three generations of women and the men who love them. When Jessica has the opportunity to steal a baby she unleashes a tangled web of lies and deceptions.

***

The Unpredictable Past – When a mysterious man, Will, moves into the house opposite hers, Elizabeth's quiet village life is turned upside down. Their friendship develops when Will helps her with researching the involvement of one of her ancestors, Edward, in the last revolution in England. This friendship sets the neighbours gossiping and infuriates Elizabeth's daughter, who is convinced Will is a con man preying on her mother, thus raising doubts in Elizabeth's mind. How can Elizabeth find out the truth about Will? Is he who he seems? Does any of what he has let slip about his unpredictable past make sense?

***

The Allotment – When Neil, an army veteran with PTSD, is persuaded to help an old man with his allotment, Neil's life changes. He meets up with other allotment holders and slowly regains confidence and the will to live and love again. Set against the background of an English Allotment, this is a heartwarming story of ordinary people, their hopes and dreams and challenges. And Beech Road Allotment oversees them all.